The Accidental Yogini: Padma

ISBN: 979-8-9860235-3-3

(Zen Barn Publishing LLC)

Dedication

This book is dedicated to my mother, Georgian, who has always supported anything I put my heart and soul into. The relationship between a mother and daughter is complicated, at best. But she's always been an atypical mother, giving me the space to be who I am without judgment yet still offering advice when I sought it. I love you, Mom.

I Do

"When you realize you want to spend the rest of your life with somebody, you want the rest of your life to start as soon as possible." – Harry Burns, *When Harry Met Sally.*

Laughter and love filled the room. This was the moment that Padma had dreamt about: her wedding day. As her husband spun her around on the dance floor, his hand gently holding the small of her back, she knew that there would never be another day to match this one, and she would do anything to stay locked in this moment forever. Glasses clinked, and the couple kissed again. He mouthed, "I love you," and she twirled away from him, her henna-designed hand clasping his strong, smooth doctor's hand. Then, flirting with her eyes, Padma brazenly released her grip and slowly walked away backward, careful not to lose eye contact with the love of her life.

Surrounded by a feminine love bubble of girlfriends who swooned over her dress, her ring, her hair, and her whole vibe, Padma realized what a big day today was not just for her but for all of her friends, as she was the first of her tribe to marry. The ladies giggled like they had as little girls, playing and planning their wedding days with their dolls. Padma recalled vividly those times with her friends. These women had always been with her for every significant moment of her life up to this point, and it was not lost on her that a divergence would soon occur as the new prince to her princess became the predominant person with whom she would create most memories moving forward. It was a bittersweet realization, as her friends had been so much of her family, not having any siblings or many cousins in her life. But in traditional Indian form, the greater community formed the base of the extended family anyway, so there was never a feeling of lack to her in that department.

Gazing over her shoulder, Padma watched her husband — wait a minute, did she say "husband?" Yes, her husband, her handsome, funny, caring, career-oriented significant other. She watched as he wiped a tear from his eye after receiving a hug and a pat on his back from his father. The men raised a glass and took a drink, hugging once again. She pondered how she got so lucky as to find a man with both wit and humor, kindness and determination. Best of all, the two aligned on all the necessary life goals. And they had a plan. They would both work for five years and then consider if they had created the necessary foundations to bring a child into the world. Once those criteria had been met, they would begin to create the family of their dreams. If they were blessed, they would have one girl and one boy. Both would follow in their father's family's physician footsteps, creating the same gorgeous life for themselves that their parents had managed to find. Padma felt with all of her heart that if they both focused on those intentions, they could manifest them with ease.

From the daydream that was becoming her actual life, Padma was pulled back into the present moment by a friend.

"Padma, earth to Padma," said Payal. "Did you hear me? When you get back from the Maldives, let's set a date for the next girl's trip."

Girl's trip, Padma thought to herself. Did she have an interest in taking a girl's trip without her husband in the foreseeable future? Certainly, what most interested her was spending as much time with him as possible. But how could she pass this information on to her best friend without hurting her feelings? How could she convey to Payal that she was not ready to discuss girl's nights or girl's trips or even a day of shopping without the presence of her other half? So, she did what she thought was best, looked her best friend in her eyes, and lied.

"Sure," Padma replied with a smile that could only be faked so well by a bride on her wedding day.

As Payal clapped her hands and jumped up and down, Padma smiled at her friend, knowing that this would probably be the first of many little lies she might have to tell her. But honestly, how did she not know that Padma would be spending every waking, breathing moment that she could with her husband? It's what the two had always talked about. Together, they had dreamt of finding their soulmates and sharing the rest of their lives with the men of these dreams. Fortune had allowed Padma to find her Prince Charming, yet Payal remained single, with no worthy marital prospects in sight. Padma could see in her friend's yearning eyes that Payal so wanted to be in the same place as her. She wished she had a crystal ball to see into Payal's future so that she could assure her that it all was coming. But she did not. And right now, at this moment, she had other more pressing things on her mind.

Padma hugged Payal and excused herself from her circle of friends to make her way back to her husband. Payal graciously shooed Padma away, attempting to ignore a sinking feeling in the center of her chest. Spending less time with her best friend soon was not lost on Payal. She understood completely what was about to happen with Padma as the bride melted into oneness with her now husband. Payal's eyes epitomized support for her friend when they could have also sunken to jealousy. Sure, there was a "why not me" pity party happening deep down, holding back an urge to cry. But she felt it was mostly the beginnings of the mourning process for what had been their collective young and single life. So Padma quickly dabbed the corner of her eye, smiled, and continued dancing with the other single ladies of their pack.

"Padma, come here, precious girl," said Uma, the mother of the bride, as she directed her daughter to join her and some friends, the elder women that are affectionately called "Aunties."

Padma kissed her mother and threw her arm around her waist, smiling at the ladies.

"Padma, please tell your Aunties about the incredible dream house that Rajesh bought for you."

"Mama, now you know that Rajesh and I bought the house together, with both of our money equally," Padma said, now forcing a smile.

"Yes, yes, of course, but we all know that soon you will be with babies, and Rajesh will be the sole provider."

"And what a good provider he will be!" One of the Aunties jumped in to add.

Padma smiled wider — something she'd learned to do when her mother's friends were around.

"Yes, marrying a doctor, one cannot ask for a better thing. Uma, you are so lucky!" Another woman added.

And as if he knew what was happening, Rajesh swooped in to save his wife. Taking her hand and smiling at the Aunties, he dropped a quick kiss on Uma's cheek, announcing that he must have his wife's time, and whisked her off and away from the conversation.

"Will you look at that," said another Auntie, "He loves you so much, Uma."

"Such respect," added another.

Uma smiled and nodded her head. For sure, she was so lucky that Padma had found Rajesh. He made an excellent addition to their small family — one that she was quite protective of.

After a few dances with friends, Padma and Rajesh were called to sit near the dance floor, where all seven of Rajesh's sisters were about to celebrate them with a Bollywood-style dance. Padma knew how many hours her new sisters had put into his dance and what it meant to them to perform it at the wedding. From the moment Rajesh, the baby boy, had told his family that he had proposed to Padma, his sisters had lost their minds creating this entertainment for their wedding. At first, they wanted to do something every day of the famous Indian festivities leading up to the actual day of the wedding ceremony, but that felt a little overwhelming to Padma. The first testament to his priority to her as his wife-to-be was backing her up on that and telling his sisters that it would be more impactful and meaningful for them to create one dance at the reception. They agreed and began the long task of choreographing and selecting costumes, hair, and makeup. Everything had to be just right as this was their only brother's wedding, and nothing was too much for this celebration.

In true traditional Indian sister fashion, the dance exceeded even Padma's most exaggerated imagination. If she didn't know any better, she would have sworn that they were all professional dancers. What she was not told was that two of Raj's sisters were friends with a professional choreographer in New York City, who they all visited several times for lessons to nail their performances down. It was a good thing that they had decided to host a seven-hour wedding-day event because this musical regalia equaled in length a major motion picture, no exaggeration.

At one point, all seven sisters, forming a lotus flower design, brought Padma into the center, revealing her as the jewel inside the lotus. Her name meant lotus, in fact, and that was a symbol that she used often instead of writing out her name. She enjoyed this as it was her understanding that the symbolism of the lotus flower equated to unrivaled beauty. Many people had commented about the significance of her name, which she was told her grandmother, Nani, had given her. Since Nani had passed many long years now, it was a way that she continued to feel a connection to her grandmother.

At the reveal of the lotus, Rajesh clapped and rushed to the dance floor to join his sisters and new blushing bride in dance and merriment. Every member of the wedding reception, the 500-or-so guests as well as the over 100-or-so additional well-wishers who dropped by for the reception, roared in excitement and joined the gaiety.

The dancing and celebration continued well into the night, as it should. And even though they'd had three days of rituals and ceremonies leading up to their wedding ceremony and reception, there were still two more days of familial rituals before the two could embark on their honeymoon and officially start their married life together. Being an only child of a rather small family, Padma had limited first-hand experience in the behind-the-scenes curation of Indian weddings. Rajesh, on the other hand, had lived through all seven of his sisters' weddings, plus various other friends. Together, the two had been to twelve wedding celebrations in the last two years alone — all friends, family, or colleagues of Raj's. So when it came to the reception, Padma was happy to leave the details to Raj's family. After all, she had the fairytale wedding of her dreams, and giving up some of the control over the party allowed for every moment to be even more magical than the next.

Padma's father's emotional speech left not a dry eye in the room. Being Swarup's only daughter and only child, he had also dreamt of this day, along with his wife, Uma. Their failure to produce more children only meant that Padma would have the best of everything, no matter the financial cost or price. Sending her to University, where she met Rajesh, an Indian doctor, had been difficult financially but ultimately incredibly significant, or they'd never be at this glorious celebration today. They knew that the most important thing in their life was the comfort and happiness of their daughter, and they were certain that Rajesh would continue the necessary steps to give Padma the best of the best.

"In conclusion," said Swarup to a room full of golden bedazzled aunties, uncles, and other guests, "I would like to thank all of you for attending this celebration and ask you to raise a glass to toast my daughter, Padma, now Patel, but always a Desingu in my heart. To my baby girl and a lifetime of happiness with the greatest addition to our family, Dr. Rajesh."

Everyone raised a glass of champagne, cheered, and reacted with an explosion of love as they watched the bride and groom kiss once more. But that was not the close of the evening. The reception only ended once the couple rode off in a horse-drawn carriage, waving and smiling back at their guests while leaving a trail of what appeared to be sparking fairy dust in their wake. No kidding, magical fairy dust was a thing that Raj's sisters had found online, and thus,

Padma was able to check off another item on her fairytale wedding list.

As the horses galloped down the lane, Padma kissed Rajesh, feeling whole and complete, just as she imagined she would feel when she was a little girl dreaming about this very day. Gazing into Raj's eyes and holding hands, she felt not the slightest need to look back.

"I love you," Padma said to her new husband sweetly.

"I love you more," Prince Charming said back.

Lovingly, they gently touched foreheads as they rode away. Padma was trotting into the future with the love of her life. They had a plan. They had the support of friends and family. And most importantly, they were on the same page about their future. Padma couldn't wait to get to living out the rest of her magical life with Raj as soon as possible.

I Don't Recall Signing Up For This

"Before I got married, I had six theories about raising children; now, I have six children and no theories." - John Wilmot.

Blood-curdling screaming filled the room. This was a sound that Padma had never imagined possible in her darkest nightmares: the endless crying of her baby girl. As she bounced her up and down, cradling her in her loving arms, she knew that as much as she loved this baby, what she needed most at this moment was sleep and rest and that she was at the point where she would do just about anything to make her stop crying.

And then it happened. The baby's crying woke their other child, Nina, who would soon require her attention. She bounced the baby up and down, singing nonsensical words and phrases to try and hush her while she listened on the monitor for Nina to call for her. Multi-tasking was her new job, and she knew that if she was her boss, she'd be fired for lack of ability to perform satisfactorily.

Padma began to cry herself. Because she was exhausted and because she couldn't determine which child to honor the most, Padma's mind began to race through endless questions and judgments:

Why was there no end to the needs of these children?

When was the last time she had bathed?

Would she ever sleep again?

How do single mothers do it?

Why do women choose to have more than one or two children?

How come men can't share in birthing half the children?

Was there a better mother out there for her kids?

Was she not mother material?

Had her mother not properly prepared her for the realities of marriage and motherhood?

And not the least of all:

What had happened to the married life she had dreamt of?

She wiped away her tears, mouthed, "I love you," put the baby down, and crept away from the crying newborn to attend to her toddler, who was now calling her name.

Raj's oldest sister had told her that the baby would stop crying eventually. If she made sure that the baby had eaten, been changed, and did not have a fever, she could put the baby down, and it would eventually calm down and fall asleep. The baby was more stubborn than she was patient because Padma had yet to see that work out in her favor. So, after welcoming her daughter, Nina, to the day with a huge hug and getting her something to eat, she once again picked up the baby and began to sing sweetly to her.

"Mommy loves you. Please stop crying. I love you. I love you. Everything is fine. You can be relaxed. You are loved. And I am going to kick your father when he eventually comes home from work. Because he's not here to help. But I love you. And mommy just needs to rest. So please go to sleep. And I'll buy you a puppy, or a horse, or a Porsche..."

Sometime many hours later that evening, with Nina back in bed after her active day and the baby currently sleeping near her on the couch surrounded by pillows, Padma had fallen asleep in an awkward position with her head fallen back, mouth fully open, snoring. She hadn't heard Rajesh come home, eat the leftover dish she'd left him from dinner, or head upstairs to shower. She awoke only from her true love's kiss on her neck and with her scream.

"Ahhhh!" Jumped Padma.

"What?" Rajesh answered her scream. "It's just me. It's just me." Raj jumped back from his wife, not sure if he should wrap his arms around her to support her or move away for his safety.

Padma took a deep breath and cringed; her neck was now as tight as a rope. She winced from the newfound pain in her neck and dropped her head forward into her hands, defeated once again. With both daughters miraculously asleep, she had found a rare moment to close her eyes and swiftly fall out herself. Sure, she wore baby spit-up-crusted clothes from two days ago and had failed to eat dinner herself, but she had been sleeping. She took that as a win. And just like that, her perfect rest had been broken, and she doubted that she would find that kind of peace anytime soon or possibly ever again.

Rajesh offered to rub his tired wife's neck while he talked, but she felt that folding the clothes was now more important. He was excited about work at the hospital and had a lot to share with her that evening about his day, as he always seemed to find the most interesting cases. And he had a knack for helping ease people's pain. He was a true healer, just like his mother. But as he began this evening to talk, he noticed Padma turn away from him. There was a time, not that long ago, when Padma couldn't wait to hear about his day and share hers. They both had looked forward to their evenings together, returning to one another after their time apart in the world. While he was still there at that time, Padma was no longer on the same wavelength. He didn't blame her. She was raising their two little girls full-time. And to him, that was the most important job in the world. Yet, he still did miss his wife's attention and perhaps selfishly felt that there should be a little something left for him when he got home.

"Hello. Padma, my darling, where are you?" Raj said, smiling at his beautiful wife.

Padma heard a distorted sound but could not focus on what it was. Folding clothes at night was her particular style of meditation, where she was able to detach and go somewhere else more relaxing for a while. Ultimately, she would much rather be sleeping, but with Raj home and excited, that prospect was over.

Him and his big dreams, she thought. *Doesn't he realize I have no more energy left for him? Doesn't he see how incredibly tired I am? Why isn't he on the same wavelength as me anymore?*

The fact was that after only a year into marriage, Padma became pregnant. They were both over the moon about the pregnancy, and although their plan was suddenly expedited, they felt that they were more than ready to start their family. Perhaps Raj even more so. Once she was pregnant, he revealed that he had only agreed to their "plan" because it was what she wanted at the time. And since he was so thrilled and they had so much support, Padma took it as an auspicious sign that the Universe was in their favor. From the moment she told Raj she was pregnant, things began their gradual change, as they always do when children come into a marriage and the balanced world of coupling shifts.

First, it began with a change of focus. Instead of focusing on their life together and their individual needs as they applied to their partnership, the focus shifted to be all about their pending child and what would be best for him or her. From moving out of the city into the suburbs to making more responsible choices about what chemicals they used for housecleaning to what foods Padma ate during her pregnancy, it was all about the baby. Not that Padma felt this was wrong, then or now, because she understood that the focus needed to be on the baby. However, Padma could see now how they had begun to lose appreciation for what had brought them together in the first place: how they just "got" each other.

Then, just a short time, married with a baby, when Padma was ready to go back to work and plug into her marketing career for another couple of years, she discovered that she was pregnant again.

All of the women in her life were nothing shy of exceedingly joyful about Padma's pregnancies. Padma had been her parents' only child, as her mother was not able to conceive after having given birth to her. This forever longing manifested as a deep and private sadness in her mother, who was more than excited to make up for that lack by being a grandmother.

Having her mother, Uma, stay with them after Nina was born had been a blessing from heaven. After a few weeks, she convinced her mother that she had a handle on the whole mommy thing and sent her back home. And although home was only a two-hour drive away from Padma, Uma would have stayed forever If her daughter had allowed her to. Padma knew this, but she also wanted to show everyone that she could do it by herself. Where that need came from, nobody was sure, least of all Padma.

Once she had the second baby, she sure wished she hadn't told her mother, "I got it," because it was obvious that she did not. And she was getting closer every day to calling her mother and pleading with her to stay with them again. Even if it was just so that she could nap a bit, Raj wouldn't mind the help either. He was from a large family and always welcomed company and help.

On his side, Raj's mom could not have been a better mother-in-law. While she was available for them when they needed her, she seemed to understand that Padma and Raj also needed some personal space in which to raise their family. This distinction was a huge feat for most mothers-in-law, especially in the case of an Indian mother and her only son. Thankfully, Raj's family was not as traditional when it came to family roles. Being a top surgeon with a career of her own, Raj's mother had somehow managed to also give birth to eight children. Padma could not wrap her head around the possibility of that with the complications and challenges that arose from only having two children and being a full-time stay-at-home mom. She wondered if she would ever get back to work now as the line of diapers, laundry, feeding, and repeated tasks continued endlessly. Secretly, Padma judged herself next to her mother-in-law's capabilities, and she just was not stacking up.

As for her sisters-in-law, well, that was certainly an interesting story. Having no siblings of her own, she couldn't wait to have other women to call her sisters. Certainly, to have not just one but seven sisters was a miraculous manifestation. Reality, however, proved quite different. While she envisioned alternately hosting holidays, having built-in babysitters, and sharing various life hacks, nobody could have prepared her for the litany of advice that would bombard her daily. There seemed to be no personal boundaries with Raj and his sisters, and she was just not used to all that came with that.

Each sister seemed to have her ideas of how to tend to Raj, and none of them were shy about sharing them. Rajesh being the baby after seven girls meant that while his mother was working at her private practice, he was being raised by several mini-mothers who micromanaged his life to the point that his every accomplishment was, in part, the result of their constant advice and support. Was this a bad thing? Not entirely. While the support that came from a big family certainly took some pressure off of her, it also created more expectations than she enjoyed having placed on her.

The first time that this situation presented itself to her was just before Nina was born when Padma took a work trip. She was worried about leaving Raj home alone for a week. She told everyone that she didn't want him to feel alone without her. But the real reason was that the interworking of the kitchen was known entirely to her, and she doubted Raj's ability to navigate it without her around. Not a problem. Raj had two meals a day delivered to the house by each sister all week, they watered the plants and fed the cat. Problem solved. Padma had a great week in Chicago at the seminar, and Raj continued to thrive back in the care of his loving family's feminine nurturing. When she eventually returned to her home, Raj was happy to see her, and Padma spent close to a week trying to find everything that his sisters felt they needed to move to a better place in the house.

One of the reasons she and Raj had chosen this particular house was for its convenient layout. The open plan meant that you could see most of the downstairs from any other point. So, if their children were playing in the living room, she could be cooking in the kitchen and still be able to see them. Or, if Raj was in his office, he could also watch his family playing. Of course, there were plenty of cabinets and closets, but there were certain things that Padma enjoyed having out — either for convenience of use or just to see them.

And yet, with this open floor plan and much space to see things, Raj's sisters still managed to find places to hide her stuff. Yet Raj's doctoral certificate was now hanging in the foyer of the house, just next to the front door, so that everyone who entered knew in an instant that it was a doctor's home. She chose not to move it but giggled as she added her diploma right above his. Sure, it was a little passive-aggressive, but it was her house, after all. And she and Raj were an equal team in it.

As time went on, his sisters' incessant mothering irritated Padma more and more. He was a grown man, after all. He was more than capable of doing things, yet nobody had ever allowed him to. This enabling of him to not be responsible at first allowed her to be in ultimate control, but now that she was dealing with raising both children full time, she relished in the idea of him helping out more. But she kept all this to herself because she had continued the family's pattern. And besides, who was she going to complain to? Her friends assumed that she was living the dream, and she didn't want to break the realities to them. Her mother refused to discuss any unpleasantries and was completely enamored with Raj in all ways. And she had convinced herself that sharing these feelings with

Raj or his family would most likely only hurt their feelings. So, just like her mother had taught her, she kept it all inside.

Sometimes, when she was doing chores at home and had little time to think, her mind would roam. Padma would recall traveling, going out to dinners, and working full-time for a company that she enjoyed working for.

She and Payal had worked for the same company, and Payal recently told her that someone else was hired for her old marketing position there. Her boss had managed to hold open her spot through FMLA as long as she could and, due to Padma's impeccable job performance, had expected her eventual return. But once Padma was ready to come back to work, she found herself pregnant again, and it didn't make sense to return only to leave again so soon after.

She and Raj talked tirelessly about whether or not she should remain home once their second was born, and both were convinced that it was better if she stayed at home, providing them with a solid foundation before sending them off to school. And although she loved being home with her daughters, Padma secretly missed the excitement she got from working with new clients and all the adulting that comes with her career. She felt a little robbed of more of this time to develop herself, yet acknowledged that motherhood and raising a family were her deepest desires. These thoughts conflicted with her daily.

At times, her flip-flopping mind was eased that she had made the right decisions. In other, more difficult times, Padma found herself romanticizing eating at fine-dining restaurants, wearing fancy clothes and looking slim and beautiful, and holding the long stem of a wine glass and gently sipping and savoring the tannins. And she missed curse words and adults laughing like children after using them. Boy, did she miss that!

The fact that these things were not better than her new mommy's life was not lost on Padma. She just thought she would have had a little more time enjoying them before the other world of being married with children would settle her down to being a self-professed, reclusive homebody. These were the many thoughts that she kept to herself because she judged that she was in no position to complain. Hadn't she gotten everything that she had ever asked for? She was living the dream.

Padma blinked and feigned a smile at her husband, who was still awaiting her presence in his conversation.

"That's great, honey," she finally mustered.

Raj pursed his lips and pulled her close to him, pouting.

"You don't even know what I said, do you?" He frowned, spotlighting the origination of the face that little Nina would often mimic when things weren't going her way. She admitted to herself that the face was cuter on her toddler.

"I'm sorry, Raj, I am just tired," Padma admitted.

"I know. I'm sorry to come home and just spill on you. I want to be more supportive of you and the girls. I need to learn how to curb my enthusiasm," Raj admitted.

"No, I want to hear about your day. I do. I want to know how things went out there in the world, and how you saved lives, and what is that on the floor?"

Shifting gears, Padma walked across the room to find something sticky, likely of lunch or dinner variety, in a spilled mess on the carpet. Without a word to Raj, she walked out of the room to get cleaner and tend to the mess.

Raj closed his eyes only to awaken a time later to Padma leaning into him, completely asleep, drooling onto his clean shirt just like Nina does when she is tired. He sighed, thinking it was cuter when his toddler did it. He knew that this phase of exhausted motherhood was temporary. But Padma did not yet understand this.

She felt defeated. She felt like a bad wife and mother. Certainly, many other women had come before her and had a more challenging time in their lives. She thought about the grandmothers and great-grandmothers in India and all over the world who gave birth at home and then got up and made dinner for the family of ten. She thought again about Raj's mother, who had eight children and a successful career. Why could she not manage this little bit of her own life? Failure, indeed.

Raj kissed his wife's head and gently lay her down on the couch, slipping a blanket on top of her. She was sleeping so soundly he did not want to wake her. He figured it was best to let her sleep right there for the time being, enjoying the deep rest. And he made it a plan to wake up extra early and attend to the girls for her so she could have more time to herself the next day. Perhaps a little rest and time would give his wife the fresh pop of energy she needed. And tomorrow, they would be able to enjoy their late-night conversations and connections again. Yes, that was the thing to do for sure.

Raj thought about fixing a snack but honestly didn't know what he wanted. Someone was always bringing him something to eat, it felt like, so he rarely had to consider what he was in the mood for. He decided instead to kick back with one of his Cuban cigars out on the patio. So, with feet up and Cuban in hand, Raj spent another hour unwinding from work in the world of medicine. Life was good. During the day, he helped people, and at night, he came home to his three beautiful girls. They had an amazing family together. Padma knew it, too, he thought. They had everything they ever wanted, and they were still young enough to carve a deeper path for their family in the world.

Light at the End of the Tunnel

"Hope is being able to see that there is light despite all of the darkness." - Desmond Tutu.

Padma awoke abruptly. The baby was crying. But where was it coming from? Upstairs? Why was she not upstairs? As her eyes began to focus, she realized she had fallen asleep downstairs on the couch. Why hadn't Raj woke her to go upstairs to bed? Ah, more realizations. He had put a blanket on her. He probably thought it best to let her rest there. But she had no time to think about that. The baby was crying.

She quickly moved to head upstairs, jamming her shin bone on the coffee table in the process.

"Oh, Mother..." Padma yelled, biting her lip to not spill the full MF word out of her mouth. She'd gotten used to shoving those words back down with a little one always nearby and quick to repeat her every word.

Running up the steps, albeit a little more slowly than usual, she went into the nursery and picked up the baby, sitting down to feed her.

They'd decided to create a new nursery for their second-born because they wanted her to have all the same benefits that their first child had. Nina's nursery had been created in typical girl colors of two-toned pinks and was still that color scheme since Nina seemed to enjoy them very much. But they wanted something different for their next child and chose a beautiful, soft green color with baby frogs as accents. Padma wasn't sure why she liked the baby frogs. When she thought about it, she realized that if someone handed her a real frog, she might most likely scream and toss it away. Yet somehow, the baby frogs didn't seem as frightening. Was it the human accents that they wore, like bowties or hats? Or maybe it was the goofy smiles on their faces. Either way, frogs, it was for the baby's little green room. And Padma found it to be one of the most relaxing ones in the house.

Of course, by the time she went to nurse the baby, her breasts were leaking milk. She had managed to stain another shirt. Or was that stain from days ago? *Mom of the year, for sure.* She was thankful that she was able to nurse her babies with little issue. At least that came easy to her and to them. It seemed that he had just weened Nina off breast milk just in time for the baby to be born. Raw was an understatement. Her nipples would never be the same. They might as well be cork. They'd make a nice wine-stopper. Yum. Wine. When was the last time she sat down, relaxed, and had a nice glass of wine?

Padma knew the date exactly. It was the week before she found out she was pregnant when she had met Payal for a brief girls' night out. She missed her bestie, and Raj had to encourage her to go out and spend some time with her friends. He teased that it would only make them miss each other more, and he was right. Sex that night was amazing. Turns out, "out of sight" is *not* "out of mind." Rajesh devoured every part of her that evening, slowly and thoroughly. It was the best sex that they'd had.

It seemed she'd misjudged the importance of a girls' night out. And, as luck would have it, she would also not have another one in over two years. She was more than due. As Padma sat breastfeeding, her only thought was sitting at Vibe with Payal and her friends, having a few cocktails, and laughing it up like the old days, the days before marriage and kids complicated everything. The longing for that simpler time developed into a long daydream, long enough for the baby to finish and fall asleep in her arms without a burp. But, the eventual fussing brought her back, and she quickly maneuvered her infant to the shoulder for bouncing and tapping. Sure enough, a loud burp blew out. The baby smiled. Padma smiled. And for a brief moment, the world was okay again.

She must have fallen asleep again in the chair with the baby in her arms because the next thing she knew, Raj was in the doorway of the nursery, and she was blinking her eyes open.

"Sorry, hon. I meant to grab the baby first, and I was going to give her a bottle and let you sleep in, but you beat me to it, I see."

Padma smiled at Raj. He sure was cute. Stupid for a doctor but cute.

"It's okay, she wanted me anyway," she said.

"Right," Raj smiled, nodded, and came into the nursery to kiss his wife. "But, now that I am awake, let me take her for you."

"Yeah?"

"Yes. And, why don't you go take a nice hot bath or shower, or whatever you want? Let me take care of the girls this morning."

Padma nodded, handed over the baby, kissed her husband, and left the room without any further conversation or debate. He did not need to tell her twice. And she dared not look back at what by now was likely his startled face. *Let him call his sister*, she thought. She didn't even care which one. What she did care about was that bath, that glorious hot bath. And because it was early in the morning, and she was still nursing, Padma made herself a "Cranberry Mocktail" instead of a glass of wine to go with her hot soak.

Anyone who says that they do not enjoy a hot bath doesn't understand the art form. One does not just run tepid water and merely sit. One does not just drop in a bath bomb and lay back. There is preparation for a hot bath. First, you have to choose the essential oils. Lavender may be most people's go-to, but Padma's olfactory sense was more refined than that. One of her company's many products included various scents, so she was privy to their fragrances because it was her job to put them into words. And not just any words, but words that would convince someone to purchase those products. Her personal favorite was "Beguiling Bergamot." Not a well-known scent, this prestigious citrus had just the right blend of light, sweet, and refreshing, with deep herbal undertones. It was the perfect scent for the mom who needs quick relaxation yet wants to emerge feeling refreshed and renewed.

Once the oil is chosen, one needs to procure the proper music and potential reading materials. In this case, there were no reading materials. Padma hadn't read a good book since baby 1. And she was less than interested in reading one since baby 2. But music, the right music, was a must. Again, nothing too soothing and mellow, yet not something that made her want to get up and dance around

Bollywood-style. Immediately, he popped into her mind: Drake. Drake, it was. Drake, it shall be.

"Drake!" She said erotically.

Magical scent, check. Music, check. Now, to set the tone with appropriate lighting. This proves difficult during the day, so closing all the blinds and creating a dark atmosphere with dimmed lights at just the right level is key. Check. Now remove any child and husband objects from the immediate area so she can float away without them in mind. Check. Cranberry Mocktail on the side? Check. Bathrobe nearby? Check. Large fluffy towel? Check. Had she forgotten anything? Just one thing: to get the hell in the tub!

She quietly hummed along with Drake, sipping her juice while pruning herself in the tub. And it was fabulous. She lost herself in a moment of relief and relaxation. The burden of constantly attending to someone was lifted, and Padma felt the usual pressure pushing on her shoulders lessen, and they slowly relaxed down away from her ears. The warm water felt glorious as it gently moved against her skin. She moved her hands gently against her body, pulling the oily water over her arms, legs, and stomach, blending the scent in. Every muscle in her seemed to melt, along with her cares, and she found herself lost in bliss with a smile on her face that hadn't been this big since her wedding day.

She did not think once about her husband or children Well, not until said man peeked his head in the bathroom.

"Hon?" said Raj.

Padma took a deep breath without opening her eyes. The image of her, with a drink in hand, hanging just out of the tub, gave him a clue that she was, in fact, awake.

"Hon," she replied without looking.

"I don't want to get you out of your zen zone here. I tried to wait, but Nina seems to want something other than what I'm giving her for breakfast, and I am not sure where that is."

"What is it that you are feeding her?" Padma inquired.

"Cereal…"

Raj didn't need to finish.

"No, babe. She won't eat cereal anymore. She's eating waffles."

Raj paused, seeking mindfully his next words.

"She won't eat it because…?" He waited.

Did Padma need to answer her husband? Hadn't she already discussed this with him two weeks ago when Nina pushed the cereal off the highchair, screamed, and cried, "I waffle!"? She was sure that she had. Ah, but that was the night he came home having repaired a perforated bowel and made some comment about not wanting to talk about food. Since he never fed the girls, it did not seem to matter. Until now. During her wonderful and most glorious hot bath.

"Babe," said Padma sweetly. "Just give her a waffle. It's in the freezer. Take one out, toast it, and put a little syrup on top."

Raj nodded and began to close the door, and just before clicking it shut, opened it up again.

"Ah, Hon, where is the toaster?"

Padma took a long last sip of her liquid bliss, imagining that there was alcohol in it that might soothe her. It would be easier for her to get out of the tub and handle this. He was only going to ask her where the syrup was, which one to use, or if he should give her a fork or cut it for her. The more Padma thought about the possibilities, the more she realized bath time was over, and she took a deep exhalation, blinking open her eyes.

"Babe, I'm done anyway. I will be right down. Just give me like five more minutes," Padma said, resolving herself to the fact that Nina was only going to want her to give her breakfast anyway.

"I can do this. I have delivered babies, and I have surgically repaired blocked valves and torn tendons. I can toast a waffle," Raj laughed. And with that, Padma, his beautiful wife, looked at him and simply smiled. Raj smiled back and headed downstairs to attend to little Nina and her current waffle addiction. What would the next thing be for her, wondered Padma. She had learned to go with the flow when interacting with her strong-willed daughter. Fighting with her or trying to force something on her that she didn't want was not going to work. Even her father couldn't get Nina to eat or do what he wanted her to when she had something else on her mind. That was the truth. Neither Padma nor Raj ran their house. A toddler was in charge of the house. And they were both at her mercy. They would both save a whole lot of time if they just gave her what she wanted. With these qualities, Padma saw so many possibilities for her daughter's future and was committed to assisting her in achieving her dreams and goals — whatever they should be.

An hour later, Padma helped Raj clean up the kitchen from the breakfasts. Nina not only wanted waffles but pancakes that morning, and Raj had torn apart the kitchen trying to find all the necessary tools to make them for his baby girl. Now, Nina sat on the floor playing with her toys while the baby slept nearby. Raj tossed the dishrag down on the counter, in the cliche way most people do to mark that they are finished with the housework. He walked over, took his wife, and kissed her. She smiled and returned the kiss. The two of them had a moment.

"Thank you for letting me luxuriate in a bath this morning. It was heavenly," Padma said to her husband, running her fingers through his hair, which sent a tingle down his spine.

"Anything for my beautiful wife," Raj replied, then continued, "In fact, I was thinking maybe you should call Payal and set up another girls' night or day out. I can have my sister, any one of my sisters, over, and we can just all hang out. You need to get out of the house. You deserve it. And besides, you're starting to smell like baby poo."

Padma laughed out loud and snorted in the process. Raj hadn't made her laugh that hard in quite a while. He laughed, too, especially after the snort. Nina peeked her head up, "Funny, mommy," she giggled, then returned to her toys.

After a full cleanup, the two retired to the living room and sat down on the couch near Nina.

"I think you're right. I need to see my friends," Padma revealed. "I miss them more than I thought I would."

"I'm sure they miss you too," Raj said. That was, in fact, true. On more than one occasion, when one of Padma's friends had come through the hospital for one thing or another, they had revealed to him that they missed Padma terribly and very much wanted to get together with her. By the time he had gotten home, he had forgotten to mention these things to her. And, certainly, most evenings, there was not an appropriate time to convey the message either. He imagined her giving him the evil eye and, with an elevated voice, questioning something to the effect of, "And when would you like me to do that?" And then he would have no answer to that question. But he did know that he wanted his wife to be as happy as he was. And she certainly was in short supply of pleasantries of late.

And so it was that by the end of the day, Padma had planned a night out the following week with her friends. Each phone call she made to each friend was better than the next. One by one, the ladies rallied, promising to create a night to remember.

That night, Padma even made it into bed before passing out. Raj's help was certainly most welcomed. Hopefully, he would remain diligent in his awareness of her needs at home while he was making lives better at the hospital. All she needed was just a little help. Time will tell. And right now, all she had was scads of time at home with her beautiful kids.

Life was good. It was good, albeit challenging at times. And she thought to herself before falling asleep that night, *what else could a woman want?*

An Unexpected Friendship

"There's not a word yet for old friends who've just met." — Jim Henson.

Six Indian women walk into an Italian restaurant. One orders the Fettuccini Alfredo. Two more of the Ravioli special. Another orders Chicken Parmesan, and the fifth, a steak, medium rare. It sounded like the beginning of a good joke, and Padma was already cracking up, having not felt this free in quite some time. She was the sixth Indian woman, and she ordered the Seafood Marinara over linguini, and it was freaking scrumptious!

Dinner with her friends took her away from the everyday doldrums of being a good wife and mother. Of course, she spent most of her time talking about the family she needed time away from. But the fussing or wailing of the baby in the background was not a thing occurring at the restaurant. Nina's jealousy over the baby also was not a thing happening in her present reality. And her amazing husband, who was trying, yet not quite hitting the mark, well, he wasn't a thing either. If anything, he had saved the day by tending to the girls so that she could go out. Okay, in fairness, three of his sisters were coming over for dinner and game night with their kids, so it was, in essence, a party that Raj would not have to prepare, cook for, or clean up from. If Raj was ever put to the task of all the work that went into a family gathering, it just might be the first thing he failed at. But it wasn't his fault. His sisters had created that story, as she recalled once again to herself.

Padma, two Pinots in, was feeling quite free to share her thoughts on motherhood that evening, although her edited version certainly was not headline-making. Instead of creating somber energy by complaining, she focused on the positive aspects and blessings of shaping her children's lives by cooking strong, healthy meals for them (that Nina would throw on the floor), providing a creative household where they had the freedom to express themselves and feel out just who they were (like the time Nina drew the history of the world on her bedroom wall in crayon), and continuing to nurture a romantic relationship with her husband (falling asleep on the couch with her head in his lap while he watched Dateline). It was all good. Maybe she would share more at another time. For this evening, it was all thumbs up about motherhood and married life, and with a little wine.

"So, I went on a blind date last week," Payal announced.

The women went crazy. Of course, they went crazy every time one of them made any announcement, no matter how big or small. They were that kind of a supportive group.

"Do tell. Do tell," Padma replied, happy to live vicariously through her single-and-mingling bestie.

"Well, his name is Kevin, and he works at a Tech company in town..." began Payal but was soon cut off.

"Blah, blah, blah," another friend, Reshma, said brazenly. "We wanna know if you kissed him and how those lips felt against yours."

"No, we wanna know if he's marriage material," said another one of the women. "I'm ready for another big wedding! It's been too long."

Had it been that long ago when they'd all run through a Hindu wedding season? Padma's wedding had been the first of those celebrations among her friends. About five months later, Reshma was married, and her wedding was one for the books. Having the wedding in India created an incredible opportunity for much of their community to go back to the motherland for several weeks that summer. Instead of a week, Reshma's wedding lasted ten full days, with visits to different temples and towns to meet with family and serve as anchor points for more partying. Padma and Raj were able to go to India for the first time together and spent an amazing amount of time there with friends and family. Although it was the wedding of all weddings, Padma was grateful that hers had not been that lengthy or expensive. Instead, she and Raj were able to go on an extended honeymoon to the other side of the world. And that was more important to her than hosting the grandiose style of wedding more customary to many in her community.

After Reshma's wedding, Sejal's wedding came the following week, so they were all ushered back to the States for a week of work and then into another wedding. Luckily, Sejal decided on a smaller venue: only 300 guests with room for about 50 more uninvited guests. They booked a beautiful but reasonable hall for the reception and completed the function in just one day, a more American-style wedding that was certainly moaned over by the Aunties, who do not like to stray from customs. Sejal and her husband were also the first to live together before marriage and purchase a home that was not in a predominantly Indian neighborhood. Suffice it to say, the Aunties usually had lots of comments about Sejal. Padma was grateful for her friend because her non-traditional ways certainly took all the attention away from her, and she was usually more free from scrutiny to push the envelope just a tad. She'd found a balanced place of being authentic to herself while honoring her family and traditions.

Between Raj and Padma's friends and family, they had been to eight more weddings in the past two-and-a-half years. Raj calculated with the amount of money spent on just those weddings, he could have opened his medical clinic. Padma calculated that for the amount of money they spent on attending the weddings, they could have put a nice deposit down on a vacation home at the ocean. Indian weddings are certainly not for the faint of heart. They could have coined the phrase, "Go big or go home." But she knew from her marketing days that the phrase had to do with Harley Davidson motorcycles. If India was to be rivaled by anywhere else in the world regarding going big, it was most certainly America. For many Indians of her generation brought up in the States, the emphasis on American culture, capitalism, and status had managed to upstage much of their heritage and roots. It felt quite natural to, say, wear both a saree and Chanel.

"Tell us about Kevin," Padma practically yelled. "I need to live through you when it comes to dating. My life is pretty fixed on diapers and bottles right now."

"Stop it. You and Raj have the best situation. Sure, with the new baby, you haven't been out lately, but you have so much more happening. I wish I were you," Payal smiled.

Padma recalled a day not that long ago when she felt the same way about Raj's sister, Meeta. She seemed to have it all — career, kids, loving husband, amazing extended family, friends, house and vacations. She and her husband managed to make it all work, and she never seemed to break a sweat.

Meeta was one of the sisters who helped Padma the most when she first had Nina. Then Padma began to notice that it seemed Meeta usually had a cocktail or glass of wine in her hand. Padma took note but didn't want to pry. When Raj mentioned being concerned his sister may be drinking too much, Padma had to come clean that she, too, had been taking notice. When Raj finally spoke to his sister about her drinking, she broke down in his arms. The full life was wearing on her more than she let on, and what started as an evening nightcap to take the edge off continued to escalate into a bottle of wine a day. With Raj and Padma's help, she was now in a program to help her alcohol dependency, but very few family members knew about this. For Padma, this was a cautionary tale not to allow herself to get that far into anxiety and overwhelm herself. Every day, she reminded herself of her sister-in-law's struggles and tried to remind herself to be aware of how she was coping — not that she always was able to have the level of awareness that she felt that she should.

Payal didn't know anything about Padma's worries or anxiety because Padma had not shared any of this with her friend. Convinced that Padma had the perfect marriage and perfect life, Payal had no concept of Padma's stressed mental state. Padma smiled at her friend and encouraged her to spill the beans about Kevin. That was a much more fun conversation to have than her anxieties about motherhood, anyway.

"So, as I was saying, Kevin works at a Tech company in town, he does that keyboard magic I don't understand. But he was easy to talk to and didn't make me feel stupid at all for not understanding his job. He was very sweet. He complimented me on my handbag, which is rare for a guy. I mean, what guy notices your handbag?" Payal continued.

"One that is a thief," one of the women said. They all laughed at her funny comment, except Payal.

"That's not funny. I mean, I don't know the guy. He could be a thief," Payal said, suddenly worried. She always tended to overreact, and her friends knew it, which is why they liked to tease her.

"He could just be a cross-dresser," stated another friend. "That's why he noticed your bag — not that there's anything wrong with that."

Payal threw her hands on her hips, annoyed. "Ladies, you cannot do this to me. Now I think Kevin is a cross-dressing thief! I mean, I don't have an issue with cross-dressing. But with my luck, he'd look better in my clothes than me!"

The girls erupted into laughter at the thought of that, mostly because they could see that story playing out. As they were cracking up, the waitress came over with a round of drinks for the women, compliments of a group of men at the bar. As the waitress pointed in the men's direction, all the women leaned over in unison to see who they were. Nobody recognized any of the four men at the bar. But Payal waved and batted her eyes anyway, then served the ladies each a drink.

"Payal, I am a married woman!" Padma wailed at her friend.

"A thirsty married woman," Payal replied, slipping a drink into her friend's hand. "And so what, you can't accept a drink because you're married? You don't see Reshma having a problem with that."

"Nope," said Reshma, sipping on her free drink.

"Besides, Padma, I waved for us all. If any of them have any interest in any of you, they have to go through me," Payal announced.

It was with mixed emotions that Padma took a sip from the drink. I mean, she needed another one anyway, so...

Once all the women were drinking their drinks, the four men approached them. One of the men was dashingly handsome with a well-groomed beard. He wore a slim-fitting sports coat and an untucked dress shirt with two buttons open for a professional yet comfortable look. His watch revealed he had money but was not from a wealthy family. He seemed confident, but Padma could tell he was doing his best to fit in. She had a way of reading people that had served her well when she worked in marketing and had not lost the gift during her time of Mommying.

The other men were both quite tall with strong features. It was good that tight-fitting clothes were back in fashion for men as they revealed their physiques quite well. These gentlemen had their button-down shirts tucked but with sleeves rolled up, no jacket, and three buttons open. It was muscle mania between all of them, which Padma found captivating. Each time either of them moved an arm in any way, his muscles would bulge so that she wondered if they would rip right out of their shirts. Well, she hoped they would, at least.

Come to find out, the man with the beard was an investor, while the other men were all football players. They were starting a business together using the athletes as the face of the business. They'd just signed a lease and were out celebrating, and it was beginning to feel like quite the party. Padma was buzzed, she was buzzed to the point that she felt perhaps she'd had one too many drinks to be a responsible adult who was still nursing a baby. Her norm these days was not to drink alcohol at all, but now that she was out and having fun, she sort of lost count. And suddenly, she had a feeling that this was all a pretty bad idea.

Padma excused herself to go to the restroom, where she took a few moments to sit in the stall and determine just how much she had had to drink. She must have fallen asleep on the toilet because she soon awoke to someone knocking on the stall door, asking if she was okay. Padma collected herself, greeted the woman outside the stall with a smile, washed her hands, and headed back out of the bathroom, where she was greeted by one of the football players, Melvin.

"Hey, there you are," he said in a concerned sort of way.

Padma gave him a weak smile and tried to get Payal or the other women's attention. But it appeared they had moved further away toward the back of the bar.

"Ah, yes. Here I am," Padma said, laughing awkwardly.

"You were gone a bit. I wanted to make sure everything was okay," Melvin said.

Padma nodded. Melvin smiled at her and put his hand on her shoulder.

"Are you sure? You look like you need to sit down or…" Melvin began, but Padma quickly interrupted him by slipping out from under his large, strong hands, just so he wouldn't get the wrong idea.

"Yes, yes, thank you for asking. It's just I have a new baby at home, and I am quite tired. She doesn't always sleep through the night and cries a lot. And I am just pretty wiped out between her and my other daughter." Padma laughed nervously. "Truthfully, I sat down in there and fell asleep."

Melvin laughed with Padma.

"I get it. My wife just had our second child, and there are times I come home long enough to say hello before she falls asleep, face-planted in her dinner."

Just then, another one of Melvin's partners walked up to them to tell Melvin that he was about to leave. Padma watched Melvin put his hand on his shoulder the same way he had hers. Suddenly, Padma felt more at ease. Melvin was just a touchy guy and also, coincidentally, a new dad. He was married. He was out celebrating work. He was not flirting with her. She had misread the situation because she was brutally out of practice. But that made her pause.

Wait, he's not flirting? Padma found herself somewhat upset about that. But this was a typical reaction because her emotions were just all over the place these days. She didn't know what she wanted from anyone at any time anymore — and that even included herself.

"Come on," said Melvin, placing his hand on her shoulder again, "let's get you back to your friends. Maybe it's time to call it a night."

Padma smiled and followed his lead back to her friends, who were all enjoying good conversation at a booth. She watched as they all talked lively and laughed. They each seemed at ease and happy. Payal was receiving attention from one of the men, which made Padma muse if her friend remembered who Kevin was now. She hoped her friend would play the field a bit and enjoy dating and being single. But she knew that the first guy to show enough interest in making her his wife would be it for Payal.

Although Melvin had hinted that it might be time to call it a night, they all continued to hang out. Glasses clinked, and more laughter ensued. And before she knew it, a glance at Padma's phone revealed it was shockingly 1:30 am. That was not good. This meant little to no sleep tonight.

"Oh, crap, guys, guys," Padma said, trying to get the word out amid their laughter."

"What's up?" Payal asked her friend.

"It is 1:30 already. I need to get home. The kids will be up in a few hours."

"1:30?!" Said Reshma, laughing. "Oops."

"Wow, I better get home too. My wife is going to kill me, "Said Melvin.

"I think I'll call an Uber. I'm way past being responsible," Padma admitted. "Anyone want to share?"

The other ladies had shared a ride, and the designated driver was good to go. So, Padma was the only one needing a ride. They all hugged and said their goodbyes, and Padma stepped outside to check her phone for a better signal to call an Uber when Melvin stepped out.

"Hey, did you already call for a ride?" He asked.

"No, but I was just about to," Padma smiled and nodded her head. "Just hand me my responsible mom award now."

"Well, if you like, I can drop you off instead of hiking it back with a stranger. My wife would kill me if she knew I let a friend do that."

"Well, she's gonna kill you for being late anyway, "Padma laughed, realizing she was pretty drunk."

"Okay, let's get you home. Besides, someone else has to enjoy this beautiful limo with me since my buddies have decided to hit another late-night party, and I am about two hours past my bedtime already. And ain't nobody gonna let me sleep in at home tomorrow morning now."

"Well, if your wife kills you and you're dead, you can certainly sleep then," Padma said, laughing even more.

Melvin chuckled, "You got that right." He then opened the limo door and motioned for Padma to get in first.

Once they were inside the limo, she managed to give his driver her address, and the two headed home. Padma decided, in her infinite drunken wisdom, to try and make normal conversation.,

"So, Melvin, tell me more about this business venture, your organization?"

"Ah, yes. Well, when I stopped playing football, which is a crazy sport, ya know? When I stopped, I needed something else to keep myself busy. So, I started mentoring kids as a Big Brother. This was before we had our kids, and I was raised to help people by a single mother who just went out of her way for me and my friends. Anyway, I spent time with the Big Brothers Big Sisters organization, and I liked it a lot. But then I started to feel like I could do even more. I started talking to people — mostly other former football players, and I created a foundation, and then we started fundraising. And our whole goal is to assist underprivileged kids to first find their passion in life. Then, once they have a goal, we either help them to go to school or learn that trade. And in the end, all we ask is their commitment to giving back to the community in their way."

"Wow, that is amazing. You must feel so fulfilled doing that kind of work."

"More than football, I can tell you that."

"Wow, I won't tell my husband you said that because he might just cry if he knew that. He loves football."

"It wouldn't be the first time I saw that happen," Melvin replied, and then they both began laughing until Padma felt a pain coming on.

"Oh man, you know what, Melvin, I just may kill myself tomorrow morning. I think I'm gonna have a raging headache!"

"Well, I hope you don't, but I'd bet you do. In my younger days, I'd chase it with a Bloody Mary before going to bed," Melvin confessed.

"Really? I think I just usually throw up!"

With that, both Melvin and Padma laughed even more. And the laughter was kind of starting to hurt her head.

There was a striking familiarity with Melvin, and It felt as though they'd known each other for most of their lives. The friendly feeling was mutual.

When they reached the house, Melvin walked Padma to the door and introduced himself to Raj, who nearly passed out from the sight of Melvin. Unbeknownst to Padma, Melvin was kind of a big-deal NFL player on Raj's favorite team. But this was one part of their lives that Padma and Raj had managed to keep somewhat separate, as she didn't love watching sports. Raj's guy crush was fun to witness and also allowed her buzzed state from drinking to go mostly unnoticed.

"Well, I'd better let you two go. But Padma, you have my number, so call anytime. And Raj, if you want to ever sneak out and watch a game, you let me know."

"You just may regret giving us your number," said Padma jokingly. "And I'd love to meet your wife sometime. Maybe the four of us can have dinner?"

"Sounds perfect. I'll talk to my better half and get back to you on that. Speaking of which, I'd better get home…"

"…before she kills you," Padma finished his sentence.

Melvin smiled at his new friend, shook Raj's hand, and headed off to his own home.

The entire ride home, Padma had done her best to ignore how drunk she was. Now that she was standing on her front porch, suddenly, her entire world began to spin. As Melvin drove out of sight, Padma turned to her handsome husband and promptly puked into his arms.

Planting Yogic Seeds

"A seed knows how to wait… a seed is alive while it waits." — Hope Jahren.

Why did it sound like she was underwater? Slowly, the sound became louder as Padma regained full consciousness. She awoke in bed with a pounding headache. Raj was not in their room, but she could hear laughter in the distance, which hurt her head even more.

After grabbing a Tylenol, Padma rounded the corner of the kitchen to witness her husband bouncing the baby while making funny noises at Nina. Nina's infectious little laugh made Padma laugh out loud, notifying her family that she was awake. Nina giggled and waved for her to come and sit with them. Raj kissed his wife on the cheek and promptly handed her the baby.

"I did my best, but I think she may want you now."

The baby seemed quite contented. And anyway, Padma was not about to breastfeed her this morning. Raj had already taken care of the morning feeding, but suddenly, Padma was aware that she had not pumped the night before. Her breasts were engorged with milk to the point of bursting. So, with a swift motion, Padma swirled around and headed for the nursery to relieve the pressure on her breasts.

As Padma pumped the extra breast milk and the baby sat quietly nearby, she had time to review the previous evening. At first, it felt good to be out with her friends, away from the never-ending story of motherhood. Yet she'd caught herself several times wondering what her family was doing at home and if everyone was okay without her.

So, was she happy being out with her friends like she thought she would be? Maybe? She needed some time away from home for her mental health. Was the confusion of extreme love for her children and an equal loathing of what motherhood was that difficult to manage? Yes, sometimes it felt so. But to the point of puking up alcohol? Padma certainly didn't like how she felt, but it all caught up with her quickly last night. She reminded herself that one night out was not a drinking problem and chalked it up to blowing off steam not to be repeated. But it was not lost on her that she needed to find a healthier way to cope with these postpartum mood swings and anxieties. And she needed to find a better way to manage her stress.

Padma was lost in these thoughts when Raj peeked into the nursery. "Hon, you have a call. It's Melvin checking up on you."

Padma smiled, suddenly recalling her new friend from last night and their short but significant connection — as if they'd known each other in another lifetime or something. Raj handed Padma the phone and stepped back out of the room.

"Hello, Melvin. Wow, I need to thank you for last night. I don't know what happened. I never really drink like that, especially since the girls."

"Oh, listen, I just wanted to make sure you were okay today. I know what having one too many feels like," Melvin admitted. "And I gave Raj my hangover remedy for you. He will probably be coming back in with it momentarily."

"Oh, please tell me it's not a Bloody Mary," Padma winced.

"Oh no. No more alcohol. It's entirely herbal, I promise you."

"Thank you. I appreciate that because I could certainly use a little remedy this morning." Padma paused, then continued, "Hey, Melvin, can I ask you a question?"

"Anything," Melvin replied.

"After your wife had the second baby, was she, I don't know, overly emotional? Anxious or depressed even?" Padma revealed her question with surprising candor. It felt good to let it out, and for some reason, to a new friend that she thought she could trust and not be judged by.

Melvin laughed raucously, "Oh, are you kidding me? Good Lord, I never know what woman I am coming home to. She is up, then really down. But we both know what we are dealing with. She still works closely with the doula who helped birth the babies and our yoga teacher, who specializes in prenatal and postpartum yoga. So, I know she is in good hands as she rides the hormonal waves out. And I do my best not to piss her off and to be supportive."

Chuckling, Padma asked, "I'm sorry, what's a doula?"

"My wife and I had alternative birth plans. We had both children at home with a midwife. This allowed my wife to have a more relaxing birth in the comfort of her home. And the birth doula supports a birthing person through labor and delivery. Then there's a Postpartum doula who supports the family, and particularly the birthing person, in the first few months after birth. We do it all!"

"Wow, I never heard of a doula before or any of this. Of course, I know about midwives, but I've thought of them as pre-western medicine. You know, I married a doctor, and his parents are doctors, so I just went with what they told me," Padma said.

"Well, we found them to be incredibly helpful, especially with understanding the postpartum period and all the things that go along with it. Don't get me wrong, we love Western medicine, but in our limited experience and opinion, these folks usually lack certain ongoing support once the baby is born. My wife and I researched things together, and it made sense to us."

"Wow. I wish I had known about doulas when I was pregnant."

"Well, I'm sure the babies are fine, and you made the best decision you could with the information that you had at the time. Luckily for me, my mother's friend is a midwife, so I knew about this for a long time, and there was no way that my mother was going to let us have a baby without at least talking to her friend Betty about it. And look, it's always about the baby — and it should be, but as my wife likes to remind me, she was the one who carried that baby for nine months and then pushed something the size of a melon out of a pea-sized hole."

Padma snorted and laughed, "Yup, that's about right."

"Anyway, I'm talking your ear off here about us. I'm sure Raj took great care of you and still is."

That was a fair enough statement, and yet, there were more questions that Padma had.

"Melvin, do you think I can get the number of your doula? I may want to talk to her."

"Sure, I'll text it right over to you. And if you don't already do yoga, you may want to consider that. Yoga has helped Melanie's body recover from the trauma of birthing babies. It gives her another tool supporting a positive mind and emotional state. I don't have to tell you how up and down you might feel from moment to moment."

Padma furled her eyebrows, somewhat confused.

"Yoga is just stretching, right? How does yoga help with a positive attitude?"

Padma knew enough that yoga had originated in India but didn't know much about it. As she pondered the thought longer, a distant memory of her grandmother, her Nani, practicing yoga or meditation or something like that came to her. But for some reason, she was having trouble recalling much about that story.

"Well, I don't know how it all works, to be honest," Melvin revealed. "All I can say is that it does. When I got drafted into the NFL, our team practiced yoga twice a week during the off-season as part of our conditioning regimen. So, when I was talking to the guys about expecting our first baby, our yoga teacher overheard and told me to check out prenatal yoga for my wife. So then Melanie started going to yoga. We both love it, although maybe for different reasons. While it does help me calm my mind when I am stressed, I enjoy the physicality of it and how it balances me out."

"You know, I think my grandmother did yoga, but I don't seem to know anything about it, and I'm Indian. Here you are, this big athlete, and you do yoga, and the brown girl over here's got nothing!" Padma joked, and they both laughed.

As Padma chatted with Melvin, Raj popped back with a blended drink in hand for Padma — Melvin's hangover cure.

"Thanks, hon. What is this?" Asked Padma.

"You shouldn't really ask that and just drink it," Raj replied.

Melvin laughed, "Yeah, maybe just drink it and trust us."

Padma handed the phone to Raj so that he could chat with Melvin while she drank his hangover remedy. She wasn't quite sure what it tasted like. It was red, but it also had a thick taste to it, and maybe a little, hmm, was that ginger? Honestly, she really couldn't figure It out and decided to stop trying. If it worked, she would just be even more grateful to Melvin, who seemed to be her guardian angel of the moment.

Padma was feeling relieved about the potential of talking to the postpartum doula about her mood swings. But the more she thought about practicing yoga, the more questions she had for her mother about her grandmother's yoga practice. For some reason, she couldn't get it out of her mind, which was now clear thanks to Melvin's miracle hangover cure. So later that day, when she had a moment, she called her mother to talk more about it.

"Hello, Padma, my love. How are my grand-babies doing today?" Padma's mother said in her heavy Hindi accent that Padma always found comforting.

"Mama, the babies are doing good. Very good," Padma replied with pride. There was no sense discussing the baby's sometimes crying tantrums with her mother, who would not understand or want to talk about any unpleasantries anyway. Padma was told that she had been a perfect baby who had slept through the night from the beginning and was a good girl most of her life. She could not remember a time when she had yelled or even spoken out of turn. Good Indian girls do not do that, after all.

"Good, good. I want to come by next week once your father's chess tournament is over. He has been using the car every day. I miss my babies. I miss my Padma," she said sweetly.

Having her parents close enough to come by for visits, yet not in the same town, had worked out very well for Raj and Padma. It gave them just enough space to not be constantly inundated. Of course, she loved her parents unconditionally and would always welcome them to her home. But it was nice to have the buffer. Even Raj's family seemed to understand their boundaries when it came to just dropping by unannounced. Now, understand that they still came by often, quite often. But at least they had the wherewithal to call beforehand.

"Mama, I have to ask you a question," Padma replied in earnest. "Nani, she practiced yoga every day, yes?"

"Yes," Padma's mother hesitantly replied.

She paused to allow for any further commentary, but none came forth from her mother.

"So, how come you never practiced it? And why didn't I learn yoga?"

Padma's mother made an air bubble sound with her lips. She waited a moment more, and yet still no response from her mother, who was avoiding the questions.

"Mommy, is there a reason why we never did yoga with Nani?" Padma pleaded to her mother.

After a long, audible sigh, Padma's mother replied, "It's nothing. Nothing to say. Nani liked to do yoga, she…uh…"

Suddenly, Padma was struck by the fact that her mother was hiding something. She had hit a cord with her mother. And that made her want an answer to these questions even more than before. She pressed on, but gently.

"Mommy?"

"It's like, we do not talk about these things, Padma. Nani did yoga, and we do not, and that is why."

"That is why?" Padma replied, confused.

"Yes, Padma, that is why. We do not — do yoga. The end. And I have to go to get dinner ready, so I will see you and the babies next week. I will call you then. Bye-bye."

And then she hung up.

She just hung up.

Shock is a lesser word than what Padma was feeling. Sure, her mother was good at redirecting conversations away from potential conflict or Padma's feelings the few times she had tried to express them. But her mother had never reacted this way before. It was not like her to shut down a conversation in such a way. Yet, had she ever really pressed her before? As an only child, she could not look to any siblings for answers. Padma was faced with an inquiry about her health and well-being in which yoga might be a supportive measure, yet her mother shut down discussing it.

Now, Nani was her mother's mother, but perhaps her father had some insights into the situation that her mother was, for whatever reason, unwilling to discuss. But she knew that she would have to wait until after her father's chess tournament was over. Right about now, he was reading and practicing all of his moves every minute of the day. Last year, Daddy had come in second place, and other than the grand-babies, chess was about the only other thing he could think or talk about the entire year. No, she would have to wait to bring it up to him. And just like that, not knowing this little family intrigue was consuming her.

This little family mystery proved to be a fantastic distraction for Padma from her everyday mother-of-two doldrums. That night, as she slept, Padma dreamt about her mother and their conversation.

"We don't do yoga," her mother said again in the dream. Then smoke filled the room, and when it dissipated, Nani was there in place of her mother, sitting with her legs crossed and her eyes closed in deep contemplation.

Padma walked up to her grandmother and attempted to awaken her, but she had no response. And then, quite slowly, Nani began to levitate up off the floor until she was hovering several feet above it. Padma slid her hand under her grandmother to prove that she was, in fact, fully levitating—no strings or lifts. Nani had a serene and contented smile. Even though she was right there, she seemed to be also quite far away.

As she began to sit in front of Nani to mimic her posture, Padma's mother grabbed her by the arm and tugged her up and away. When she looked back, Nani was dissolving further and further away until she was no longer in view.

Padma looked at her mother, who simply repeated, "We don't do yoga."

Yet evidently, some of them did.

The Plot Thickens

"With a secret like that, at some point, the secret itself becomes irrelevant. The fact that you kept it doesn't." — Sara Gruen.

This family "secret" regarding her grandmother's yoga practice had lit a fire under Padma that she had not felt since she ran her last successful ad campaign. So after Raj left for work and her morning routine of feeding the girls, cleaning, and starting the laundry was complete, Padma dove into the archives of her family photos. She knew that she had some pictures of her grandmother somewhere. But she could not remember exactly the nature of the photos or even where she had stashed them. When she sat to think about it, she had a very vague memory of what her grandmother even looked like, having only spent time with her maybe twice when she was a little girl. Her grandparents died when she was very young, and from that point on, Padma's family rarely ever brought them up. As a kid, she was good with that. She had her things going on, and soon, the memory of her grandparents slipped into the distant past. Suddenly, however, she felt like she needed to understand her roots better, particularly because there may be a tie-in to a practice that could help her feel better.

She pulled another box down from the second-floor storage closet. "Ah-ha," she said out loud. That was the box she had been looking for. Among her Girl Scout badges and soccer trophies, several handfuls of black and white photos were grouped and secured with white lacy ribbons. She remembered the day that her mother went to throw the photos out. Uma had told her daughter that she didn't want to remember sad things, and since her family was all gone, she didn't want the reminder of them with the photos. Padma asked her mother if she could keep them, and Uma passed them along to her daughter, who neatly tied special ribbons around them and placed them in this keepsake box, never to be opened again until today.

One by one, Padma unraveled the packs of photos to flip through them. The first batch appeared to be random photos in no particular order or reference. Who the people were in the photos was completely lost on Padma. She neatly retied the ribbon and went to the next bundle. This went on until Padma finally came to the right bundle.

There, hidden with photos of unknown people, were two photos of Nani: one of Nani and Uma at her parent's wedding and the other of her kneeling at the feet of a man whose face had been cut out of the photo. Padma had no idea who the man was, but she knew it was not her grandfather. What her grandmother was doing was confusing to Padma, but she had a feeling that it may hold some relevance. She didn't know why. She just did.

Padma pulled the photos out and put them on her dresser so that she could bring them back out when her mother came to visit. She understood that was a risky endeavor since her mother hadn't wanted to see the photos again, but it seemed necessary nonetheless.

After she had found the only photos she had of Nani, Padma found another bit of time later that evening after dinner, and once

Rajesh was home to help out, she retreated to the office so she could do some research on the computer.

A quick search revealed that there were two yoga studios in Padma's little town: a hot yoga studio and a Hatha yoga studio. Hot yoga sounded, well, uncomfortable. She already felt like a hot, sweaty mess most days, so why pay to bring about more suffering? The other studio appeared to be interesting enough. They offered a beginner's package where you pay for one class and get the second one free. And they described themselves as offering many modifications for beginners in their all-level classes. And bonus, there was even a beginner meditation series that was about to start in a week.

Padma sat back in the office chair and made an air-burp sound with her lips. If she went forward with the yoga thing, would she be going against the wishes of her mother.? Yet, her mother was not forthcoming with any significant reason as to why they did not "do" yoga, and without any particular reason, Padma felt there was nothing concrete to preclude her from, well, "doing" yoga.

She tapped her fingers on the desk a bit more, puckering her lips out and in several times. Padma was deep in thought when Raj peeked his head into the office.

"Can I help you with something, hon?" He asked.

Padma shook her head. She was still deep in thought.

"Ah, you are doing that thing you do when you are focused, in the zone, and onto something," he said.

Padma turned to him and smiled. "I have a thing?"

"Yeah," he said, walking to his wife and planting a deep, wet kiss on her lips, then continuing, "You are very sexy when you are in this zone."

"Hah," Padma laughed. "Sexy is something I do not feel much of these days, not with dripping boobies and hair that hasn't been washed in six days."

Raj leaned over and planted another deep kiss on his wife. This one stirred something within her that had not been awakened since just after they conceived baby number two. Agh, and just like that, with the thought of the new baby, the moment of excitement was over.

Padma leaned back and wiped her lips. Raj smiled. He understood this as his window now being closed. Truth? That window was closed a lot these days. But he understood it all too well. He correctly thought it best to change the subject.

"So, what are you into?" Raj asked inquisitively as he shifted the uncomfortable urge that had risen in his trousers so that he could sit on the edge of the desk.

The move was not lost on Padma, although she pretended not to notice. Having children helps you pretend not to notice lots of things that you don't want to deal with. Perhaps she'd learned that from her Mother.

"So, I was talking to Melvin, and he told me that his wife, among some other things..." Padma decided not to reveal the midwife or doula stuff at this time. That was for a later discussion. She continued, "...she does yoga, and that it helps her with her mood and emotions."

"Really!" Raj said a little too enthusiastically.

"Really," Padma concurred, noticing Raj's interest. "And so, I remembered that my Nani used to do yoga. I don't remember seeing her do it, but I remembered something about her and yoga."

Raj was nodding, listening intently.

"So, I asked my mother about it..." Padma stopped deep in thought, keeping Raj hanging, but he couldn't take it. After a long pause, he interjected, "And?" which brought Padma back into focus.

"Oh, and she didn't want to talk about it. She just told me that Nani did yoga, and we do not do yoga."

Raj seemed confused. "And when you asked her why?" he probed.

"Yeah, see, that's the weirder thing. I asked her why, and she said, 'We don't do yoga, that's why'."

Raj laughed. "That isn't an answer."

"I know!"

Raj folded his arms into his chest. He was also up for a little puzzle-solving. Truthfully, they both loved a good mystery; it was one of the things that brought them together. He recalled the days they'd gone to escape rooms together. And then that reminded him of the time that they had sex in one room, not realizing that they were on camera. This thought revitalized the urge in his trousers again, causing him to re-shift. Again, this was not lost on Padma, who was now confused about the timing of this new arousal. Another thing best to ignore, she thought.

"So, what are you thinking about that?" Raj asked, trying to shift attention away from himself.

"I don't know. There's something my mother isn't telling me. We don't talk about difficult things, so there is a hidden story there. What it is, I don't know. It's not like I have a lot of people to ask. I don't have a big family like you," Padma said.

"Your dad?"

Padma nodded her head, "Yeah, gonna do that after his chess tournament next week. Mom said she was coming by, and I was going to reach out to him, and then I was going to probe her more. I even found a couple of pictures of my grandmother."

Padma picked up the two photos she had found and handed them to her husband. He looked at the first one and smiled, then slid it under the second one with the cut-out person.

"Hmm," he said.

"Hmm," Padma replied.

"Who's that?" Raj asked, pointing to the man with the cut-off head that Nani was at the feet of.

"Indeed, who's that?" Padma replied with a judgmental tone.

Raj and Padma sat nodding their heads in unison, Padma puckering her lips in and out.

"Well, whoever it is was probably her Guru," Raj said, handing the photo back to Padma in a very matter-of-fact way.

Looking at her husband, Padma paused and then looked back at the photo, "Her Guru?" She asked.

"Yeah, well, she is bowing at a man's feet, that is a traditional *pranam*, where out of respect, one bows to his teacher and touches the teacher's feet."

Padma was surprised, although she shouldn't have been. Rajesh was well-traveled and understood a plethora of things, in addition to being a handsome, life-saving doctor. That still did not make her want to have sex with him right now, but it was never bad to remind herself what she loved about him.

"Really?!" Padma said in a way that showed she had learned a deep and significant truth.

Did Nani have a Guru? And does this have something to do with why her mother did not want to talk about yoga? Does having a Guru have anything to do with yoga at all? The plot was certainly thickening.

Raj changed the subject back to Melvin. "So Melvin brought up yoga for you, huh?"

"Well, he suggested that since it had helped his wife, it might be something I would want to look into," Padma said. "He does yoga too. He said that his whole team had done yoga."

"Really?!" Raj said the same way Padma did when she learned a deep, significant truth.

"Really," Padma said, then started giggling.

"What?" Raj asked.

"Hah, I think you have a man crush on Melvin," she teased her husband.

"And what if I do?" He said.

And with that, Padma could hear the baby starting to stir on the monitor, so she stood up, kissed her husband, and began to walk away. Without turning, she replied, "I like it. It means Melvin and I can be friends."

"After Melvin and I," Raj yelled as Padma disappeared around the bend.

That evening, Padma had another yoga dream. In this one, she and Raj were practicing yoga with Melvin and his teacher. Raj insisted on practicing next to Melvin, so Padma took a literal backseat and practiced behind them both. Raj kept watching Melvin and doing what he did. Padma seemed to move instinctively as if she already knew what to do somehow. In one posture, although she was looking down, Padma saw a man's feet step up in front of her. It was the same foot as in the picture with Nani. It was even in black and white. Padma slowly began to pick her gaze up, noticing the bare leg and up to the small cloth he wore around his waist. But when Padma started to look at his head, it was cut off, just like in the photo.

Padma shot up straight in bed. Her sudden movement as her dream came to an abrupt stop did nothing to shake Raj. The man slept like a woman who had just given birth to quintuplets. She shrugged it off and got out of bed, slipping into the nursery to check in on the baby and to Nina's room to watch her little girl sleep.

Nina slept deeply, like her father, and most likely as she had when she was a little girl herself before there were babies and motherly responsibilities. Her little snore was adorable, and Padma gently blew her daughter kisses and blessings for nothing but happiness and love to come her way.

As she did this, she was struck by a memory of her grandmother, who had snuck into her bedroom one night to share a mantra that would bring her good luck, abundance, and joy if she sang it. Nani taught her this sacred Sanskrit phrase. Padma closed her eyes, trying to recreate the mantra, but it seemed lost in the fog of the past. She hummed, then stopped, then changed the pitch, hummed, then stopped. Even as much as she did, she could not remember the sacred phrase that Nani taught her to chant. She could barely remember that she had even forgotten it.

The mantra seemed like another important piece of this puzzle that Padma was trying to put together about yoga, her mother, and Nani. If it wasn't the middle of the night, with a baby about ready to wake up and be fed, Padma would have hopped back on the computer to do more searching. But for tonight, it would have to wait. Tomorrow was another day, and Padma couldn't wait to do her best to crack the codes to the mysteries that she'd found her family involved in.

There's a New Sherlock in Town

"I'm not a stalker...I'm just an unpaid private investigator." - Unknown.

The yoga studio appeared to be harmless enough. Padma watched as many smiling people walked in and out. She sat with the stroller at a nearby cafe, watching. One by one, and sometimes in small groups, people seemed to bounce into the studio excitedly and then eventually exited, all smiling. She was trying to get a feel for why her mother may not like the family to do yoga. As she watched all the different people come and go, she couldn't find one that did not seem joyful as they left. And anything that made people happy couldn't be a bad thing, could it?

She had sat there for two hours, chores be damned, as the baby slept. Nina had gone with one of Rajesh's sisters on a playdate, which gave Padma the ability to sneak out with the sleeping baby. Each time the baby wiggled or made a noise, Padma would gently rock the stroller back and forth, lulling her back to sleep. It was working, and she found herself thinking she should hang out at the cafe with the stroller more often.

In between watching the clients come and go to yoga, Padma scrolled through the studio's website on her cellphone. She recognized the teacher named Ashanti. She was tall and thin, with wild dreadlocked hair, wearing a flowing shawl that not so much as hid her beautiful, most likely non-mommy body but somehow accentuated it. Padma twisted her lips as she watched Ashanti hug a few people as they came into the studio with her. All the people looked so cute. Padma paused to notice what she had managed to throw on for today's P.I. excursion. Of course, sunglasses and baseball cap aside, Padma did have on black leggings, mostly because they were the only comfortable things she could wear these days as the baby fat hung to her like sap on a tree. Above her waist was an actual atrocity. Padma did not even match. Yes, it's difficult to imagine what does not go with black leggings, yet somehow Padma managed to find the one thing that did not, and unbeknownst to her, baby spit-up ran down her unevenly buttoned-up front. She was a total mom mess. This was her life.

Padma looked up to once again judge herself compared to the well-color-coordinated people who came in and out of the yoga studio. They must have worked hard on those outfits, she thought. She couldn't even remember the last time she had put thought into creating an outfit. Comfort was about her only concern. Well, comfort and coverage, because right now she did not like very much about her body, least of which was her constantly full and leaking breasts. Why they were a fascination to Raj, she couldn't even consider.

Once the class was in session, Padma decided to walk by the front windows of the yoga studio to get a closer look. She took her time, going slowly, and used the baby as an excuse to park right outside the front window. As she bent over to look in the stroller, pretending to care for her infant, she turned her head, peeking inside. She could see the hardwood floor of an expansive room. Ashanti stood in front of the room, flanked by two plants on either side of her and what appeared to be an altar behind her. The yoga mats were lined up in two rows with ample spacing between them. Everyone but the teacher was seated in the same yogic posture Nani had been seated in the dream. Although their backs were to her, she imagined their eyes closed in meditation. Ashanti walked around the room, waving her hands through the air as she spoke and occasionally placing them on someone's shoulders and appearing to massage them. What she was saying was another mystery. But soon, they began to all move and stand.

Padma managed to watch the class for some time before Ashanti finally looked directly at her, smiled, and waved. Realizing that she had been caught standing there gawking at the class, Padma shrieked and went running forward, jerking the baby's stroller and waking the baby, who then began to cry. She dashed off to tend to her in the car and to make her way home. In the time she watched the class, however, it looked interesting, like a meditation in movement. Each student stepped here or there, moved the arms this way or that, and Ashanti walked the room, offering brief but what looked like very intentional adjustments to the students. Padma was struck by the serenity and joy in the faces of the students as they practiced. She could see why Melvin and his wife enjoyed yoga classes. And this stumped her even more over why her mother was so deeply against this practice for her.

She would continue to ponder these and other questions regarding the yoga mystery until several days later when her mother called to let her know that she would be by in two days. This was perfect. It gave Padma enough time to reach out to her father to pick his brain before her mother's visit. She knew that she needed to call him at just the right time, when her mother was out running errands and not home, to intercept the call so that he would be more free to talk to her about her dreaded yoga stuff.

And so, the following day, she managed to catch her father at such a time.

"Hi, Daddy! Congratulations," Padma said in the sweetest voice she could find.

"Ah, I came in second place again! Can you believe it? Again, I lost to this Charles Danning man. This is his fourth consecutive victory. They should not let him into the tournament anymore. It is making it so nobody wants to do it anymore," her father said in his lilting British accent. Padma doubted this was the case and more a factor of her father's bruised ego. But that was not important this morning. Right now, she needed to butter him up for deeper inquisitions.

"Oh, Daddy, I know you played extremely well. You gave this Charles man a run for his money," she said lovingly.

"No, he beat me quite clearly and in eight moves. I never saw it coming," her father said frankly.

"Well, there's always next year."

"Yes, yes," said her father. "Next year."

Padma could not fane excitement about chess any longer. She needed to know what he knew about yoga and Nani. The question fell out of her mouth before she even knew it.

"Daddy, why does Mommy not want us to do yoga?"

Silence came from the other end of the phone.

"Daddy?" questioned Padma.

"Yes, yes," said her father. "I heard your question. Padma, why does this matter to you? Did your mother not explain that you don't do yoga, and that is why?"

Had her father given her the same nonsensical answer her mother had? Really? This was not like him. He must have been coached by her mother already.

"Daddy, that is no explanation. That is a statement posing as an answer. I think they call that something." And if she didn't have baby-brain, she could have used the big adult word there for more impact.

Her father took a deep breath, then continued, "This is none of my concern. Frankly, it is not interesting. There is nothing to tell. Let it be."

Ah, "Let it Be," powerful words by another Brit, Padma thought. One that had a lot less to worry about in his life than she had right now.

"Daddy, now you know me better than to tell me to let something be. You know that only makes me want to understand more," Padma said. "I do not mean to be disrespectful, and certainly would not ask if I thought it would hurt Mommy or you, but it just seems so important for me to understand right now. Someone suggested that I try yoga and…"

"Don't do that," her father said, cutting her off. "Don't do that. Mommy would be very upset if you did that."

Did he sound scared?

"Yes, Daddy, but why would Mommy be upset about it? I need to understand this. If you know, you owe it to me to help me to know. I won't stop until I do."

Padma had put her foot down harder than she ever had with her father. She didn't even know she had it in her to be so stern and direct. It must be motherhood that had given her this new, surprising superpower.

"Agh, Padma, okay. I will tell you something, but then you must let it go, and you must not press your mother…"

"…but…" Padma tried to interject.

"…uh, uh, uh. No, if I tell you, then you must respect that, is that okay? You must promise me."

Padma did not want to accept that, but in any argument, there must be a compromise, and she thought to herself, I *can always change my reply later and blame it on my hormones. I am his only daughter, and that is not enough for him to disown me.*

"Of course, daddy." She lied. She was getting better at it as time went on.

What Padma's father told her was, quite frankly, a bit underwhelming by today's standards. She was expecting a much deeper revelation, something intriguing and possibly embarrassing.

"So, Nani was the only woman in her town to be allowed to practice yoga with the men?" Padma asked in confirmation.

"Yes," replied her father.

"And she was devoted to her Guru?"

"Yes."

"And if it wasn't for her arranged marriage, she would have preferred to stay at his ashram instead of performing her duty to marry a man in the village, Grandpa?"

"Yes."

"So it seems like a sad situation for Nani. But she married and raised children with Grandpa. She did perform her duty."

"Yes, but…"

"But…"

There was another long sigh on the end of her father's phone.

"You don't understand, Padma. Those were different times. Your duty was to your family — 100%. To have another man be more important than your husband in your life was not, as you like to say, 'cool.'"

"Okay, I can understand that. I can see where that would be problematic for both of them. Nani's heart was split. But she did what she knew to be right for her family, and she respected Grandpa fully and raised a family with him despite her wanting to be more involved in her spiritual practice. And for Grandpa to feel that her whole heart was not with him despite what she did would be difficult. It's a sad story for both of them."

"Yes, that is true," her father replied.

Padma was torn. Being keenly aware of the misfortunes of many women — some forced into worse situations than marriages against their wishes. Women's rights and voices were meaningful values to her, and she felt strongly that her grandmother had not been allowed to speak her truth for much of her life. And that truth was still being withheld by her mother, who refused to talk about the issue.

"Okay, daddy. I understand where this could be difficult for my grandparents, but why does it make mommy so upset, and to the point that she says, 'We do not do yoga.'?"

"Padma, I am done with this story," her father said. "I do not know your mother's feelings, but I honor her wishes."

And with that, her father changed the subject back to Charles Danning, chess, and the babies, the three things he did want to talk about. Padma, being the well-behaved daughter, did not press any further, at least not that day. But she knew in her heart that she would not accommodate her father's wishes to bury it because it felt important to acknowledge this issue so that her family could heal and move forward.

When Padma told Raj about the conversation that evening, he seemed to understand it better than she did.

"I remember hearing a similar story once about the Guru in a neighboring town. In those times, mostly men did yoga, and women were not allowed. This particular Guru, though, decided to let women practice with the men. Now, the men, they didn't like it very much. But this made him even more popular with the women, who flocked to stay at his ashram and to serve him. The unfortunate part was that this particular Guru used that for his gain and became abusive, forcing himself on the women sexually. Because they trusted him completely, they continued to go along with his advances and did not talk about it. That was, until one day, many years later, when a new woman came to the Ashram and refused his advances. When she left, his abuse was finally revealed. And you know what they did?" Raj asked.

Padma leaned forward towards Raj, mouth open.

"What they did was remove the women from the ashram, and then all the men came back to practice with this Guru," Raj finished.

"What? Wait, were charges brought against him?" Padma asked.

"No, as far as I know, he continued to teach the men until he died. And, even then, many of the women came to his funeral and wept for him. It was quite a twisted affair."

Padma sat back, considering all of this.

"Do you think something like this could have happened to my Nani?" She asked her husband.

Raj bobbled his head a moment. "Well, it is possible. Or it is possible that this and similar stories got out to the many towns and that any Guru who had allowed women into the ashram's credibility was then questioned with regards to women. It could be that your grandmother's teacher didn't do anything inappropriate but that he was perceived as doing so because of the wrongdoings of another teacher."

Considering her family's consistency about not talking about anything difficult, this could be the reason her mother did not want to discuss yoga and how she had misconstrued what was happening with her mother and her guru. Again, it only made her feel sad for Nani and her family. And it made her want to fix the issue with her mother by mending the misunderstanding.

"You know, you can't change the way your mother feels if this is so," Raj said.

"I know," Padma replied in a knee-jerk way.

"Do you?" Raj smiled at his wife. "Why am I doubting that you do?"

Padma wrinkled up her nose at him. He knew her all too well.

"But if I have the chance to try and make her understand it was incorrect thinking…"

Raj stopped his wife, "We don't know if it is or not. Could he have been an abusive Guru? Yes. Could it have been a misunderstanding of another Guru? Yes. And how could you ever know the truth now anyway? He is gone, your grandmother is gone. All that remains is your mother, and your relationship with her is the most important. You could consider stopping chasing this story. Perhaps, as your father said, it is time to let it go."

Frankly, Raj's comments shocked Padma. How could he be so dismissive? The entire story reeked of misogynistic bullshit, and he should know it having seven sisters and a mother of his own.

"Are you kidding me right now?" Padma asked, obviously irked with her husband.

"What?" Raj said. "I am just saying that you don't want to upset your mother any more than she already is about this."

"No," Padma doubted that was the whole truth. "What you don't want me to do is give my grandmother, and possibly the women who were taken advantage of by their Gurus, a voice. You don't want me to go down this rabbit hole of feminine empowerment because it's uncomfortable for you."

"Wow," Raj responded, throwing his hands up in the air. "How can you think that of me? Perhaps Melvin is right; yoga may help you with these mood swings."

"Oh no, you didn't!" Padma said, shooting up from her seat and walking out on her husband. But at the same time, she wondered, was he right? Was this just another time that her hormones had gotten the better of her mental and emotional state? Was she so bored that she was looking for conflict and excitement where there was none? These days, she always second-guessed herself.

That would be the worst argument of their marriage so far. Padma felt horrible, and so did Raj, but neither one wanted to initiate a peace treaty. Raj was deeply hurt by her accusations. Padma was so fired up by the entire story that she felt a deep, unexplainable need to continue to pull it all apart and ultimately make things right for everyone involved.

Padma took the two pictures of her grandmother and framed them together, placing them in the foyer next to the other family photos. She knew her mother would see them tomorrow and most likely have an adverse reaction to them, but she was too fired up to care at the moment. The time for not speaking up was over. The time for giving a voice to women who didn't have a chance to use theirs was at hand. And if Nani was either abused physically by her Guru or mentally by her family, it was time to heal those wounds.

Cupcakes & Family Secrets

"The world isn't all cupcakes and rainbows." **Trolls**, the movie

"Ho'o Pono Pono," said Payal.

Padma looked at her friend, deeply confused. "What's that?"

"It is ancient Hawaiian. It means to make things right," said Payal. "I read it in Cosmo. When something has a bad energy around it, and you want to fix it, you say this prayer, it's like four sentences, like..." Payal needed to check her phone first to verify through a quick search. "Yes, here it is. First, you say, 'I'm sorry,' taking accountability for your part in the situation. Then you say, 'Please forgive me,' obviously asking for forgiveness. Then, 'Thank you,' meaning you are thanking them for the opportunity to learn and grow and be better because of the situation. And then you follow it up with, 'I love you'."

"Wait, so you don't say Ho-popo?" Padma asked.

"No, it's Ho'o-Pono-Pono," Payal clarified, over-articulating the words. You don't have to say that word. Or, maybe you *can* say that word. Or you can say the four sentences."

Padma was more confused. Payal tended to read and not fully comprehend something new, then confuse the entire thing. She decided not to harp on that aspect with her friend.

"Okay. And what does that do?" Padma asked.

"It makes it all right," Payal explained.

Padma blinked her eyes a few times. Was it her mommy's brain, or was Payal not making sense?

"And how does that make it right?"

"It shifts the energy."

Payal seemed quite excited to know this information. "It's like really good too. It works. I did this when Kevin cheated on me, and I really was so mad at him, and I just didn't want to take him back, and so I said those sentences, well, I think I started with 'I love you,' and then I did the others and then, you know, we got back together, and I forgave him, and we were good. It made it all right."

Padma paused, considering how to approach her response.

"Payal, I love your enthusiasm for this, but I think you are confusing what's happening. I mean, how did that make anything right? Kevin, who cheated on you, then broke up with you completely for this other woman."

"Yeah, like eventually he did. But initially, after I said the Ho'o Pono Pono, we got back together and worked things out."

Padma blinked her eyes some more as if somehow that would assist her in finding the right words to illuminate the conversation or her friend.

"Payal, you stalked Kevin on social media until he finally blocked you. I fail to see how that set anything right."

"Well, if the Universe felt that we weren't supposed to be together, then I guess mission accomplished," Payal said, smiling, then tapping her fingernails on the kitchen counter.

Just before her mother arrived, Payal had come by to see her and the kids, so she shared the yoga mystery with Payal to get her thoughts on it. Payal's response was to Ho'o Pono Pono it. And while it was a nice thought, she wasn't sure what it meant or exactly how it worked. And she was certain that her friend didn't either.

Padma rubbed her forehead and decided to move on with the conversation because it just wasn't helping. Yesterday, there was no question in her mind that she would confront her mother about Nani and yoga. Today, she was pretty exhausted from the baby being fussy and not sleeping well, leading up to a marathon tantrum. Just when she thought she was making headway and finding a schedule, the baby decided to remind her who was in charge — second to Nina, of course. Today, she wondered if talking to her mother about this family issue was even important or not.

"When was the last time you washed your hair?" Payal asked her friend, a bit disgusted with Padma's appearance.

"Seriously? Do you have any idea...No, of course, you don't. Never mind," Padma said, dismissing her friend and turning to wash the dishes.

"I didn't mean it I just was asking. You are glowing. Full Mommy Glow! Did you want to wash your hair? I can watch the kids if you do." Payal did not know what to say to her friend at this moment. She did, however, feel a growing need to run out the door. She could see the anger and exhaustion in her friend's eyes, and it was not a good look on her.

Then, without warning, Padma threw the dishrag down and began to laugh a full belly laugh that felt simultaneously real and unreal. She looked like a supervillain from a comic universe to Payal. It was either a lack of sleep or hormones, but either way, her friend was certainly in need of assistance. Now she understood why Raj had asked her to stop by.

Wiping hysterical tears from her eyes, Padma continued to giggle, "Oh, man. I honestly don't know if I am happy or sad, pissed or elated. I am just so tired. So. Incredibly. Tired."

Padma folded her arms on the table and collapsed her head down, sighing. Payal did not know what to do for her friend. She felt an overwhelming need to do something. She just did not know what.

"Look," Payal said, patting Padma's head awkwardly, "Why don't I watch the kids and you go lay down upstairs."

Padma did not move or make a sound. Payal put her hands up in the air, confused. Had Padma already fallen asleep? Was she ignoring her? Had she died standing up?

"Padma?" She said.

Slowly picking up her head, Padma gazed, eyes glassed over, obviously half asleep. Payal helped her friend up and to the couch, where she lay down and immediately fell asleep. Payal felt good about that — until the baby started to wrestle around in her bassinet, seemingly uncomfortable. Panicked, she realized she had no actual skills to care for an awake baby. Nina, thankfully, was down for her nap and supposed to be down for...

"Uh-oh," Payal said, realizing Nina was standing next to her, gazing up with a smile.

"Uh-Oh," Nina said, repeating Payal.

"Okay, Okay..." Payal said, shuffling her feet around, looking over her shoulder, and feeling completely inadequate. Nina started shuffling her feet like Payal, giggling, mimicking Payal's funny dance. Padma lay unconscious in the other room. The baby wrestled around as if to awaken at any moment. Nina continued to mimic Payal.

"Oh, Okay, this is fine. This is fine. No, this is better than fine! This is great. We are great," Payal said, trying to convince herself.

"Great," giggled Nina, still shuffling her feet with Payal.

So that they did not disturb her friend, Payal rolled the bassinet out of the room with Nina in tow. She moved them into the kitchen, far enough away from the sleeping mommy monster in the other room. She grabbed Nina and propped her up in the high chair. Nina watched Payal as she searched around the kitchen for something — anything — to help out.

"All right," Payal said, clasping her hands and sitting in front of Nina. "So, what about a snack? Do you want a snack?"

"Cupcake," Nina said, giggling.

"Cupcake? Alright," Payal said, jumping up and moving about the kitchen, searching the counters for any sign of what might look like a cupcake, cake, or any pastry in general. Alas, nothing.

"Okay, Nina, where does mommy keep the cupcakes?"

Nina smiled at Payal, then giggled.

"Ha, Okay. Well, let's try this. If you don't tell me where the cupcakes are, then you won't get any cupcakes?" Payal stood tall, placing her hands on her waist, giving Nina the best stern look she could muster.

Nina, giggling uncontrollably, repeated, "Cupcake!"

Payal began looking in cabinets and drawers, searching for the elusive cupcake. Even in the pantry, there were no cupcakes to be found. She was beginning to think that Nina was messing with her. Was she old enough to do that? Finding a granola bar with chocolate chips in it, Payal rationalized it was the best possible current substitute. Maybe if she sold it the right way, Nina would buy it. Time to bring out all of her best collegiate and corporate marketing strategy — on a toddler with the upper hand.

Bringing Nina the granola bar, Payal said, "Alright, I found something EVEN BETTER than a cupcake! I found you this chocolate chip bar. And it is even yummier and better than any cupcake. So, you know, this is your lucky day because not everyone gets granola chip bars, but you do! You get one, Nina. Because you are a very special girl, and you want to keep being a very special girl, and you want to eat this scrumptious and nutritious snack, and let mommy sleep, and just enjoy it. Because it is so good..."

Payal continued to "sell" Nina on the granola bar. Nina watched and listened with the patience of a senior monk. Then she watched Payal open the granola bar and hand it to her. Nina looked at Payal and the granola bar, then Payal again.

"Cupcake," Nina said, frowning while pushing Payal's hand, along with the granola bar, aside.

The kid was not going to win. Payal knew that as an adult, she had to hold a strong boundary. Plus, there were no cupcakes, or she would have caved and given the kid three already. She was beginning to understand why Padma was so tired. Parenting, it turned out, was exhausting, and she had been playing one for about two minutes.

"But I told you, these are better than..."

"NO!" Shouted Nina at Payal. And then came the tears.

Leaning down to hug her, Payal replied, "No. No, no, no, no, no, no, no, no, no — no. It's okay. It's okay. You don't have to eat this crappy granola shit — Oh..."

Payal jerked her body up and threw her hands over her mouth. Nina wiped her tears from her eyes, looked at Payal, smiled, and added, "Sh-i-T," emphasizing the T.

Payal swirled around with her hands on her head. And then, when she thought it could not get any worse, the baby began to scream. No, scream was not the right word. This was a sound she had never heard a human being make before. Was it coming from the baby? Had a 7th-level demon taken over the body of the baby? Seriously, what the fuck?!

Nina continued using her new favorite word, "shit," demonic sounds spewed from what looked like a baby, and Payal did the only thing she knew how to do. She cried, too. And for a moment, it worked. Nina stopped cursing and watched curiously as Payal cried as if pondering her next move. The baby stopped screeching, seeming to observe Payal. When she realized that they both were intensely watching her, Payal amped up her dramatic cries. She knew that to an adult, they wouldn't have passed for an actual cry. But the toddler and infant either bought it or were thoroughly confused by it. She recalled an acting class that she took fondly, considering that she should have stuck with it instead of quitting. Her parents thought that the class would never be of any use. Hah, she was proving them wrong!

"Hello," came the voice of an angel from the foyer. Payal swirled around just in time for Padma's mother to arrive in the kitchen.

"Payal, dear, hello!" Payal ran to Padma's mother and threw her arms around her.

"Oh, thank goodness you are here, Uma. I have never been so happy to see you — or any adult, ever," said Payal.

"Hmm, is that a compliment?" Padma's mother replied.

"Oh, I am so sorry," Payal said. "It's just, the baby was crying, and Nina was crying, and I was trying to let Padma sleep, and... She paused for a moment, put her hand on her heart dramatically, and took a deep breath. Then she finished with a quivering lip, "...it was just a lot."

Padma's mother looked at her grand-babies, who seemed content and at peace, and then back at Payal, who seemed a wreck.

"Dear, if whatever was happening here was too much, I suggest you stay single and do not have children," Padma's mother said, laughing, then hopped over to Nina with arms outstretched. "Come to Gramma, little one. Gramma has missed you so much. Give me a big kiss."

Nina wrapped her arms around her grandmother, and they both squeezed tight. Payal felt relieved. The baby watched on. When Nina finally let go, she looked at her grandmother and said, "Cupcake," just as cute as possible.

"Cupcake? Now, you know you don't get any cupcakes, Nina. Where are the apples."

Payal snapped her fingers as if she'd just remembered the code to the vault and said, "Apples!"

Padma's mother took an apple out of the refrigerator, cut it into slices, sat down, and ate it with Nina. Nina gladly took the apple slices from her grandmother and chomped on them, smiling. Padma's mother, seeing an open granola bar on the table, asked, "What is this?"

"Oh, I was trying to get Nina to eat something healthier than cupcakes," Payal said.

Chewing with her mouth open, Padma's mother said, "What is healthier than apples?"

Nina took an apple slice into the air and giggled, "Ap-pal."

Padma's mother motioned to Payal, "Come, Payal, sit down with us. Tell me how you are doing. Have you met a nice man yet?"

Payal sat down at the other side of the table. The baby was eerily still, Nina was happily chomping on apples with her grandma, and Padma still slept in the other room. She could relax.

"Well, not quite. Dating is not easy these days," Payal told her.

"Oh, I know. My friend's daughter, Pravi, thought she met a very nice man; they dated for several years, and she was ready to be married, but he was not. Finally, after living together and sharing their lives, they broke things off. Pravi is devastated. I understand he is dating someone else already. I suppose he will string this one on for a few years until she presses him. Boys these days don't want to grow up, be men, and raise families. They want to run around and play. What do they call it, 'Peter Pan'?" Uma's smiled and hummed, "Mm, Mm, Mm."

Payal nodded her head. She could relate to the story of Pravi wholeheartedly.

"That sounds familiar. I went through something like this with my ex, Kevin..."

"Kevin," Padma's mother interrupted her, "That was the boy's name."

"Wait, what? It can't be the same, Kevin, though. My Kevin wasn't living with someone...he..."

Payal stopped talking because the gears in her head were moving faster than her mouth. She was revisiting the many times Kevin had not answered her back, called her at odd hours, made strange excuses for not being able to get together, and the time he had cheated on her. But had he cheated on her? Or had Payal been the one he had cheated on Pravi with? Suddenly, she felt sick to her stomach.

Padma's mother, still chewing with her mouth open, replied, "It is of no concern. Payal, you need to find a nice man. Someone ready to get married and not string you along. Maybe your mother and father could arrange something for you if you are having trouble."

"Arranged marriage? Do they still do that?" Payal asked.

Padma's mother's eyes widened with glee.

"Yes, they do. Not as much as they used to, but certainly in some situations where the children are having trouble finding a partner on their own. And, I am sure if you asked your mother, she has someone in mind already."

Payal was shocked, "Already?"

"Yes. Any good mother already has an option for her child to marry. Most do not need it, but perhaps in your case…"

Mid-sentence Padma appeared, wiping her eyes, smiling. Padma's mother smiled. Payal was relieved again.

"Hey, I was hoping you would sleep more than that," Payal told her friend.

Padma waved her friend aside, "Oh, please, that was the loveliest 10 minutes of rest I've had in a while." And with that, the baby realized that mommy was back and mealtime was upon her, so Padma was back on duty.

A few hours later, once dinner was done and the kitchen was cleaned up, Padma sat down in the living room with her mother. Raj had taken Nina up to read her a story and put her to bed. The baby was quietly sleeping for the moment.

She had decided not to bring up her grandmother or yoga that evening. They were all having a lovely visit, and she figured if it hadn't been an issue up to then, she could let it go now. Perhaps she would revisit it, but suddenly, she felt less fired up about the injustices of her ancestors than she had a couple of days earlier. That's what life can sometimes do to you. Some days, you are just happy to have a 10-minute nap or a nice meal. Perspective. This was one of those days.

Unfortunately, she had forgotten about framing Nani's pictures, including the one where she was kneeling at her guru's feet. And somehow, even though the lights were dimmed, and they had come from the kitchen to the living room, the picture caught her mother's eye, and she went to the accent table where it sat and picked it up.

"Where did you find this?" She asked her daughter, less reactive than Padma thought she would be upon seeing the picture.

"I'm sorry, Mommy. I found that and just wanted to connect to Nani."

After a long, silent gaze at the photos, Uma sat them back to rest on the table and came back to sit by her daughter. She said nothing for some time, deep in thought. Padma enjoyed the silent time and did not press. And when her mother was ready, she began to talk.

"Your Nani was a good mother. She did everything that she needed to do. She made sure that we were fed, we went to school, we were taken care of. She always did well with her children and her family. But."

The "But" hung in the air for what felt like an extended period to Padma, who hung on the very word, awaiting the continuation of the story.

Finally, she continued, "But, her first love, the most significant thing in her life, was her Guru. And no matter what she said or did for us, it was obvious, even though she was silent about it, that her love for her Guru went beyond any other love that she could have for her family."

Padma remained quiet as she listened to her mother talk, for the first time, in this way about her mother.

"One day, it was Hanuman Jayanti, the celebration of the birth of the monkey god, Hanuman. This was a big celebration day at her Guru's temple. My father went to work like every other day, and my mother took us to the temple. It was a lovely day. We chanted together sacred mantras, and we danced together so playfully, and the food, the lovingly created food, just kept coming. It was such a beautiful community event. And I suppose that I was about six or seven at the time, and I just enjoyed all of the activities. It felt very loving and beautiful. I think we all loved it so much that when we came home, it was all that we could all talk about. Nani told us that my father would be tired when he came home and to let him rest. This was not anything new; this was the way things were when my father came home. It was normal to us."

Padma's mother took a long sigh, rubbed her hands together, and paused. Padma reached over and held her mother's hand. They smiled at each other, knowing it was okay to leave the conversation there or to proceed, yet both understood it would be said.

"So, I think I was so very excited about the puja and the celebration that when my father came home, I just wouldn't stop talking about it. And my father went a little crazy. He started yelling at all of us." Uma paused again, and Padma gave her the space to continue.

"My mother sent us all to bed. All night long, I heard him yelling at Nani. Calling her names. Saying horrible things about her and her Guru. He forbid her to take us children there ever again. And," Uma stopped, putting her hands over her eyes. Sobbing, she finished, "I heard him hit her."

Padma's mother fell into her lap. She had never seen her mother so upset and, at the same time, never so open about her feelings. It was so unlike her mother. And the compassion she was feeling in her heart for her welled up so that she too began to sob.

"Mommy, I am sorry that happened to you and Nani. I am sorry that you are still holding onto so much sadness about this," Padma consoled her mother.

There was a part of Padma that felt glad that they were having this honest sharing, even though it was bringing up so much sadness for her mother. It felt like a deep healing was already taking place.

The women hugged and sobbed for some time until it began to subside. There was a moment when Padma's mother touched her face and smiled at her in a way that she had never done before. She would never forget this moment with her mother when she felt closest to her.

"Padma, I want you to know the reason I never let you do yoga is because it reminded me of that night and how every moment after that was never the same in our house. My mother's love for her Guru only grew more and lessened for my father. And his disdain for this situation only amplified as time went on too."

Padma needed to say something; she wanted to fully understand the story while she had an opportunity to.

"Mommy, when I was a little girl, we went to India, and we visited Nani and Nana, and they seemed, well, normal, I guess. They seemed like every other Indian family I knew."

"Yes, of course," Padma's mother explained, "They would always keep up appearances. And, you know, divorce, this was not a thing. This was not something that was done. You married for life, and that was it. Your purpose, as a woman, was to raise a family. And what would it look like for others to see someone's wife spend all her free time in the presence of another man, a man who dressed half-naked, a man who took her in as a woman to practice what only other men did? This was not the way."

Getting up from the couch to stretch her legs, Padma's mother sighed and shook out her arms for a moment to relieve the stiffness in her joints. Padma took the time to stretch out on the couch, knowing that it was getting late and she was incredibly tired, but she had no intention of asking her mother to leave.

"Mommy, why don't you stay the night? We have the spare bedroom for you, and you can go home tomorrow sometime. It is getting late, and the baby will be up in a couple of hours," Padma said.

Her mother nodded yes.

"I should call your father and let him know that I am going to stay so that he does not worry," she said, beginning to walk away until her daughter stopped her.

"Mommy?" Padma called out. Her mother turned and smiled at her.

"Mommy, do you think..." She found herself pausing because she suddenly found herself uncomfortable with the next question she wanted to ask. Searching for the right words, she decided to simply state the most obvious in the gentlest way she could.

"Do you think that Nani was having 'relations' with her Guru?"

Without hesitation, her mother answered, "No, no, no. It was not like that. The Guru relationship was pure love. It was not about sex acts. It was a Divine love. And I think that is what bothered Nana the most, you know. How could he ever compete with that?"

With that final remark, she walked out to call her husband. Finally, receiving the answers to the mystery, she found herself with mixed emotions but was satisfied to put the story to rest—at least the mystery part.

Date-Night Snorting

"Good friends make each other laugh. Best friends go for the snort!"
- Unknown.

Date night. Raj and Padma joined Melvin and Melanie at a Restorative Yoga class and then went to dinner. It was their first foray into yoga, and Melanie had assured Padma that once she took this class, she would be hooked. With her mother's blessing and the babies well attended to at Raj's parents' home, they could enjoy a night out with their new best couple friends. Padma was both excited and nervous about the class but knew that it could not make her feel worse than she already felt about herself.

Between her exhaustion and the mental fluctuations from both lack of sleep and hormones, Padma was ready to try anything. She had been reading up about yoga, and several notable places, such as the National Institutes of Health and Boston University, claimed that studies showed that yoga had positive results in helping with mood swings, anxiety, and other mental issues. Now that she had a friend in Melanie, another new mom who was working through many of the same issues as she, Padma felt better about approaching Raj with her own experiences.

Raj had not been surprised to hear Padma disclose what she had been going through. Several of his sisters had experienced similar postnatal issues after their pregnancies. He was more concerned that Padma felt the need to hide what she was dealing with from him and not talk about it. That need to keep things in and feel as though she had to suffer alone went deep for Padma, and she knew that it would take time to feel completely different. But, just the little positive feedback and support she'd received from Raj about this already made her feel better about opening up more.

Melanie had mentioned the Restorative class to Padma at lunch a week prior, and she didn't have to think twice about it. She Venmo'd Melanie the money, and the tickets to the class were booked. Even Raj was excited about attending, although probably mostly because Melvin was coming.

Their yoga studio was in Melvin and Melanie's hometown, which was about a twenty-minute drive from theirs, so it was not the studio that Padma had previously stalked or the teacher who had waved to her through the window! This one was tucked away in a small office complex. If you hadn't been looking for it, you would never know it was there. From the exterior, the yoga studio looked just like another medical office. But once you walked through the front door, the serene ambiance immediately felt welcoming and relaxing to Padma.

The studio was decorated in dark purple and green colors, had many live plants scattered about, and was carpeted. A large Buddha statue and many other small nuances made the space feel more like being in a friend's living room than out at a business. The cozy feeling was also mirrored by the other students and the teacher, who herself seemed like a normal woman like her and not a magazine cover model.

Jodi, Melanie's yoga teacher, helped them gather all the props that they would need for what she called "Heaven on a Bolster." Padma liked the sound of that. Right about now, she would have taken "Heaven on a Rock," and it probably would have had the same effect.

With the lights dimmed and soft ambient music playing, Jodi instructed everyone to lay down on their backs, supported by the bolster. She then came around and assisted everyone individually with other props to alleviate any discomfort so that they could rest and enjoy. Padma hadn't even heard Jodi come by and inquire about her comfort. She had already fallen asleep. Raj waved Jodi on, whispering to her that his wife was dealing with a new baby and toddler at home and that she would most likely sleep through most of the class. Jodi nodded that she was okay with that. She let Padma sleep through the first two poses before she came over and gently woke her to move into an entirely new position.

Restorative Yoga was lovely. Each posture was held for about 15 minutes, and Jodi guided them on breathing and relaxation throughout, or so she was told. After sleeping solidly for the first half-hour, Padma was able to enjoy the rest of the class without falling too deeply asleep. She found the instructions easy to follow and the poses extremely comfortable and relaxing. After the class, the foursome went out to dinner, where they had more time to talk.

"Well, what did you think?" Melvin asked the couple as the four of them sat in the softly lit restaurant.

"Honestly, I feel great," said Raj. "I didn't think I would relax that much. I thought I would be a little antsy, but I wasn't."

"Yeah, I feel you. I felt the same way when I first heard we were doing yoga at training. I was like, 'Huh? Come again?' But truthfully, it is so relaxing," Melvin replied.

"And how about you, Padma? How do you feel?" Asked Melanie.

She had caught Padma with a mouthful of bread, so motioning with her index finger to hold on, Raj jumped in with more questions.

"Is this the same kind of yoga you do in training?"

Melvin shook his head, also with a mouthful of bread. He and Padma started laughing, then both tried, unsuccessfully, to swallow the bread, then eventually spit it out rather than choke on it. Melvin had to wipe his eyes from the tears rolling down when he was done wiping his mouth.

"Oh, Lord. What timing!" Melvin announced, still laughing and wiping his eyes.

"Padma, I can't take you anywhere!" Raj feigned seriousness.

"Yes, Melvin, seriously!" Melanie jumped in, then bounced her elbow off Raj's arm.

What a comfort to spend time with people who weren't pretentious.

"Melvin, I swear it feels like we have known each other forever," Padma said.

Melvin nodded his head and reached for Melanie's hand. "I was just telling Mel the other night that, for some reason, I feel like I know you, Padma. Like, I know this sounds weird, but from a past life or something."

"Padma told me the same thing. She thinks you two may have been cousins," Raj shared.

"The weird thing is that I don't know many of my cousins very well because they are all back in India. So it feels strange to say that you feel like a cousin of mine because I don't have much to go by on that other than to say it just feels like that. Does that make sense?" Padma asked.

"It does to me. I don't have the same connection, but I can say that it just feels good to be with you. You feel familiar to Melvin, and so you feel like family to me already," Melanie shared.

Padma reached over to hold Melanie's hand.

"I'm so glad that you feel that way. It is sometimes strange for men and women to be friends. I don't want this to be that way for us," said Padma.

"Never," Melanie replied, squeezing Padma's hand.

"Man, if the guys on the team hear any of this, I may have to give my Super Bowl ring back!" Melvin laughed, and the others joined in.

"So, what was that yoga question?" Melvin replied once the love-fest was over.

"Oh," Raj said, "Yes, the Restorative, is that the same yoga you practiced with the NFL?"

"Oh, no. Ours is more athletic, I would say. We do lots of standing postures. We start with this series of postures called Sun Salutations that warm us up, and then we move into other postures. It kind of gets more challenging, and then toward the end more stretching, then a short relaxation at the end."

Raj and Padma nodded their heads in unison, listening.

"Ashtanga?" Raj chimed in.

Padma jerked her head to look at her husband. Raj's knowledge of things seemed to pop up out of nowhere sometimes. And, by the way, what the hell was Ass-tango?

"Our teacher calls it Vinyasa, but I think it is a variation of that. I think Ashtanga is more 'traditional' if that's the right word. But I don't know for sure. I just do what they tell me to, and I always like it," Melvin said.

"We had some family friends who used to practice Ashtanga, and one or two of my sisters had practiced for a while with them. My sister, Sangeeta, I think, still practices daily. She moved out to Colorado, so I don't get to talk to her as often, but she had a daily practice and said it helped her stay focused and agile," Raj said.

"I didn't know that," Padma said, smiling at her husband. The details of his family would take a lifetime to catch up on.

"Yes, Sangeeta. Didn't I mention it when we started discussing yoga?" Raj replied.

"No. You didn't, but that's okay," Padma was not interested in getting into this or that in front of Melvin and Melanie, and anyway, it was a minor exclusion.

"So, Padma, how do you feel after the class? Now that you don't have a mouthful of food, I can ask," Melanie said, smiling.

"Ha," Padma said, chewing, again pointing a finger up to alert them to wait a minute before she could finish.

"Make sure to fully swallow that," Melvin laughed.

Padma was able to swallow her mouthful successfully in time "Thanks, Melvin. Yes. Well, I have to admit, I feel pretty happy right now. I don't recall feeling so upbeat in the last — year?" Padma giggled. "But I feel very calm and just happy. I think being out with the two of you also helps."

"True story," Melanie agreed. "You know, I love being a mother and having the ability to be home and raise the children, but the times when you get to go out and speak to other adults and have a nice meal prepared for you, those are like magical moments."

Padma certainly was on the same page about that. Not that they went out very often these days, but she was starting to feel that they needed to happen more.

"We should make this a regular occurrence. Go out for something—food, shopping, nail appointment—something every..." Padma began to say before getting cut off by Melvin.

"...week. Every week, I make Melanie an appointment for something just for her. That's in addition to yoga. I feel it's important for her to take care of herself so that she can care for the kids. If not, I see them all grumbling more in some way. It's all about balancing it out."

Padma, again, agreed. "Hmm, I like the sound of that," Padma said. "Raj, how about getting in on that with Melvin?"

"Sure," Raj said, slipping a kiss to his wife, "Anything for my goddess."

The goddess's comment surprised her so much that she snorted, then immediately tried to hold it in, only to wind up snorting again.

Melvin and Melanie both began laughing. This made Melanie snort as well. With Raj and Padma joining in, the group was having a full-belly laugh, with intermittent snorting throughout. Then suddenly, and with the assisted thrusting of his stomach, Melvin farted.

The fart put the group over the edge. Padma's stomach hurt so much from laughing, but she could do nothing to stop it. Everyone in the restaurant took turns looking over at them, mostly smiling. Except for one well-dressed couple in the corner looking sternly at them, the other diners chuckled along in good humor. Eventually, their waiter returned to the table.

"I had to come back over and see what all the merriment was about. Please tell me it's not the food!" He said with a grin.

"It's just…" Padma began but couldn't get a full sentence out as laughter took over.

Melanie decided to help her out, "She snorted…" but fell short of finishing her sentence as well.

Padma snorted again. Melvin pointed in Padma's direction, gesturing to the waiter, the source of the laughter, attempting to draw attention away from his fart. The fact was, he was puckering up his ass-cheeks so tight, he could have held a football with them and ran in for a touchdown.

"Oh," the waiter started to chuckle. "Sometimes it just takes something little to start it all off. You guys are so fun! I'll be back with a little something for you."

With that, the waiter scooted off, and the four comrades in crime began to slowly wind down, wipe their eyes, and regain composure. It was not easy, and none of them wanted to. But alas, they were in a public place.

"Maybe next time we do this at one of our homes," Raj offered.

"Love it! Let's do a game night, too," Melanie said.

"Yes!" Padma was all in, "We can take turns at houses."

"Deal," Melvin said.

With that, the two couples clinked glasses and cheered.

"To regular gatherings and meetings of the mind," Raj said, lifting his glass again.

What a joy to have found such rare friends that you can laugh and be real with, they all thought individually, but at the same time.

Later that evening, Padma found that she was able to handle the baby's fussing a little better. She didn't feel her normal terror of her insecurities arise. She simply picked up the baby and rocked and sang to her sweetly. Somehow, the baby also seemed to pick up on Padma's more relaxed energy because it did not take as long for her to calm down.

This change in her energy field and emotions seemed to last for just about three full days. Was it the yoga practice that had helped boost her mood or a dinner out with friends? Perhaps it was a little of both, but Padma decided to return to a yoga class soon now that she had this jumping-off point. The relaxation she felt in her body and mind from that one practice was extraordinary. She wanted — needed — to try it again and see if it made a consistent difference. And, if so, make it her weekly thing, just like Melanie.

The local Hatha Yoga studio did not have a Restorative class on its schedule, but there was something called Gentle Yoga several times a week. After talking with Raj, she registered for the Wednesday evening class at 6:30. Two more days until her class, and Padma was looking forward to it. But before she went, she wanted to let her mother know about it.

Uma took the time to read about the studio that her daughter was interested in, and seeing that there was no Guru responsible for the facility, she felt more at ease. The studio appeared to have quite a nice blend of Eastern and Western philosophies and practices. The teachers all looked nice enough and funny, though they were all women. This certainly contradicted the norm she knew of from India of most yoga teachers being men. That made her feel even better about this particular studio for Padma. Convincing herself that her daughter was not her mother and that this was an entirely different situation, Uma gave her full approval to Padma to start a yoga practice there.

On the evening Padma was to begin her yoga classes, Uma visited the local Hindu temple to pray, just for good measure.

First, she walked over to Lord Ganesha, the elephant god known as the Remover of Obstacles. She lit incense and placed a candy by his feet that she pulled out of her pocket as an offering. She checked to ensure that she and Ganesha were alone before speaking to him out loud.

"Okay, Ganapataye," she said, using another of the god's names. "I know you. It has been some time since I've spoken directly to you, but I know you." Uma began. She cleared her throat and continued.

"Okay, so you know me too. Let us be friends again. As my mother loved you, I ask for you to be in my favor and to hear me now. Clear the path for my daughter, Padma, so that she may enjoy the many benefits of yoga without needing to find a Guru. Always be with her when she practices yoga. Remove any teachers not of the highest integrity from her path. Be with her to steer her when I cannot be. Watch over her, always. She is my light and my love. I cannot lose her as my father lost my mother."

Uma wiped a tear from her eyes. "Yes, I know it is not the same. Yes, but yes, it is perhaps the same or similar. You know what it is that I mean."

This was the sort of line that her daughter would poke fun at her for saying, but it conveyed a deep truth for her. Sometimes, things, although seemingly quite different, have a similar essence as this felt to her. And often, it is all just too difficult to explain. This was another reason why she chose to try not to focus on difficult things — so that there was no miscommunication furthering the issue.

Uma took a deep breath and removed a second candy from her pocket. She had thought to save it for her ride home, but upon second thought, she gave it to Ganesha as another gift.

"Well, you certainly do get the best candies, don't you?" Uma said to Ganesha. Was that a smile of recognition on his face? She looked at the god from another angle. Was he smiling? Why shouldn't he? He had a pile of candy and a lot of money on the offering plate at his feet. What was not to be happy about?

"Okay, we have a deal then, yes?" Uma continued. "You watch over Padma, keep the bad teachers away from her, keep her safe, and I will, okay, yes, I will come more often, and I will bring you more candy."

Did he smile again?

"Do not smile like that at me. I see what you are doing. That is very sneaky, Ganapataye."

Uma threw her hands up in the air, flustered, then reached into her pocket for the next piece of candy that she had convinced herself she would have *after* dinner, and she tossed it down on Ganesha's offering plate. Uma folded her arms across her chest. Silly Elephant got all her candy.

"Okay then," Uma finished and walked away.

Ganesha smiled.

Once in her car, Uma reached back into her very deep coat pocket and revealed yet another piece of candy. Tearing it open, she popped it in her mouth. Then, giggling, she drove off. She giggled because this particular piece of candy had a nut inside, unlike all the others. Maybe Ganesha had three pieces of candy, but she had the best one!

That night after dinner, when Uma began the dishes, she reached into another pocket, this one in her sweater, and once again, uncovered another nutty nugget and popped it into her mouth.

Where did the candles end? Only Uma knew the answer to that question. And she was never going to reveal those secrets.

Dipping a Toe In

"Meditation is my thing. But I'm not going to lie: sometimes I go into my closet and lock the door so no one can find me." - Gwen Stefani.

Padma signed in for the yoga class, received a studio mat, and walked into the wide-open yoga room. She wasn't quite sure what to do, as she had arrived first before anyone else. She tried to recall how the mats were set up during her day of discovery when she looked in through the window but couldn't remember. Besides, she had spent another restless night with the baby, leaving her with a frazzled brain again.

Both Padma and Raj had become concerned with how difficult it was to soothe the baby and had taken her to their pediatrician, who diagnosed her with colic. Her advice was tremendously helpful, and since then, they'd taken several steps to assist them, and many were working.

Padma had realized that whenever she ate dairy, the baby seemed to have a more difficult time after feeding on those nights. She attempted to cut as much dairy out as she could but had succumbed to a nice block of aged cheddar yesterday for lunch, which led to a challenging night with the baby. It was another layer to her bad-mom guilt — even though the doctor had comforted her and said that she was doing everything that she could to help her baby be more comfortable. But then, the good doctor didn't know about the aged cheddar, only Padma did, and it was also playing a part in her mental state at the moment. Somehow, though, she had made it to the class and was hoping that it might make her feel better somehow.

Ashanti strolled elegantly into class. Padma envied her slim, tight figure and got caught staring.

"Hey, love, is this your first class here?" Ashanti said, smiling, either unaware or ignoring Padma's glaring eyes.

"Is it that obvious?" she replied, shyly smiling.

"Well, the studio mat may have given that away. Let me help you set up. Is this your first yoga class as well?"

Padma was realizing that Ashanti had a lovely British accent. She had quite the Scary Spice vibe going on.

"Yes, well, no. Kind of?" Padma said. "I only took a Restorative class a couple of weeks ago. But this is my first real class."

Ashanti smiled, "It's all yoga at the end of the day. But it's good. Restorative is an amazing intro to yoga. So, what brings you here to us?" she inquired, arranging Padma's mat and props.

Padma giggled nervously, "Ah, my mental health?"

Ashanti smiled and laughed, "You know what they say: many people do yoga so that they don't smack people."

Padma looked at Ashanti, surprised, "Seriously?"

The teacher laughed, then shook her head from side to side. "Well, not really?" She said more questioning than stating. "I was joking, but there is a little something to that!"

Padma laughed, relieved. It may not have been encouraging, but it was comforting that the yoga teacher also had conflicting thoughts.

"Well, I just had my second baby not that long ago, and she is colicky, and there are days when…" Padma paused but didn't need to finish, Ashanti did for her.

"I get it, sister. I think any mom gets it. Listen, this is your time. Although we love our kiddos, this is our time to reconnect with ourselves. So, give yourself this time completely. And then, tonight, you'll have more energy for them."

"I will take me some of that!" Padma said, nodding.

"I've set up some props so that you can lay down and rest before class. We have at least 15 minutes before we start, and this gives you time to relax. Lay down, and we will be starting before you know it," Ashanti said, then guided Padma into position, leaving her to rest with soft music playing.

Ashanti was not kidding. What felt like thirty seconds later, she was awoken by the clinging of bells and Ashanti's voice guiding everyone to slowly come into a comfortable seated position. From there, she began the class.

"I would like to start our practice today with some pranayama techniques. These are the yoga breathing methods, and they have many benefits. But first, because we all came in from different places and all have a lot on our minds, let us use these practices to relax and focus on the present moment…

"If it's comfortable for you, close your eyes and begin to feel the sensation around your nostrils. Feel the air flowing both in and out. Notice how each part of the breath feels in your body. Do not try to change your breath, just be a witness…inhale…and exhale…

"Now, begin to slowly pump the abdomen by stretching it forward as you inhale, holding it for a moment, then pulling it inward on the exhale, holding it squeezed back to the spine before the next inhale. Do not rush. Slowly pump the belly in and out, and let the mind focus on the breath and the movement…"

Padma liked the belly breathing. She remembered this from the Restorative class, so she felt more confident with it this second time. Whereas at the first class, she wasn't sure of the belly movement, in Ashanti's class, she was watching her breath with intent and noticed it and the belly slowly moving in and out to a hypnotic rhythm. She was not sure how long she'd been focusing on the breath, but eventually, Ashanti's voice came back.

"Now, for those who wish to move to our Yogi breathing, on the next inhalation, take the breath from the belly to the chest and expand the whole body cavity outward. Still pause, this time feeling the breath upward more toward the neck. When you exhale, release from the chest down to the belly and pull it inward, holding it tight before the next inhale. You should feel the ribcage expanding and contracting to help this total body breathing occur. If it is too much, return to the simpler belly breathing."

Padma tried to perform the new Yogi breathing but was having some difficulty with it. She seemed to feel the breath get stuck somewhere, making the exhale a little more choppy than the inhale. But she stayed with the technique until Ashanti guided them to stop.

"On the next exhalation, I would like you to let go with an audible sigh, returning to your natural deep breathing."

Padma inhaled but stopped short of the verbal sigh. She heard the others in the class. It sounded amazing, but she was not sure she could do it. It also sounded a little erotic, and that made her uncomfortable to do amongst strangers.

"You have another chance for those who wish to give it another go, inhale, and let's all release it with a verbal sigh... AHHHHHHHHHHHHHHHHH!" Ashanti said, the class mimicking her sigh.

Again, Padma inhaled and held it in. She just couldn't get herself to exhale with sound. This made her think about how she sometimes stifles her voice when making love to not sound so, well, into it. Surprisingly, Padma now had herself questioning why she did that when in intimate situations with Raj. Her mind quickly took onto that line of inquiry and got lost in it until Ashanti started moving everyone into Child's pose, a position she recalled from Restorative Yoga, only this time she was not hugging a huge pillow. Now, her forehead was resting against the mat with her arms at ease at her sides. What a glorious stretch for her back.

Ashanti came by, "Would you like a little assisted stretch?" She asked Padma. Padma was not sure what to say or do, so she lifted her head and said, "Okay."

Ashanti gently pressed somewhere along her lower back, which allowed her buttocks to press into her heels. The teacher held her while asking her to breathe more deeply. Padma did what she was asked and felt herself melting like butter in a warm pan. She didn't even know Ashanti had left until she heard her from the front of the room.

The class was guided at a very slow pace, with most of the postures on the floor. Perhaps the poses were held a minute or so before moving to another. In each one, Ashanti guided the students to breathe either into the belly or with Yogi's breath while holding the postures. This was not difficult for Padma as all of the poses were gentle, but she did feel a lot of stretching. She even felt a large pop in her hip joint when they moved into the Supine Pigeon posture. It released some tension there that Padma was not aware she even had. She smiled, giggled, and then immediately wanted to cry.

Cry? Wait, wasn't yoga supposed to help boost her mood? Why was she starting to cry? Then, after a few tears, she felt better. What the heck was that about?!

Padma felt unsure about what to do next. The brief emotional release started her mind working overtime as she lay on her back. Was she doing something wrong? Could she have hurt herself? Had anyone seen her cry? Her mind was frantically racing when Ashanti came over to her.

"Are you okay, Padma? Can I help you?" Ashanti said, concerned.

Padma, unaware that she had been holding her breath in with her emotions, quickly opened her eyes, which had been held tightly closed to not let any more tears leak out. When she did, a last tear gently rolled down her cheek. Ashanti seemed to understand completely. A glance around the room also keyed her into the fact that others had moved into another posture. How long had she been sitting there holding things in?

"Got it. Just stick it out here, seated or lying down, and rest. Work on your breathing, as it is more important than the movement. And if you feel like joining us in any other pose, please do. Remember, this is *your* practice," Ashanti said with a wink, then walked over to the next student to check in with him.

Padma took a couple of deep breaths. Her mind seemed to respond quickly to the breathing as her thoughts quieted, and the frantic emotion soon receded. She was able to join in the rest of the yoga practice, which seemed simple yet offered some surprising challenges to her out-of-shape body. When it came time for the final relaxation, she fell asleep, only to be awakened by the sound of bells and the others sitting back up.

"Thank you for taking this time out of your busy day for yourself. Remember, wherever you go, there you are! So, since we are going to be in any place physically, always give yourself the gift of being there fully. Om, Shanti. Shanti. Shanti. Peace, peace, peace. Namaste," said Ashanti, bowing her head with her hands at her heart in prayer.

Padma placed her hands at her heart and also bowed her head with the other students, but she did not repeat "Namaste" with them, mostly because she didn't realize she was supposed to.

As students were rolling up their mats and heading out, Ashanti came back to check on her again.

"Padma, thank you for coming, I hope you enjoyed tonight's class."

"Ah, yes. It was really lovely. I'm sorry I sort of zoned out in the beginning. Something made my mind click into overdrive, and I got distracted," Padma said.

Shaking her head in acknowledgment and smiling, Ashanti replied, "I realized one day that I had control over my mind. It was an amazing discovery. It changed everything. I soon became aware when my thoughts were flying here or there, and I was better at stopping them and reclaiming my focus. Remember, there is a real you who is in control of that small mind. And..." Ashanti placed her hand on Padma's back, "it's okay to cry." Patting her back, Ashanti winked and walked away.

It was a brief exchange, but one that made Padma feel seen. When she got back to the desk to return the yoga mat, she noticed a few people chatting while putting on shoes and drinking some water. One of them acknowledged her.

"Hi, I'm Rachel, is this your first yoga class?" she asked Padma.

"Ah, well, my first class here, yes. I only did one other class before, so I am new to all of this," she said, swirling her arms around to reference all of the studio.

"I hope you enjoyed it. I love the people here. Everyone is super friendly, and it is not competitive. You can move at your own pace, and there's no judgment," said Rachel. "And this is Max," she said, referring to the man that she was sitting next to.

Padma waved hello to Max, and he waved back. Then the two got up, said that they hoped to see her again, and left the studio. Padma watched them exchange a smile and a nod, then head off in separate directions. Later, she would come to understand them as "yoga buddies," people who had met at yoga and had come to be very good friends. It reminded her of Melvin and their short yet significant relationship that, while not founded through yoga, had that same common thread. She smiled, recognizing all the nice people who were suddenly coming into her life.

When she got home, Raj greeted her with a kiss, interested to know how she felt after the class. She chose not to share her cry with him or the reason why it came on but told him she felt really good. He sounded happy and encouraged her to go each week.

"Well, if I am going to make this a thing, I think I should buy my yoga mat," she said.

"Yeah?" Raj asked. "Okay. Want me to get you one?"

"No, I can get one. Let me ask around first and see what I should get. I noticed a lot of different ones at the studio. I wouldn't know where to start."

"Kind of like golf clubs," Raj said.

Padma looked inquisitively at her husband.

"Aren't they all the same?" she asked.

Raj had a good laugh at her expense. Certainly, she had to be kidding. But then he realized, how would she know?

"Yeah, for sure. Most people have clubs specifically fitted for them. It's a whole thing," he said.

"So you got those clubs of yours 'fitted' for you?" Padma asked, "The ones that sit in the garage all the time because you never have time to use them, and they probably cost like a million dollars?"

Raj laughed, "Yup, those."

Padma walked over to her husband, threw her arms around his waist, and pulled him close.

"You know what? You work a lot. If I get a night out, you should get a day out to golf."

Smiling, then kissing his wife, Raj replied, "Yeah? Wow, you know what? You're right! I need to make more time for myself, too. We should both have some 'Me Time'."

Although he couldn't be sure that it was the yoga talking, Raj was pretty certain it had a part in Padma's good mood. Medically speaking, he had no explanation for this phenomenon, yet he couldn't ignore that there was something different going on with his wife's demeanor this evening. Perhaps he should look more into it and read some articles on yoga studies. He made it a point to make time to research more and to reach out to Sangeeta. After all, they were overdue for a connection, and this was the perfect reason to call his sister.

As the sun went down on another evening at the Patel home, Padma found ease in dealing with the baby, and both of them even managed to grab a little more sleep than usual. Was it due to her yoga practice? Or possibly the baby massage that the doctor had taught her? Who knew for sure? But she was starting to see a value in yoga. And if dipping her toe in had this sort of positive effect, Padma was hopeful that a full swim would reveal even more benefits.

Birthday Blowout

"Man is not worried by real problems so much as by his imagined anxieties about real problems" - Epictetus.

"I cannot believe my grand-baby is four years old today!" Uma beamed, skipping around Padma's kitchen.

Neither could Padma. Where had those four years gone? Oh yes, to the mists of time, years that she would never get back, just like her pre-mommy body. Why couldn't she be more like her friend Reshma, who had a baby and sprang back so quickly that nobody would have believed she had been pregnant if they hadn't seen her with their own eyes?

"Padma, let me help you, my dear. What would you like me to do?" Uma asked her daughter.

It was clear that the party was taking its toll on Padma, who looked weary and stressed. Parties were supposed to be happy occasions. She wished her daughter had taken her up on paying for a caterer, but Padma and Raj didn't want to make every birthday such a huge affair. They had decided to keep it a small event at home with just the intimate family. Padma forgot just how big that actually was, however, and she was now awaiting some seventy-five guests, or more, which is normally the case with their family celebrations. The tent arrived the day before with the tables and chairs, which the rental company set up, thank goodness! And even though Padma did decide to have most of the food catered, there was coordinating all of that, getting together the party favors, fixing up the games and events, and, of course, Nina's gift, a little bike that Raj had been working on getting together that week. So, the small, intimate celebration indeed looked like a regular American wedding.

"Mommy, if you can just watch the babies for me, that would be a huge help. I know where everything needs to go and be, and it is just easier for me to do it all myself."

That was not entirely true. Padma did need help, but she wasn't in the mood to listen to her mother's constant upbeat chatter at the moment. She wanted everything to be right for her little princess's birthday party, and that meant she had to tend to many things for the past several weeks, forgoing her own self-care time with relaxing baths and weekly yoga. She was surprised how quickly her body felt tight from missing out on the yoga classes at the studio, and she was very much looking forward to getting back just as soon as she could.

What she hadn't noticed as much, although it was not lost on Rajesh, was how anxious and emotional she'd become as well. Her mood swings were back full-tilt, and it was almost a regular evening occurrence that she would have either a crying breakdown or be more than a little curt with him. He had offered to help more with party planning, to have his sisters help, and even to pay for more help for the event, but Padma insisted she could handle it all on her own, and yet it was obvious to everyone but her that she could not. Raj was just hoping to get through the day, and then he could send her to the spa with Melanie next week, followed by her regular yoga regimen. He had already purchased the spa package. But with her moods and stress over Nina's party, there hadn't been a good time to tell her that it was coming up.

With just under an hour before the party guests were to arrive, Padma sat in the middle of a pile of goody bags, half-full and half-sorted piles of favors, ready to be placed in bags. She had just recounted, for the fifth time, and realized she was going to be short about twenty-five bags and was sitting there trying to figure out what to do when she felt the emotions welling up inside her. She had already put on her makeup and was holding back tears from creating a mudslide down her face, but it was getting more and more difficult to contain. She knew that she was at the point where just one more little thing was going to put her over the edge. She just was not sure what it was that was going to do it.

And that's when her phone rang.

Padma recognized the number because it was the entertainment company she had booked. Three Disney princesses came to the party to make up all the little girls, give them tiaras, and sing songs with them.

"Hello?" Padma said, worried.

And, yes, her worst fear had come true.

"Mrs. Patel, I am so sorry to tell you this, but one of our princesses has contracted a virus, and the other two scheduled to come, well, they were with her just two days ago. I'm afraid we won't have anyone else to send to your party today. I realize this is not the news you wanted to hear today, and I've already refunded your money. I would like to extend a free event to you for another time. Again, our sincerest apologies."

She placed the phone down, and the floodgate to the waterworks opened on full blast. As tears streamed down her face, Padma grabbed the items next to her, the goody bags, and began to tear at them, throw them around the room, and scream. It was quite the site — candy and little purses were flying everywhere as sounds that could have been from hungry hyenas came out of Padma. Amid her adult tantrum, Payal entered the room and ran to her friend.

"Padma! Padma, what is it, dear, what is it?" Payal said frantically as she grabbed her friend in a strong embrace.

Padma reached for Payal and sobbed into her shirt for some time. The two women sat on the floor rocking back and forth, Padma crying, Payal very concerned. Finally, when the outburst subsided, Padma revealed the state of affairs, now made even worse by the whole goody-bag situation.

Payal was at a loss for words. Maybe it was her gaping mouth, but Padma started laughing uncontrollably, which troubled Payal even more. But rather than worry, she decided to laugh with her friend. After all, if she could cry with her, laughter certainly felt the better emotion to share. Two of Raj's sisters walked in to see the women laughing amidst a room strewn with the remnants of the goody bags.

"What did we miss?"

Padma wiped the tears from her eyes.

"Oh, the Disney princesses aren't coming, and the party favors are destroyed. It's okay, though, I didn't have enough anyway." She said before launching into another hysterical round of laughter and throwing herself back on the floor.

Payal looked at Rajesh's sisters, awaiting a response. They both looked about the room and took a few moments to consider the options before starting to whisper to each other. Payal leaned forward but couldn't make out the conversation over Padma's sinister laughter.

So it was when Padma's laughter subsided that Meeta spoke.

"Okay, this is the plan. We can gather up, re-sort the bags, and make random collections for the favors. Or, we can put all the favors in a bowl and let the kids take a couple of their choosing on the way out. How does that sound?"

Padma looked at her sister-in-law. What was her choice? She shrugged her shoulders. "I guess."

"Okay then. We will figure this out," Meeta continued.

"It isn't going to be a princess party without all the princess things, though," Padma said.

Raj's sister Sangeeta then spoke, "Well, perhaps we need to redefine what a princess is!"

Padma looked at her sister-in-law and softened. She stood up and smiled at Sangeeta and Meeta.

"Yes! Let's redefine what a princess is!" Padma announced, not fully understanding what that meant but liking the idea of it all.

Payal came over as the four women stood for a moment, smiling at each other.

"Oh my, we have some work to do," Meeta finally said. "Go fetch the other sisters," she motioned to Payal but then stopped her just short of leaving the room.

"Wait, wait, wait. You cannot go out like that," Sangeeta said, motioning to Payal's blush-pink blouse that was now stained with Padma's mascara and other makeup.

Padma threw her hands over her mouth and pointed at Payal's blouse.

"Payal! I am so sorry!" she said, then realizing if her friend's clothing looked like that, then she must look even worse.

Whirling around to take a peek at herself in the mirror, Padma realized that the mess on her face was going to need a bit of work, too. Horrified, she turned to face the woman, trying to hold back more tears.

"No, it is okay. Go wash your face. Do not attempt to put anything on; we will work with it," Sangeeta said. "Meeta, go get the sisters, tell them to split up into two teams. Half to run home and gather all their makeup and some jewelry, the others to come here to work on the goody bags. Payal, please take Padma upstairs and, well, fix yourselves."

Padma hugged her sister-in-law. Now, this was what she imagined family was really about.

"Go, go, go, please, we can hug it out later. We have a half an hour!" Sangeeta said.

And with that, all the women scattered, moving with purpose to shift the energy and prepare for the party for Nina. The little one had no idea what was happening and never would know of the last-minute change of plans, for the party resulted in a perfect day for everyone.

Each sister paired with one or two little girls and put on some makeup and jewelry from what they had gathered. There was enough gold among them all to make it work. There was even a tiara for little Nina to wear from one of her sister's weddings. After the little ones were made up, Sangeeta and some of Raj's other sisters taught the little girls traditional Indian "princess" dances, and the little ones ate it all up, as did the Aunties and other guests.

Watching the immense support system that had come to her rescue, Padma felt truly blessed. With all the people in their lives who would have helped, why had she tried to manage it all on her own? There was some outdated belief within her that if she was a good mother, she had to do it all and be it all, especially since she did not work outside of the home. But the reality was that she could not do it all. She was not Wonder Woman. And she knew that she was going to have to rely more on the other women around her in the future. But that old pattern of hers of feeling somehow like an incompetent mother by not being able to manage everything ran deep. Yet she knew it was time to let it go.

When the party was over, and most of the guests had left, Raj's sisters and mother, along with Payal and Uma, all gathered Padma and brought her to the living room to chat. Concerned, Padma thought she was about to be reprimanded. But the women had something else in mind.

Sangeeta began, "Padma, dear one. I'm going to tell you a little secret, something that you need to hear. Something all women need to understand. It is high time that we all help each other, for we are stronger in numbers. We gain our strength through our feminine energies when we come together. Our families need us to band together. Our communities need us to thrive. Even our country needs us to stand up and make ourselves known. We have to start this within ourselves, one at a time. We have to realize we are individually strong and capable, yes, but together, we can move mountains, we can create real change."

Padma nodded her head. All the other women smiled and leaned in to hear more from Sangeeta.

"Look what we did in such a short time together, and just for a little party. Please know that you never have to feel alone, ever. Whatever you are going through, trust me, other women are either going through it or have been through it. We can help each other. We need to help each other because we are so much stronger together."

Rajesh's mother came over and hugged her daughter, then squatted down in front of Padma, placing her hand gently on her knee.

"Padma, dearest. I think of you as my eighth daughter. I know you have a beautiful mother, but with me, you have two to call on for wisdom. For certainly, we each have our wisdom to share," she said, nodding to Uma, who smiled back before continuing. "So I want you to know that if you need help, or just someone to listen, or to come by to watch the babies, or even helping you find a professional to talk to, we can do it. And, there is no shame in that."

Padma began to tear up. Raj's mother handed her a tissue and stayed with her until Payal came over and sat with her friend, placing her arms around her.

"Padma, I hate seeing you in such a way. Although I do not know what you are going through, I understand what it feels like to feel alone in pain and difficulty. And we have always talked about our deepest secrets, haven't we? You can share anything with me. And if you need me, you can call me, and I will be here at a moment's notice — because we all know I have no life of my own."

With that, all the women, including Padma, began to chuckle. It was good to break the heavy yet sincere words with levity, as only Payal could do. Padma felt this was a good time to speak up.

"I want to express my deepest and most sincere love for you all. I am so blessed to have so many women in my life, I truly am. I have always been able to run with things myself, and it is difficult for me to sometimes ask for help. I often think I should be able to handle these few things on my plate, and yes, I do feel shame for not being able to," Padma confessed, looking at Raj's mother.

"You know, Padma, every woman is different. This postpartum stage is so difficult for many. I have to admit, after two or three of my children were born," she stopped to look around the room, then in a joking way continued, "I will not say which ones as they are all present here, but after several births, I felt this deep well of emotions."

More chuckles and heartfelt smiles came before she continued.

"There were days I did not want to get up and feed the babies or even take care of myself. But I had lots of assistance from my family and many friends, and of course, after the first few babies, then you have built-in little helpers! And it gets easier. So my only advice to you is to have many more babies, and you will soon have your team of assistants in the home!"

Everyone started cheering, "More babies!"

With a nervous laugh, Padma said, "Oh no, I believe we are done. Raj and I talked about it, and I think that we will stop with two babies." She looked at Raj's mother, "I am not you. You are such a strong, accomplished woman. I can't even imagine you having a down day. But I understand what you are saying. Even so, how did you do it? How did you have eight children and manage to be a physician?"

"I would also like to know this," Uma said with great interest.

Several of the others also chimed in. Certainly, this question had been on many of their minds throughout the years.

Raj's mother sat back in a chair, threw her hands up in the air, and shrugged her shoulders.

"In this case, I wish that I had a deeper wisdom to share with you. I just did it. When I was tired, I slept. When I needed a break, I asked for help to get one. When I had to go back to work, I let the other family members jump in. You know, we have a very big family, Padma. I have seven siblings, and Raj's father has five. With all the Aunties and cousins and children, there seems to be a plethora of assistance, admittedly, sometimes more than one wants at times, but yes, always someone to help. And you have to learn that you are married into this fine mess! You and Uma now have so many more women to count on in your life than each other. And while we do not come close to the bond you two share, you will find great strength in leaning on us when you need to."

"I am so glad that you say this," Uma said, "Because I need someone to come and clean my house with me every week. And maybe to cook — and help with the laundry."

Everyone began to laugh again.

"I am not kidding!" Uma said, then laughed. For certain, if anyone had offered, she surely would have taken them up on it.

The women sat and chatted for some time, sharing stories of good and bad times and how they had reached out to one another. Padma was truly touched, and while she knew that she could lean on so many, she was wondering if Raj's mother's idea of talking to a professional might be a starting point. She still felt it difficult to completely share. Those ways of holding in the difficult things were a family trait that ran very deep in her. So after the women broke up and everyone began to leave, she asked her for a recommendation, and Raj's mother said that she would reach out to a friend and have a name for her by the next day. But before the evening ended, Sangeeta came back up to Padma with one last thought.

"And get back to your yoga! Raj told me it was helping you with things, and I know you felt good after going. It is a way to bring all the parts of you, body, mind, and soul, together. It is a great method of unifying within you and creating an inner peace and calm that helps you navigate your world."

Padma already knew this to be true and promised Sangeeta that she would put yoga back into her weekly schedule as a non-negotiable, parties and social events be damned.

What started as chaos ended in a deep blessing of love and support. Padma was certain that there was more working through these situations to come, but she also knew that with all the amazing women in her life, she would never go it alone again. And maybe, just maybe, that was not such a bad thing after all.

That evening, before climbing into bed, she paused at the bathroom mirror, gazing into her weary eyes.

"It's time to let go of the shame about asking for help," she said to herself.

She took a deep breath and smiled. Already, she felt lighter for just giving herself that permission.

Yogini in the Making

"Yoga is not about touching your toes, it's about what you learn on the way down." - Jigar Gor.

"Inhale," said Ashanti, "breathe in the good new energy. Now exhale and blow out all the old energy that does not serve you."

Padma allowed herself to receive good, positive energy and then imagined any negative energy leaving her like black smoke. Fifteen minutes into yoga practice, she already felt like a new woman.

"Inhale again, "Ashanti said, "and press through your arms, lifting your heart upward toward the sky into Cobra pose. Be careful to drop the shoulders down from the back of your head, and keep that neck long. Now, exhale and smile because it's just yoga, darlings. Don't take it so seriously!"

The class laughed in unison.

The vibe at Laughing Lotus was a beautiful blend of chill and will. Through the right effort and relaxation, Padma was finding the class levels perfect for her mom's body. She had permission to draw back and relax when she needed to take a pause or to push herself to her edge when she felt the energy was there for it. She'd had various gym memberships in the past, and in comparison, the yoga studio felt quite non-competitive and unlike any gym she'd been to. There was also more of a community feeling, as if they were family, at Laughing Lotus. Padma had only been going for two-and-a-half months consecutively and already felt quite comfortable with the friendships she had made there. She wished the location was closer for Melanie to attend with her, but on occasion, the women would switch and visit each other's studios as yoga buddies. It was always nice to change things up. And meeting more friendly people through yoga was certainly not a bad thing.

Padma had also started a weekly therapy session and was feeling that the conversations with her therapist, along with the weekly yoga practices, were helping her to both understand and balance her moods. Yoga, in addition, was assisting with her physical discomforts due to recent pregnancies. She was feeling stronger and more at ease in her body. Ashanti was her favorite teacher. She exuded warmth and nurturance, a truly authentic teacher with a knack for understanding what she was feeling without ever asking her a question.

Uma was aware that Padma was attending regular yoga classes, and as time passed, she felt more at ease with the idea. But her daily prayers to Ganesha continued. She'd even purchased a small statue of Ganesha that she kept in her car, and she could pray to him for Padma from wherever she was. She didn't feel it necessary to share this with anyone, as she had many mixed emotions running through her. She understood Pamda when she talked about how everything that was happening was supposed to be so that their family could heal from the wounds of the past. Yet those old wounds had not ever healed for her, mostly because she had kept them hidden in the dark for so long. She was not like her daughter. Her daughter was strong-willed and open to new things. Uma didn't quite feel that she could change her ways. She was an old dog, unwilling to learn new tricks. Giving her daughter space was hard enough.

"Okay, so next inhale, raise those hips to the sky, push through the arms, and let the head hang. Give me a big sigh and let out anything you need to. Feel into this Downward Facing Dog," Ashanti said.

Then, coming over to Padma, who had already given her permission for hands-on adjustments, placed the palms of her hands along the small of her back and gently pressed Padma's hips up and back. Immediately, she felt ease in her shoulders and was even able to press her heels closer toward the floor. They didn't touch the floor, but according to all the teachers, they never needed to. This was something Padma was working through because somewhere in her beginner's mind, she felt she needed to have her heels flat for more security. Through this practice, she was somehow also learning to trust.

She didn't want Ashanti to leave. The support of the teacher in a yoga class is magical. Padma noticed that with just a simple gesture, her body was suddenly able to move much deeper than it had moments before. Alas, Ashanti gently released her touch and moved away from Padma with the grace of a butterfly.

After class, Padma sat on the bench, putting her shoes back on and preparing to exit the warm studio for the cold winter awaiting her outside.

"Hey, Padma, thanks for coming to class today. I enjoyed practicing with you," Ashanti said, sitting down next to her on the bench.

"I assure you," Padma said sincerely, "the honor was entirely mine. I love your classes. I always feel so much better at the end."

"Ah, thank you. Hearing that never gets old," Ashanti said, smiling. "Did you see the upcoming retreat to India I posted on the message board last week?"

Padma had not seen the post. Usually, she rushed into class from dinner and then headed right back home to put the kids to bed. She relayed this to Ashanti.

"Well, I just thought perhaps you might be interested in going with us. It is a year away, and we are going to be taking a real pilgrim's path. I saw you with us in a dream."

"Wow, you know, as a Marketing person, that is a fantastic method of recruitment," Padma laughed, hoping Ashanti would also. But truthfully, she didn't doubt that Ashanti was being authentic by sharing the dream.

"Hah! I never even thought of it that way. I suppose I should consider how I say that a little more in the future," Ashanti replied.

"Oh, honestly, I was joking with you. But as for the journey to India, well, it hasn't been on my radar. With two small children at home and having difficulty sometimes managing that, it may not be in the cards for me right now."

"I hear you, Ashanti said. "It is difficult to leave my children when I travel, but there's something about Mother India. I've been there three times, and each time is more magical than the last. I find if I release and allow Spirit to guide me that, I am taken to deep places that allow for healing to occur where I didn't even realize that there was something that needed to be moved to another level.

"I decided to take a group with me this time, and I am allowing my intuition to guide me as to who is right to come with us and who may not be ready for the journey. I feel like there is something within you ready to open, and India can be the key to allowing that sacred flowering within you. I see you embodying the wisdom of your name on a whole other scale.

I see you embodying the wisdom of your name on a whole other scale. What did Ashanti mean by that?

"Take a look at the flyer or website, and think about it. I have a meeting coming up next week to discuss what is happening, and I would love your presence there if it feels right to you. And, if not, then okay." Ashanti finished.

Padma promised to look into it. But a big retreat to the motherland felt a bit extravagant to her. She thought about what Rajesh would say about the trip and pictured him booking her tickets and putting her in a limo to the airport. She laughed a bit out loud, considering it. Raj would do anything for her and to support her well-being. If he thought a yoga retreat in India would be good for her, he would be sending her right off.

Now, Uma was another thought entirely. Although she was considerably more tolerant of her newfound love of yoga, the idea of Padma going on a yoga retreat to India could very well restart her mother's former fears about it as they pertained to Nani. Certainly, her yoga classes at Laughing Lotus were quite different and less threatening to her than an ashram in India, which would most likely be Guru-based. Although, she did not know that to be true.

After pondering Ashanti's invitation, Padma decided that a yoga retreat was not that important to her at this time. Her life was pretty full right where she was. So, she left the studio without checking the message board and felt good about heading home to her family, refreshed and energized from her practice that morning.

When she got into the car, she paused to check her messages and emails before heading home. Laughing Lotus's email about the yoga retreat to India popped up first. She chuckled. Now, it seemed the Universe was being a little pushy with her. But she simply deleted the email and went about her evening activities, tidying up around the living room, running the dishwasher, and removing little pieces of food tucked into all the places that Nina could find to press them into with her dainty little fingers. This was an evening game that she was sure Nina played on purpose. Padma continued cleaning up the house. At some point, her cell phone began to ring. A glance revealed it to be Melvin, who she had not spoken with for what felt like ages. Enthusiastically, she yelled, "Melvin!"

"Padma!" He replied with the same vigor. "I miss you, girl, how are you?"

"Very good, Melvin. Very well. Had a lovely yoga class today, came home and spent time with the family, cleaned up, and prepared a late dinner with Raj, who should be home soon. What more can a girl want?"

Padma and Melvin giggled.

"Well, I am not sure what a girl may want, but it does sound like a lovely day," Melvin said.

"To what do I owe the pleasure of your call?" Padma asked.

"Well," Melvin began, "I just saw an email from Laughing Lotus come through."

"Oh."

"Did you see it?" Melvin inquired.

Padma had to think. Had she seen the email? Even though she was feeling better these days, it didn't take away the frazzled evening mommy brain. Then she recalled sitting in her car checking emails and the blast about the trip.

"Oh, yes, the yoga retreat," Padma said, lackluster but also curious why this little retreat didn't seem to want to go away today and kept coming back into her consciousness.

"Hey, that was not the response I was thinking I would get," Melvin said.

Padma took a deep breath and sat down on the couch. "Honestly, I just can't see myself going away right now. There's too much going on here at home with the kids and life."

"Got it. Well, for what it is worth, Melanie and I are going to go to the meeting next week. We are thinking about going to India to celebrate our anniversary, which is around the same time. And it sounds like something we both need," Melvin revealed to Padma.

"Well, it sounds lovely to you. I just don't think it's in the cards for me. But, if you two decide to celebrate your anniversary another way, I am sure Raj and I would join you if it was closer to home and easier to manage."

It was not lost on her that the Universe wanted her to take a look at this yoga retreat. And she was beginning to wonder why she was being so dismissive of the idea. She and Melvin caught up a bit more and then hung up just about when Raj was coming home late from work.

Rajesh walked into the house, dropped his bag, and went right over to Padma, giving her a long hug.

"Just who I needed to see," he said, squeezing her a bit tighter than usual.

Concerned, Padma held her husband tight until he released the grip. She didn't say a word and waited for him to speak. Raj sat down at the table and began to share about his day.

"Today was rough. There was a car accident on the highway that brought in two families," Raj paused, trying to find the words to continue. Padma handed him a glass of water and held his hand, waiting.

"Agh, okay. We worked nonstop for hours in the ER. My entire staff poured themselves into these families. In the end, the mother of one vehicle and two of the children from the other died."

Padma gasped and began to cry.

"Two broken families," Raj said, crying into his hands.

These were the moments that Padma dreaded. Not only was Raj upset, but the story stirred thoughts in her mind that something like this could happen to their family.

"I have to ask," Padma paused, "How did it happen? The accident?"

Raj looked at her and shook his head. "We can't be sure, but there is a theory that one of the children dropped something, and the mother reached around to hand it back to him, taking her eyes off the road for a couple of seconds and just long enough to veer into the other lane."

"Oh, no," Padma shook her head and wiped her tears.

"I couldn't wait to come home to my family and to kiss you and the girls. We did everything that we could," Raj said, laying his head in Padma's bosom.

Each time she put the babies in the car, Padma's motherly instincts reached new limits. Aware that anything could happen, she chose to believe that the Universe was looking over them and then, with the awareness of a hawk, watched with the eyes in the back of her head for any emerging dangers. When she reached her destination safely, she felt she could take her first breath again. For this reason, she chose not to take the girls to many places and stay in their safe little abode more often than not. She realized on one level that hiding out was not going to work forever and that even at home, things could go wrong. But for some reason, she just wanted to shelter them as long as she could and create the sense that all was well.

Rajesh and Padma went up to check in on the sleeping girls. Nina lay in her bed with her favorite stuffed animals surrounding her. She lay on her back with her arms up. Her little body rested diagonally across the bed as if it wanted to take up all the space that it could. Every few moments, her little fingers would twitch. She must have been deep into a dream, and it would be a shame to wake her.

Rajesh tiptoed over to Nina and kissed her gently on her forehead. He waited a moment or so before turning back to his lovely wife, hugging her, and stepping out of the room. Something within him seemed to soften after seeing Nina and validating that she was okay. He smiled and hugged Padma at the waist as they moved into the baby's room, only to find her sitting up in her crib as if she were waiting for her parents to arrive.

Padma giggled, and Raj ran over to the crib and picked up his baby girl, swinging her around. The baby laughed and kicked her feet and arms about.

"Not too loud," Padma said lovingly, "Don't wake Nina!"

"Oh, who cares? If Nina wakes up, we can have some family bonding time," Raj said, whipping his baby around.

"And not too fast because she can spit up," Padma said.

Raj stopped spinning and gripped the baby around his hip, turning to his wife.

"I know what you're saying, but after what I've seen today, I'll take a little spit up and my kids awake past bedtime."

Raj bounced over to Padma and kissed her rapidly all over her face. The baby and Padma giggled. She understood what he meant, and although she sometimes went through a lot to put the kids to bed, at the end of the day, Raj enjoying his family was more important than getting them to sleep again.

"Life is too short, Padma. You know? You think you have more time to do things, to be with your family, to say the things you wanted to say, but sometimes you don't have the time you thought. We have to live large every day. We have to love more all the time. We should not let life stop us if something is important in our heart," Raj said as he sat on the floor with the baby, gently rubbing her belly.

Padma nodded her head. He was correct. In an instant, anything can change. The possibilities are endless. But instead of focusing on what wrong things could happen, it was more important to focus on making space for what was in one's heart, where all the really important things sit.

As she watched her husband play with the baby, she looked into the depths of her heart to find what stood out as the most important things. Her family came in at the top of this list. Without them, she had no life. But what lies beyond that? What significant things sat in the hidden spaces in her heart?

She left Raj to play with the baby and went downstairs to make a cup of tea, then sat tall on the living room floor, crossed her legs, and closed her eyes. She took a few deep breaths in and out of her nose, relaxing her mind and calming her body. The body part was easy, for that was forever tired and easily relaxed. But the mind, the constant chattering of data, like a computer that just ran and ran on its own without an operator at the helm, was the tricky part. Even as she tried to meditate, she realized that not focusing on her thoughts only brought more awareness to how many of them there were.

Padma took a long, deep breath out of her mouth, like a sigh, just the way Ashanti taught them to take the surrender breath, which she now confidently joined in with at class. It did help, momentarily. And then, the thoughts were back. She took another deep breath and began to visualize a blue sky with white billowy clouds. As she breathed, she could see the wind gently moving the clouds. She had an idea to place her thoughts on the clouds and let them gently roll out of her mind.

Her first thought was of something dangerous that could rip her family away from her. This fear seemed to nag her all the time, creating anxiety and restlessness. As she sat with the thought, she realized how much that fear was controlling the rest of her. Thinking about losing what was most important to her tensed her body, she now realized. She felt more thoughts invade her mind like a swarm of ants on a freshly dropped piece of fruit. Her breath quickened, and her chest constricted. She realized at some point that she was almost holding her breath as the painful glimpses of this potential situation overcame her.

Taking another surrender breath, Padma returned her mind to the image of the sky and placed that awful fear on a cloud. Immediately, it turned into a black storm cloud with lightning and a thunderous charge. She focused on deep breathing and releasing the cloud out of her mind's eye the way Ashanti taught her. And as the cloud moved away, the sun came back out, and the blue sky was restored. At that moment, she recognized that, sure, anything could change in an instant, but more so, that she was the one steering the ship of her mind, just as Ashanti had told her on that first day after class.

With her now in control, she quickly shifted her thoughts and reality. A more peaceful sense came over her body, she felt more relaxed again and focused on staying present with her breathing. This proved a great tool in regulating the fears that gripped her and releasing their power over her.

Soon, a sense of calm overcame her in a way she had not felt before. She realized that she was both present in the here and now, yet not engaged in any distractions. She felt herself hover in this blissful place for some time, and truly, she had lost track of linear time and had no real understanding of just how long she'd been there until Raj came back downstairs into the room. She could sense his presence, but he remained quiet. Padma brought her awareness back to her breathing and into her body, slowly moving and stretching, and finally opening her eyes to see her loving husband also in a meditative posture with his eyes closed.

She sat still, watching him until he started to move about and awaken as she had. When they locked eyes, they both smiled. Neither one moved any closer to the other but simply held space for each other. Again, there was no sense of time in this space.

Most days are not perfect by any stretch of the imagination. Life is complicated and messy. For a mom, it can get out of hand as you navigate managing the house, kids, and partner, tending to everyone's well-being, and still getting in your self-care. Padma was starting to understand, however, that most of the things that created stress or complicated her life were her creations and that just as she gave them power, she also could take it back.

Now, this was not something she had mastered. She wondered if true mastery would ever come to pass. But at least she had some tools to help her now, and she was seeing very positive results in just a very short time. Would this change who she was? No, she would always be Padma, the good girl who wanted to make everyone happy and have everything just perfect. But would these tools of yoga and meditation assist her in not losing her mind in the process of living? It sure looked like it.

It wasn't the slow, passionate love-making between her and her husband that evening that helped her sleep so deeply — although it probably helped. What helped her sleep the best was the knowledge that life was precious, and at least for that night, she had everything that she needed right under her roof. She would take it.

An Important Decision

"Courage is feeling the fear and doing it anyway." - Oprah Winfrey.

"Wait, let me get this straight: you're getting married, and a nayan has found your mate for you?"

Padma's mouth was wide open. Payal had just told her that she was engaged, and it was an arranged marriage through a matchmaker or nayan. She'd met and spoken with him online but not in person. Currently, he was working out of the country and would be back in the USA next month, when they would meet and then have their wedding ceremony. This was an unprecedented situation nowadays, as most young Indians preferred to find their mates and marry on their terms, having first fallen in love with their partner. Payal was trusting someone other than herself to find the love of her life.

"I don't know why you're so surprised, Padma. You know I want to be married, and it's just not working out for me as it did for you and our other friends. I mean, I know I am a great catch, but for some reason, there are no fish in the waters around here," Payal told her friend over FaceTime. "Furthermore, you should close your mouth before a fly gets in it."

Slowly closing her mouth, Padma had no other words for her friend. It was easy for Payal to see her friend's dismay at this decision, so she tried to make jokes to lighten the mood.

"You know what it's called when Indian parents throw their kid a surprise party?" Payal asked, laughing at her joke before the punchline.

"Wait, what?" Padma asked, confused and not realizing the line was a joke.

"It's called an arranged marriage!" Payal continued to laugh, barely getting the words out.

"What?" Padma asked again, still confused about what Payal was saying.

"Oh my god, Padma, it is a stupid Indian joke. Why are you reacting so strangely? I mean, where is your faith in the Universe?"

Padma felt that the idea of an arranged marriage was outdated, and she truly felt that her friend deserved more. Her friend deserved the same kind of mutual love that she had found. There were no guarantees that you would hit it off in an arranged marriage. What if she was not attracted to him? What if he was abusive? The more she thought about it, the more questions she had.

This was her go-to personality trait, though, the one that she was working so hard to let go of. The one that focused on the worst-case scenario and not the positive possibilities. In the past, she would have let her mind continue to run wild and create anxiety and stress until it became out of hand, however, through the mindfulness that the yoga practice brought into her life, she got better at catching herself when she began falling into these old patterns.

Padma took a deep breath, exhaled, smiled, and softened her face. She needed to be more positive for her friend because she had already decided the wedding was happening. And there was no reason to focus on the possible negative aspects. She stood up taller and shifted her reaction.

"You're right, Payal. You are right. I'm not being a good friend to you right now. I realize this is a huge step for you, and I see that you are excited about it, so I promise to do whatever you need. Just tell me what you need," Padma said, forcefully smiling yet still meaning what she said.

Padma recognized how quickly energy shifted just by changing her thoughts. She saw it every day, and the more she caught herself, the quicker everything shifted for the better. The fact that bad things happen was not lost on her. Raj reminded her of these things often as he came home and shared what he had experienced at the hospital. But she found choosing what to focus on made life much nicer. Was she living in a fantasy? No. Because most of the time, life was truly unbelievably great. And, when something challenging happened, she was learning that she could figure it out with a little help from her family and friends.

All of this was an enormous change to her thought process, and it had come about in just a few short months of regular yoga practice, combined with a few counseling sessions. She enjoyed the community she was getting to know at the yoga studio. Generally, everyone was very nice and open about their life and positive changes since they had started practicing yoga regularly. The teachers were all welcoming and supportive of the journey, too. Even when she found herself crying on the mat, which did happen, there was a nurturing hand suddenly rubbing her back or supporting her in some way.

It was a shame that she hadn't practiced yoga until recently. She tried not to hold any negative feelings toward her mother for keeping her away from the practice when It was clear that her grandmother would have wanted to teach her. This nagging annoyance in the back of her mind only crept in when she watched other students who had been practicing longer at the yoga studio be able to go deeper into postures than she could.

The yoga teachers always reminded them that yoga was not a competition and they needed to work at their own pace and ability. This is why many modifications were taught in the classes. Maybe it was her driven nature, but Padma couldn't help but notice the more advanced positions and wished that she could do them with as much grace and agility as some of the other more practiced students. Competition was certainly alive in the yoga studio, even if only in her mind. Again, this was a work in progress.

"Well, that is more like it, sister! I need you to be my maid of honor! I need you to stand up for me, to help me get dressed, and to help me pee during the reception," Payal joked.

They both laughed. Padma had chosen to have only one drink for her wedding reception so that she would not have to put any of her friends in the position of helping her to the bathroom in her monstrously large dress. Other friends had not been so kind, and she had all too many memories of awkward incidents in bathrooms at various weddings.

"Oh my goddess, do you remember at Sejal's wedding…" Payal began and then couldn't finish due to laughter.

Padma joined her in laughing because she recalled it all too well. For some reason, the way Sejal's dress was made, there was no easy way to hike it up so that she could relieve herself. To make matters worse, the bathroom stalls in her reception hall were so tiny that they couldn't fit another person in with her. So, Payal and another friend hung over the top of the stall, reaching down towards the dress while two others went under the stall onto the floor and used a broom to push the fabric upward enough for the two perched above to hold it. Sejal had to unhook a piece underneath her dress to allow her to sit on the toilet. With all this effort, Sejal still sprinkled pee on her dress, the floor, and some of her friends. They spent about forty minutes in the bathroom between the incident and subsequent clean-up. That evening, Padma had to shower the bathroom stink off her before climbing into bed.

"Promise me that we can practice going to the bathroom before you purchase your dress!" Padma said, laughing.

"Deal! I do not want to create those kinds of memories. I have too many other things on my mind."

"The book?" Padma asked.

Payal nodded, then picked up what appeared to be an antique bible, about four inches thick, with papers spilling out in all directions. Since grade school, she'd been gathering all the ideas for her perfect dream wedding into this book. Padma was allowed a small glimpse here or there throughout the years but had never seen the full scale of its contents. And there it was, the book that Payal had been adding to for about thirty-five years, looming in the distance, threatening to spill into her life and take over everything. Where were they to begin?

"Wow," Padma said, "*That*, there are no words for that."

"Let me tell you, this book is worth some money, baby. I could write a best-selling wedding-planning book with the contents of this manual," Payal said.

"Well, maybe let's get through this one first. But I have a question: does your nayan assist with the wedding planning?" Padma said.

"Oh, Padma. You really should know these basic things. No, the nayan only serves as the go-between in the matchmaking. She is my mom's friend and my fiancé's Auntie. It took her about three minutes to put us together. She has a long client list. And if you are in the community, she has you down on that list. She knows everyone! She is amazing."

"Wow, do you think I was on her list? I feel like that is kind of creepy to stalk unmarried people," Padma said.

"Oh, stop. This is about me. Who cares if you were on her list or not? You've been married for like forty years…"

"…Five," Padma corrected her friend.

"Okay, for like five years. Who cares. This. Is. About. Me!" Payal said, screaming at the end, "I'm getting married!!!"

Padma felt obligated to scream with her friend. This alerted Nina, who came bounding into the room and began to join in on the screaming, considering it a game. Padma scooped up her little one so Payal could see Nina through the camera.

"Guess who is getting married, Nina? Auntie Payal!"

"Yay!" Nina said, clapping with her mother. In reality, she just wanted to join in the revelry; she had no concept of weddings or the situation being celebrated.

"Listen, Payal, I doubt we will get any real conversation in at this point, so let's plan like dinner or something to talk more about what you want to do for the wedding."

The women made a plan and said their goodbyes, Padma turning her focus back to her little girls and creating an afternoon of play. The girls loved the yoga poses that she was teaching them.

The baby watched and smiled whenever they did a little family yoga. Nina was still a little young for the kid's yoga classes at the studio, so she figured she would channel her grandmother's energy and show her a couple of fun things here and there, just enough to spark her imagination and interest in yoga. She certainly wanted to give Nina the opportunities that were not given her. Whenever she thought about her grandmother's passion for yoga, she wondered if she should dive deeper into the practice.

Maybe that's why she found herself online that evening, reading details about the India yoga retreat with Ashanti and the Laughing Lotus crew. Melvin and Melanie had already put their deposits down. Aside from the yoga, it would be a fun and exciting trip because she would be traveling with her good friends. And even though that was a huge bonus, it was not what was fueling her interest at the moment. It was the ability to truly heal some of the ancestral wounds still energetically tied to her, originating with her grandmother, the Guru, and yoga.

The more she thought about the situation, the more she felt driven to return to India. She considered visiting the ashram where her grandmother lived at the end of her life. She found herself researching how close to that area the retreat was and if it might be possible to check it out.

India is a large place. With over a billion people, 28 territories, and 121 languages, it is one of the most varied and spiritual locales. When one goes to India, it is truly a full-sensory explosion. From the various herbs and culinary traditions to the smell of incense wafting in from local temples, one can be overwhelmed with the fragrant aromas.

The majority of the population, approximately 80 percent, practice Hinduism. In that religion, numerous representations of gods and goddesses, deities, and spiritual symbolism combine to create an explosion of color — particularly red and gold. The sparkles and bling of India are surpassed by none.

Visually, the only thing that stands out amid all the color is the natural landscapes that reveal her authentic beauty. The sacred rivers, such as the Mother Ganges, which have been elevated to the status of a Goddess, flow with unmatched beauty. In the north, the Ganges flows eastward from the base of the Himalayas into the Bay of Bengal. It is a pure cleansing essence. Framed by snowcapped mountains, the Ganges is known to be the goddess of purification and forgiveness. Many walk into her waters, seeking freedom from the heavy energies of the past and to elevate their spirit.

From the overwhelmingly beautiful natural setting in the north, India changes drastically as you travel south. Certainly, the cliffside cities of Varkala and Goa promise a refreshing coastal vibe. And, of course, in the middle, between the mountains of the north and the sea towns of the south, India does not disappoint. The decadence of the Taj Mahal, a memorial built to honor an emperor's diseased wife, is now listed as one of the Seven Wonders of the World due to its stunning architecture and is an absolute must on the list of attractions for one to visit while traveling to India.

As luck would have it, the yoga retreat did have a few of those locations on the itinerary. But, the places that interested Padma were the ashrams in Rishikesh. Known as the "yoga capital of the world," Nani's ashram was located a short distance from the city of Rishikesh." It certainly was not on the list, but Padma still pondered if she could sneak away there anyway during the retreat. Well, there were many questions, that being just one of them. Others were:

Should she go to the ashram? What was she truly looking for there? Would it destroy her mother if she went? All of those questions just left her with a whole bunch more.

Padma pushed herself back in the chair and rubbed her head with her hands. Certainly, this was an opportunity, and something moved her to dive into it. She just needed to determine whether it was that important to her. At the same time, she continued to tell herself that it was not, something in her kept coming back again and again to these questions.

Just then, Raj passed the office and saw Padma rubbing her head. "What's up, sweetness?" he asked, coming over and planting a kiss on his wife's cheek.

"Ah, well, you want to know?" Padma replied, smiling.

"Of course I do!"

She took a deep surrender breath and started to talk. Those breaths were becoming an important staple in her life. Rajesh knew it, too, and chuckled. He was starting to enjoy her deep exhales as they warned him that something deep was brewing in her mind, and she was about to reveal it to him.

"I am thinking about going to India on this yoga retreat," Padma told her husband, then squinted. "What would you think about that?"

Raj shrugged his shoulders. "Okay."

Padma leaned in. "Okay?"

He shrugged his shoulders again, "Yeah. Okay."

She threw her hands up in the air, a little annoyed.

"You mean to tell me that your wife, the mother of your two little children, the one who manages the household and takes care of everyone, including you, could just take off for two weeks to India, and you have nothing more to say about it? Like, am I that insignificant?"

"What?" Raj said, confused. He truly thought supporting his wife with whatever she wanted would be welcomed. "How did this turn around?"

She glared at him, unamused at his grin. He folded his arms across his chest and glared back at her.

"Padma, seriously. If you want to go to India, I'll support that decision because we have many supportive friends and family to assist us while you're away. No, it's not the same as you being here, but we can manage."

She folded her arms across her chest and tried to hold back a smile. Of course, he was right. Why was he always — no, usually right?

"Well, I'm considering it. But I have some concerns and questions. I need to sit with it a little more before I decide. And I probably should talk to my mother about it."

Raj shook his head, listening intently. "How do you feel that will go, talking to your mom about it?"

She smiled and nodded her head. He smiled, then changed to a grimace, considering Uma's possible reaction.

"Well, let me ask you, what is your primary purpose for the trip? Is it to get away? To dive into yoga? Or to look into your grandmother's history at her ashram?"

How did he know what she was thinking? Because he knew her.

"Well, first of all, I do not need to get away from all of this," Padma said, opening her arms, referring to everything in their home.

Raj chuckled, "Of course."

"Yes, so having said that, yes, I like the idea of immersing myself in yoga, seeing if I can go deeper and where it could take me if I had the time to focus on that. But..."

She paused before launching into the real reason behind the intentions.

"But..." Raj waited.

"I can't explain it. It's like," she paused, seeking the right explanation for her feelings. "I understand what happened and why my mother feels she lost her mother to that Guru. I feel like signs are pointing me to go there. Maybe it is to heal the origins of our family's wounds. Or maybe it's to discover something else for myself. I never thought I would need to return to India on some finding-myself trip, yet there's something to that.

"And, also, it's like, I have these strong roots in India and yoga, and yet I don't fully understand them. I think I need to connect to Nani and to that somehow."

Padma finished with another surrender breath. She had gotten it all out, all of her thoughts on going to India on this retreat. It was out there. That was how she felt. And she now also felt relieved. And with the relief and the honesty, she felt even more certain that she needed to go to India on the retreat. In the process of answering Raj's question, she had convinced herself to go.

"Well," Raj said, getting up to kiss his wife again. "I guess that settles it. You are going to India."

Padma smiled. She felt good about it.

"I'm going to India," she said out loud.

Now, the only thing left was to say it to her mother.

Mothers and Daughters

"The mother-daughter relationship is the most complex." - Wynonna Judd.

Several months before the India trip, Padma had taken to a daily home yoga practice to prepare her body for more rigorous and frequent practices. Although Ashanti had promised her that she only needed to work at her level and pace, even in India, she felt a need to be, well, better at it. The old competitive nature was still rearing its ugly head for Padma. She just couldn't help herself. Whatever she put her mind to, she needed to do to the very best of her abilities. And yoga was certainly something that she knew she could understand better.

Of course, a home practice is trickier than going to the studio, where there is soft lighting, ambient music, and a teacher to guide you. At home, she was lucky to have a spot where she wasn't stepping over toys, listening to mumblings on a baby monitor, and watching herself in the mirror. Melanie had suggested she not use the mirror, but how else was she supposed to know what she was doing?

Normally, she had time about an hour to practice when the girls took their afternoon naps. With the baby and Nina fast asleep, she rolled her yoga mat out and slid into the child's pose position, stretching out her arms in front of her and placing her forehead on the ground. She took several deep breaths and enjoyed marinating in the moment of silence, where she could connect with herself on a profound level. She only managed a few postures some days, losing herself in the moment of being present. Other times, she felt a wave of energy move through her, propelling her into the Sun Salutation series, a particular arrangement of postures done to promote a fiery, uplifting energy. There was never a plan when she got on the mat. She simply allowed herself to connect and feel where she needed to be at that moment. She came to know it as her intuitive guidance. And that was the biggest plus to having a home practice.

Somewhere into the practice that day, Padma's cell phone went off. Although she had it on vibrate, she could not avoid checking it. Uma had left her another message, making it three since she had spoken to her mother several days ago.

She pressed on with her yoga practice, not wanting to ignore her mother, but unable to find the right words to say after revealing that she was going to India on the yoga retreat. Uma cried. Padma didn't know what else to say or do. Her father called Padma to discuss the trip and her mother's feelings about her going. And although she listened to him, she also told him she needed to listen to herself first.

Besides, she told him, what if her going to India could put the issues to rest for the family and heal everything from the past? Swarup couldn't see how that could happen from a yoga retreat.

What he could see was how going to India was affecting his wife, who had thrown her car Ganesha statue in the trash and discontinued any prayers, having felt as if the gods had truly abandoned her in her time of need.

Padma found the whole situation silly. Maybe her mother failed to see that the gods *were* in her favor, protecting Padma and guiding her to India. Just maybe the gods had better judgment than her mother had. She wished she could convince Uma to take yoga classes with her because she could see that her mother could benefit.

On this day, on the mat, she chose to work on some hip openers and strengthening postures such as lunges, Goddess pose, and pigeon. She moved into whatever felt natural next, remembering some of the sequencing from previous yoga classes. She knew to start slow and gradually progress, to keep postures simple in the beginning, and to move toward more complex ones. And she certainly did not forget the final relaxation because that was her favorite part of the whole class. When she lay down and closed her eyes, she could feel all the energy in her body coursing through her in tingles and pulsations. The sensations made her feel vibrantly alive and very grateful. As a bonus, if the babies were still sleeping, she would allow herself time in meditation at the end. Her alarm clock was usually a moaning child, and then she would gently rise and, feeling refreshed, head back into mommy mode with newfound vigor.

At dinnertime, Nina sat in her chair and the baby in hers as Padma danced around the kitchen, tossing random food pieces onto their plates. Nina giggled, grabbed a noodle or a piece of chicken, popped it in her mouth, and danced in her chair. The baby smeared the contents as if making a masterpiece of food finger paint rather than eating. This was normal. Padma was okay with it all.

In the middle of the dance-and-eat game, Padma's phone rang again, this time through her iPad that was docked upright in the kitchen. Although Nina couldn't read, she knew it was her Nani and announced it out loud. Padma decided to answer, as this was as good a time as any.

"Hello, Mommy," she said with a smile.

"Nana," said Nina with a slight scream.

Uma smiled at the site of the babies through the video on her mobile phone.

"Hello, my grand-babies," she said, beaming from ear to ear. "What is for dinner tonight? What did mommy make you?"

Nina picked up some random pieces of food and held them up in the air, but they were too far for Uma to see, which did not stop her from leaning forward toward the camera anyway. This created a funny super closeup of Uma's nose, which sent Nina into a full laughing fit. Padma thought it was funny, too.

"Mommy, you are too close to the camera. We cannot see your face," she laughed.

"Oh, what is it to you? So what about my face? I can see you," she said, then added, "Anyway, I am glad that you picked up finally."

"Yes, yes, I am sorry, Mommy. It seems like there is always something going on when you call, and then I get busy and, well, anyway, here we are now. How are you feeling?"

Padma thought it best to divert the query to another thing entirely, as she wanted to avoid any possible argument with her mother. She was in too good a mood today for that.

"I am okay. I am fine. Your father is fine. We want to come see you tomorrow. Is that okay?"

"Oh," Padma said, "Sure."

Her mother had caught her off-guard. Was tomorrow a good day for a visit? She couldn't even think at the moment. Instead, she decided to simply go with it. It was overdue anyway.

"And Daddy is coming too?" She asked.

"Yes. Daddy wants to see his grand-babies, too," Uma said.

After a couple of other pleasantries, Uma said goodbye, leaving Padma to wonder what tomorrow's visit might hold. Surely, she had no idea, but she was hoping for the best.

That night, she decided to make some of her mother's favorite snacks for the following day. Believe it or not, her mother loved all things tacos. And tomorrow was Tuesday, so Padma put together a Taco Tuesday and nachos bar to die for. She asked Rajesh if he could come home for a bit to see her parents and eat with them, and he was able to accommodate the request. She felt since her father and husband would all be there, the conversation had a better chance of going smoothly. She did not want to fight with Uma. She wanted her mother to be happy. But she also wanted her mother to accept her decision to go to India on a yoga retreat, which was quite different than the intention of any past trips there. She was hopeful that they would come to a good resolution. And the tacos would certainly help.

The next day, Uma bound into the kitchen, surprised to see the spread.

"Happy Taco Tuesday!" Padma said, giving her mother a huge hug.

Uma grinned and held her daughter tightly, perhaps a little too much so. But it was all because she loved her so very much. Above all, she wanted a nice visit and not to fight with Padma about going to India, doing yoga, or even worse, visiting Nani's ashram. No, she vowed to avoid that conversation entirely.

The women released their embrace, and Uma's eyes caught a glimpse of the sweatshirt Padma was wearing. Padma hadn't thought about it when she grabbed the shirt that morning. Honestly, it was clean and close by. It was a pink, cut-neckline sweatshirt with a drawing of a blue lotus flower with a figure of a woman meditating on top. Uma tugged at the shirt.

"The lotus flower," Uma said. "Did I ever tell you how we came to your name, Padma?"

Her daughter stopped short, puzzled. Suddenly, Ashanti's voice came into her head:

I feel like there is something within you ready to open, and India can be the key to allowing that sacred flowering within you to bloom. I see you embodying the wisdom of your name on a whole other scale.

"What? No, I don't believe so. Please," Padma motioned for her mother to come to the taco bar, "tell me."

"Well, it begins with the story of how your father and I just started dating. I was a lonely girl in India, and I was working at a local grocery market. Your father came in and was selling some lotus flowers. They were exquisite. I caught your father watching me, but I was very shy, so I ignored him. The next time he came in, he asked my name, and we started a friendship.

"Each week, he would come in to sell beautiful lotus flowers to the owner, and each week, he would give me one. Eventually, he built up the courage and asked me to go out with him. We didn't have any money, so it was a very simple meal of samosas on the riverside.

"Well, you know the rest, how we were married and moved to the United States to start our family. When you were born, the only thing I could think of was how we met with those beautiful lotus flowers. And I thought about that symbol and how these two poor children from India found their way to America and to a new life together. We grew just like the lotus flower out of a challenging situation and created this amazing life together. You are our sparkling jewel, and you mean more to us than anything else in the world."

Padma teared up. She had never heard that story before. The women embraced until Swarup broke them up.

"Now wait a minute, that story is incomplete and incorrect," he said sharply.

Uma slapped him on the arm. "Stop making fun, that story is entirely correct."

Padma loved to see her parents poke fun at each other.

"Tell me the story, Daddy," she said teasingly at her mother's expense.

"You be sure to tell the truth and not make up a story again," Uma scolded her husband.

"When do I do that?" He asked, winking at his daughter, knowing full well his propensity to embellish.

He continued, "It's the part about me watching you. That is not entirely true. I noticed you watching me first."

Uma slapped her husband again, lightly, on the arm, "I think perhaps your memory is going. I certainly did not watch you."

"But you said you saw me come into the market," Swarup said, with another wink to Padma.

Uma sighed, frustrated, "No, I saw a person, a man person, bringing in flowers. I noticed the flowers and not you at all. Just a person with beautiful flowers."

Padma was enjoying the little banter quite a bit. Nina giggled, too. Even the baby gave a quick chirp and smile, which Uma decided to use in her favor.

"You see, the baby even disagrees with you," she said.

Swarup popped a piece of cheese into his mouth and, without skipping a beat, replied, "Hmm, funny, the baby made the sound after you tried to tell us you noticed just a person, but not me. Do you know why? Because I was the person, and even the baby knows you are the one who was checking me out," Swarup spun around and shook his tush back and forth, creating more laughter from the grandchildren and forcing a snort from Padma.

Uma slapped her husband several times and shooed him away, then turned to Padma, "You see how men like to turn things around?"

At that moment, Rajesh came into the kitchen.

"Uh, what's going on here?" He said, smiling because Padma was smiling. It was a good moment to be walking in.

"We were talking about how I got my name, and my parents cannot seem to agree about a tiny fact. But, actually, Mommy, it does seem like you saw Daddy first when he came in with the flowers. I mean, he had a handful of flowers, so he probably stood out, and you saw him first."

Uma put her hands on her hips. Nina giggled again, and the baby chirped a quick laugh. Padma started laughing as she led her mother to the table.

"Mommy, what is so wrong about it? I think it's cute."

"Cute? What is cute? Okay, okay, I saw the person, that person, your father, and that is all. I *saw* him. So what? He came to *watch* me and then to give me flowers and to talk to me," Uma said as she began to create her hard taco.

Swarup sat down next to his wife and gave her a big, fat kiss on the cheek, ending with a lip-bubbling. She recoiled, flinching her shoulders up toward her ears. Nina and the baby laughed. When Uma looked at her husband, he wiggled his eyebrows up and down a few times at her playfully. Uma, releasing her guard, finally began to laugh. Raj decided to lay the same kiss on Padma, and soon, the entire table was smiling, laughing, and enjoying their time together on Taco Tuesday.

When the meal was over, Swarup took his grandchildren into the living room with Raj to play on the floor while Padma and Uma cleaned up the kitchen. It had been a very enjoyable meal, and neither woman was particularly thinking about anything else at the moment. They cleaned up mostly in silence, smiling and hugging each other when they locked gazes.

When they were finished, Padma wiped her hands on a dishtowel, folded it, and placed it on the sink. Uma took a big "Surrender" breath and sat down at the table again as if to indicate that she had had enough of the exercise of cleaning for the day. It was at that moment that Padma realized her mother chose to sit in the kitchen, alone with her, instead of heading to the living room with the men and children. A sudden sense of uneasiness came upon her as she pulled out the chair and sat down across from her mother. She folded her hands and waited to see what Uma had on her mind.

Uma rubbed her hands together in deep thought. She knew that she must have one more talk with her daughter and yet was unsure how to begin. Certainly, she did not wish to create disharmony on such a gorgeous day, and the last thing that she wanted was another fight with Padma. Someone had to break the silence, and she knew it had to be her.

Uma began, "Okay..."

But that was it.

Padma smiled at her mother, reaching across the table to hold her hands. Uma gazed up at Padma and smiled back. Did they need to say anything? Love was a silent language that all understood when they quieted enough to hear it. Anything and everything that she felt was out of a deep love for her daughter, something that she had never felt from her mother, although she had seen her mother exude that kind of love to her Guru.

Time had allowed Uma to feel into those issues with her mother and to realize that her relationship with Padma was completely different and always would be. Of course, there were times when she wanted to grab her daughter, shake her, and wake her up from whatever slumber her mind had taken to. Daughters can always test their mothers, can't they? Perhaps it was because Padma was an only child, or maybe it was just her nature, but they had never had any long or bad fights like some of her friends did with their daughters. No, they had it much easier, and their relationship was certainly strong and true. There was only one last thing that she wanted to say to Padma, and so she did.

"I am sorry, Padma. I want to give you my blessing. Go to India, have a fabulous time. Do the yoga there. I am okay."

Uma smiled as a single tear ran down her face. She had been holding on to so much grief for so long, and she was ready to let it go.

Padma wiped the tear from Uma's face and smiled. Relief washed over her body, and she felt the bit of tension that had arisen since she had revealed that she was going on the yoga retreat to subside. She and her mother sat, holding hands for a moment or so before she spoke, but words were not necessary. When authentic love is present, you can sit with someone forever.

"Mommy, I love you. Thank you. I will enjoy India," she said, finally. "But I do have one last question for you. Because I thought that Nani had named me, or now I cannot remember why I thought that."

Uma paused, took a breath, and looked into her daughter's eyes, smiling.

"Yes, it was her wish to name you Padma. But the story we told you tonight is true. We named you Padma to honor our own story, but yes, Nani had a part in it, too."

Padma smiled. That was enough for her.

The rest of the visit with her parents was wonderful. The children certainly enjoyed all the attention, especially Nina, who had already figured out how to manipulate everyone in the room with just a smile.

As Padma sat, enjoying the family time, she watched her own two little girls and took some time to contemplate what her relationship with her daughters would be like in another twenty or thirty years. She certainly was trying to be the best mom she could. As an only child, she didn't know how to raise *two* little girls. She had always been given 100% of her parent's attention. Nina had that for a short time, but now she shared the spotlight with baby Zoya. Padma never wanted either of them to feel slighted. She knew that she would make a point of giving special alone time to each of them to cultivate individual relationships with her daughters as well as family time. No matter how busy life got, she knew that those two little faces would always be the ones she would go to bed thinking about the most. And if they were happy and healthy and good people, then she would know she did a good job at being a mother. She felt so blessed to have a good role model for that in Uma.

Intentions

"When your intention is clear, so is the way." - Alan Cohen.

She couldn't wait to open the gift box from Ashanti. She knew that if she brought it into the house, she would first have to tend to the girls, so she parked down the street from her house, placed the box into her lap, and looked at the wrapping. The gold box weighed a pound or so and was tied with a beautiful red ribbon. A card with an elephant on the front was tucked inside the ribbon, and Padma slid it out and opened it up. It read:

Welcome to the India Yoga Retreat. I am excited for you to join us next month in our adventure together to the Motherland of Yoga, where we will immerse into the practices of yoga and meditation through a journey of the five types of yogic practice: Karma, Raja, Hatha, Jnana, and Bhakti.

To prepare for the travel ahead, on the night of this New Moon, open the contents of the box and create an altar where you can come to meditate, journal, or reflect upon what intentions you are creating for this journey. Setting clear intentions creates a powerful pathway for you to align with that same energy. Continue your ritual daily until we depart on the night of the Full Moon.

Thank you for trusting me as your spiritual guide.

In love, Ashanti

Padma read the note twice before gently unwrapping the ribbon and opening the gold gift box. Inside was another note with several items. First, there was a box of Satya Nag Champa cone incense with a small holder. Although she typically did not light incense at home, she did enjoy the smell of it in the studio. Lifting the box to her nose, she took a long whiff and smiled, immediately feeling connected to the yoga studio and the relaxing vibes it exuded.

The box also included a pink stone, a clear stone, a red candle, and a small statue of a goddess seated on a lotus flower. There was also a cloth at the bottom of the box. Padma scanned each item, one at a time, feeling them for understanding, before picking up the note inside, which read,

Padma, I have chosen these items for your home altar. Please choose a place at home where you can come to the altar daily for your retreat intentions.

Place the altar cloth down first to create a sacred space. Then, place the other items on the cloth in any way that feels appropriate.

When you come to the altar, light the red candle and incense. The incense is a gift for your goddess, and the light represents your spiritual essence being present. The two stones are rose quartz and clear quartz. Rose quartz is a stone representing love in all forms, and the clear quartz amplifies positive energy. If you like, you can hold one in each hand while meditating, or they can sit on the altar.

I have chosen the goddess Saraswati for you. She is the Hindu goddess of knowledge, music, and creativity. In yoga, she is revered as the Sushumna Nadi or Central Channel, in which the kundalini energy rises upward through the human body, assisting in spiritual liberation. Her mantra is:

Om Aim Sarawati Namaha translated as Salutations to the Goddess Saraswati.

Or, if you want to learn her Gayatri Mantra, which is translated to obtain success in business or any educational pursuit:

Om Aim Vagdevyai Vidmahe

Kamarajaya Dhimahi

Tanno Devi Prachodayat

Chant to her once, three times, or 108 times each time you light your candle and incense. Call her into your space, both externally and internally. Invite her to guide you from home to India and back safely. And ask her to reveal to you the knowledge and wisdom that you need at this time in your life. You can wear white to connect with her more closely. And if you want, you can put fresh flowers on the altar. That is up to you.

In Love, Ashanti

Padma picked up the goddess Saraswati statue. She was depicted as a beautiful woman sitting on a lotus flower with a dove at her feet. She was playing the Indian instrument, the veena, which looks similar to a guitar. Saraswati wore a white sari with gold stars and trim and a red blouse, also trimmed and adorned in gold.

Well, I am not just dipping my toes in now, am I? This feels like a full plunge.

She smiled. She loved her gift box from Ashanti and felt it very accurately represented what she needed to focus her energy on for the trip. Gently, she placed all the items back in the box and tied the ribbon back on top, enjoying the thought of opening the box for a second time as if it were the first.

That evening, after the little ones were asleep, Padma searched for the exact location to place her altar. Preferring a place where she could leave it out and have it to herself was going to be difficult, considering her little one loved to get into all of her things. But she eventually landed on a spot in her bedroom. A small antique table from India that was in her father's family made for a perfect base. The low stacking table, which was once part of a group, was hand-painted and decorated with little flowers and other ornate shapes into a mandala-type decoration. The cloth that Ashanti had given her to place down was lovely, but Padma decided to put the items all on the table itself to continue to enjoy the decoration. Once she put the other items on the table, she wove the altar cloth between them, careful not to have it too close to the candle.

That evening was the night of the new moon when the sky was dark, and just a tiny sliver of the moon appeared, mostly unseen to the naked eye. This is an auspicious evening, as the new moon represents new beginnings, and in Hindu and many other spiritual traditions, holidays and celebrations often fall or begin on these eves.

She had done a little research on Saraswati and found that she is celebrated as part of a major Hindu festival called Navaratri, or the Nine Nights of the Goddess, two times a year — once in fall and again in springtime — on the night of the new moon. During Navaratri, the divine feminine is celebrated for nine nights in her three forms: the destroyer goddess, Kali; the goddess of wealth and good fortune, Lakshmi; and Saraswati. Each goddess, in her principal aspect, is honored for three nights each, with feasting, dancing, and other celebrations. As luck or divine timing would have it, Navaratri also began on the eve of this new moon. Padma felt this to be another auspicious symbol in her journey.

Most of Padma's friends, or at least their families, belonged to the local temple. Although her family also did, it was more for the social aspects and events. She didn't have prayer rituals or regular attendance at the temple but always enjoyed putting on a pretty sari, glamming it up, and going to parties there.

Rajesh had shared that sometimes he just went to the temple for the amazing food. This was certainly an unquestionable truth, as Rajesh loves his food and enjoys being taken care of by women. And at the temple, there are certainly plenty of Aunties to cater to him and, at least before they were married, discuss their daughter's availability with him as well.

Hypnotically gazing into the candle flame, Padma softened her eyes, relaxed her body, and began to breathe slowly. She decided to keep her eyes slightly open in a tratak or trataka, which means gazing meditation. She positioned Saraswati close to the candle so that it lit her features up, but the dancing candle flame had her more enthralled.

As she took several deep breaths, Padma allowed her mind to release the day. It was getting much easier than it had been in the beginning. Early in her practice, she sincerely felt she'd never get to a place where she could let go of the constant worry and chatter in her mind, let alone actually feel calm and serene. Yet, it wasn't taking her as much time to get to that sweet place these days. Daily practices surely do assist in building upon that energy, just as Ashanti and the other teachers at Laughing Lotus taught.

She felt the energy of the moment and allowed her mind to focus on the flame's shifting energy. At first, she noticed colors, mostly orange and yellow, but then more blue in the middle. She realized that the more focused her mind became, the more still the flame was, and whenever she caught herself thinking about something, the more it swayed or danced. Was it her breath making it do that? Or was there a connection to her brainwaves?

Soon, she was seeing shapes and patterns in the flame. She swore a woman was dancing in the flame. Was it Saraswati? Kali? Herself? She was not sure. The feminine figure moved like a Bollywood dancer, arms and hands in mudras, knees bent, and feet pointed outward, lifting her legs, moving gracefully yet powerfully. Was she dancing with the flame? Or was she the flame itself? Shakti, the divine feminine creative force of the Universe, surely was dynamic, and she couldn't take her eyes off of the dancing figure.

She was not sure that it was telling her anything, nor did she think about the image until well after the meditation. Captivated by the movement and energy, Padma found herself immersed, and time seemed to stop or pause while she was in the meditation. It was difficult to tell how long it took her to return to the present moment in her body. She began to take a few deep breaths to feel back into herself and how to find her intention for the trip.

At the top of the list of things was to heal family wounds, especially as they were connected to her Nani and her Guru. The second intention related to Ashanti's quotation about embodying the wisdom of her name on a larger scale. She was named after the lotus flower, a favorite symbol amongst Hindus and Buddhists. Surely, she had thought about that but never as deeply as to uncover a deeper layer. She loved that Saraswati was the goddess of knowledge and that by inviting the goddess into her journey with her, she was asking for that deeper wisdom piece to land for her.

And then there was the yoga connection. She was turned on to yoga to assist her post-natal body and mind, and she found it to be an uplifting practice. She wanted to understand it more and also to share the trip with her new yoga friends, who also seemed to be stoked about this practice and the healing benefits that they received from it daily.

A male yoga student at her studio named Bob told her that he'd had a hip replacement, and he touted yoga as the one tool that enabled him to cycle again and give him the range of movement he never thought he'd have back. An older woman with COPD named Xin claimed that yoga breathing helped ween her off of her medicines and that her doctors had no way of understanding how her symptoms had gotten better to the point where she was no longer experiencing the issues she was diagnosed with. The list went on and on. It seemed like everyone at the yoga studio had a positive story about yoga and how it had helped them.

And then there was an intention to get in touch with anything else that was lying asleep within her true heart. A cord had been struck there several weeks ago, and although her days were busy, in the late hours before she fell asleep, she would often wonder about these secrets. She loved her family and her life so very much that she could not imagine what else could fill her heart up even more. And yet, was there not always room for more love?

Finally, she considered traveling with her new best friends, Melvin and Melanie. They had both become a significant piece of her life today. How funny that they'd met at a bar. Melvin, her guardian angel, had thought enough to ensure she got home safely. And Melanie, instead of being jealous, became a fast friend to her and Raj. With their love and authentic friendship, she was excited to see how their adventure would create lasting memories for them to share.

Rajesh was a little envious that the trio would be spending so much time together on vacation. But he also knew that this was a trip for Padma. He had been to India many, many times before, and he had other obligations to care for at home so that she could have this for herself after all the long, sleepless hours that motherhood had brought her the last several years. Perhaps one day, they would go as a family back to the homeland. That was certainly something that he would enjoy.

So, intentions for the trip. She had many, it seemed. Could she wrap them up in a sentence or two so that it would be easier to recall and restate? Did she need to? She decided to spend a little time journaling and see what would come about.

Opening the new journal that Rajesh had gifted her, Padma decided to break it in on the auspicious eve of the new moon as she was creating these intentions. The leather-bound journal was green with a laser-engraved tree with a woman sitting underneath it next to a deer. The deer was one of her favorite animals, and on the day she told Raj that they were expecting dear Nina, they'd taken a drive to the local petting zoo, where she had bottle-fed a baby deer. It had also become a symbol for their family, one that she could take with her on her expedition.

She journaled for some time about the meditative experience, about the Divine Feminine, and her intentions. The words fluidly moved from her brain to the pen and paper without much effort. Before she realized it, she had written five full pages. She stopped to stretch her fingers and rub her wrist before going back over what she had written. She liked what had come up, and she took several more moments before picking up the pen again to finish out the intentions. Padma wrote:

My trip to India will be healing, journeying to my family's homeland, revisiting where my mother's heart broke, and healing the wounds of the past created from misunderstanding. With the assistance of Saraswati, who I welcome with me on this journey, I will uncover the deeper wisdom of who I am and my purposes here in this life.

And then, because it felt right, she finished with:

Om Shanti Shanti Shanti

This, of course, meant peace and peace and peace. She knew that from yoga classes. And so, her intentions were now official.

As Padma closed her journal and blew out the candle, she realized that an hour and a half had passed since she had sat down to do this ritual. Raj had not stuck his head into the room to ask any questions. The babies had not awoken and needed her. She had a full hour and a half to herself and for this purpose. The Universe was surely smiling on her that night. It usually did. But it was only recently that Padma was realizing it.

Bon Voyage!

"Life is either a daring adventure or nothing." – Helen Keller.

"Padma, we are over here," waved Melvin from their departure gate at the main airport terminal.

Seeing her friends, Padma began skipping like a schoolgirl toward the gate, rolling her carry-on and holding a white carnation. She had just said goodbye to Raj and the girls in the car. She thought that she was going to cry, but Nina handed her the carnation and said, "Hab trip, Mama. I will be good," and instead, she smiled, hugged her daughter, planted a kiss on the baby, and tapped foreheads with her husband. Then, with a smile, she twirled out the door and into the airport, only looking back maybe twice.

Airport check-in was easy-breezy as she liked to be early. Not as early as Melvin and Melanie, but early nonetheless. Her TSA pre-check allowed her to skirt through airport security rather quickly, and before she knew it, she was rolling up to the gate with Melvin and Melanie.

"Oh my god, I am doing this!" She screamed, giving them both hugs.

"You are! We are! Oh my god!" Yelled Melanie, hugging her again. "Pinch me; I can't believe we are headed to India. And you've been before?"

Padma took a quick sip of the Starbucks she gifted herself for the long flight and nodded her head.

"Yes, a few times when I was young and then again more recently for a friend's wedding. Mostly family things and not a lot of, say, exploring or enjoying the different places."

"Well, you are going to see some things this time," Melvin said. "I think we are hitting many of the main stops, according to Ashanti, the Taj Mahal, Rishikesh, New Delhi, Varanasi — I can't even remember it all. But I am excited!"

"How many of us are there, do you know the final count?" Asked Padma.

Melanie nodded, "I think Ashanti said there were about thirty of us. Some folks left yesterday and various other times. Not sure who else is on our flight with us."

Thirty people. That felt like a good support group to travel with on this journey. Padma considered that no matter what was happening, someone was bound to be around and handy to assist if need be. Although, she was hoping that this was not going to be necessary.

Padma felt a buzz she hadn't felt in a long time. Traveling was always a fun adventure for her, first with her parents and then with her friends. India was quite a destination to travel to. Normally, the trip took a full day from start to finish. It was a pretty exhausting travel route to go to Asia. This was her first adult trip that did not center around sun and fun or drinking and dancing. No, this trip was quite a different kind of adventure for Padma.

There were about thirty-four international airports in India and over 100 domestic ones. Normally, a trip to India was one long international flight of about fourteen or fifteen hours, nonstop. And that non-stop was a biggie. If you had a layover somewhere, that could add five hours or more, easily, to the trip. Padma was careful to try and book the non-stops when it came to travel, as they did this time. They were taking a direct flight to New Delhi, which meant no smaller flights on the first trek. They'd be traveling by bus and train most of the remainder of the trip throughout India, with one small flight somewhere in there, if she recalled correctly. However, the door-to-door time from when she left her home until she reached the hotel in New Delhi would be approximately twenty hours, going through customs, getting bags, and then transferring. That was a lot of travel.

For this reason, Padma stocked up on snacks and reading materials and also ensured that her phone was fully charged so she could listen to music, guided meditations, and even look through her photos. She felt ready for the long haul to India and knew that when she arrived, even if she hadn't slept and felt exhausted, it would still not be as difficult as when Zoya had colic and didn't sleep for more than a couple of hours at a time off and on for months. If a mom can live through that, then a simple trip to India is of no consequence.

The flight was full, so the thoughts of having any legroom to spread out died quickly. Melvin took the aisle seat in the row, Melanie in the middle, leaving Padma the window seat. She was happy to be able to lean into the window if she felt like falling asleep, although, at the moment of embarkment, she was certainly wired to the hilt. Of course, the Starbucks she had at the airport was also not helping. She and Melanie chatted away about all things motherhood and wife-ness and were so engrossed that they hadn't even realized the flight had taken off so much for listening to the safety video.

Padma rationalized it was okay, as she'd heard it so many times before. As a young girl, she even memorized the United Airlines drill and could recite it with the flight attendants, much to her parents' joy. Sometimes, it even got her a little gift or extra snack from the crew. Yes, the good girl she certainly was.

About two hours into the flight, the meal was served. Padma had not thought to ask for any particular meal, so what came was chicken parmesan with a side salad, chocolate pudding, bread, and butter. She scarfed it all down before realizing that she hadn't even tasted any of it. She was so used to cooking for the kids and eating as she went that she'd forgotten the art of savoring food. Mentally, she made a note to eat slower for the rest of the trip, as they were certainly going to be eating some amazing Indian cuisine.

Following the meal, the flight crew turned off many of the lights, leaving the plane quite dark. She decided to try and watch a movie on the personal screen in the seat-back and realized that many movies she'd earmarked for date nights with Raj that never materialized were now available. So, with delight, she tagged them all in her playlist, hit play on the first movie, and in what seemed like just a moment later, woke up to the flight attendants putting the lights back up for the next meal. She was more tired than she thought, as she had slept about six hours! That was more than any usual night at home. Feeling rested, rejuvenated, and ready to go, Padma suddenly realized that there were still several hours to the flight left.

Melanie was still sleeping. Melvin thought it best to let her rest through the meal. It was difficult to talk across Melanie, so she and Melvin made several hand gestures in an attempt to communicate before laughing and giving up. She must have signed something hilarious because Melvin was having a fit, trying not to laugh out loud and wake up Melanie. Of course, when Melvin started laughing, Padma started laughing. And soon, the two were both working to hold in the laughter. It was all going okay until Padma snorted.

Melvin's laughter burst out quite loudly, much to the disapproval of those across the aisle who gave them both dirty looks. Melvin's eyes opened wide, and he gave Padma the "cease" gesture so that they didn't get into any more trouble together.

Padma decided to put in her earbuds and listen to a little music on her phone for a while before, again, falling asleep. It turns out that traveling without kids across the world is quite a breeze for moms with small children. They simply sleep through the flights. Padma woke up to the sound of the captain alerting the passengers to prepare for landing in just about thirty minutes.

Melanie rubbed her eyes and looked about, dazed and confused.

"What time is it?" She asked Melvin and Padma.

"It's about 7:30 in the morning, our time at home," Melvin said, checking his watch.

"Huh?" Melanie reacted, then continued, "So what time is it?"

"Well, that depends on what reality you are asking about," Padma answered, friendly. "At home, it is 7:30 am. That means at Greenwich Mean Time, it's about 12:30 in the afternoon. But in reality, where we land in India, it will be around maybe six in the evening the following day. And it's all true!"

Padma was happy with herself. Knowing time-zone changes was another gift of hers that she used to delight fellow travelers. Only Melanie did not seem delighted. She still seemed confused. Padma wrinkled her nose as Melanie glared at her.

"No?" She said to Melanie.

Melvin jumped in, "She's not a morning person. Add in the time change, and she will be jet lagged and sleep another day, most likely."

That was a thought Padma hadn't had yet. By the time they landed and got to the hotel, it would be well into the evening in New Delhi. And that meant sleeping again before their retreat started the next day. Anxiety crept up as she considered for a moment what it might be like to not sleep and be incredibly tired the next day. She took a few deep breaths, closed her eyes, and remembered it was all a journey. It would all be okay.

Melanie had already closed her eyes again. She was not thinking about sleeping or not sleeping. She was just sleeping. It was great to have Melvin there to attend to the adulting so that she could just drop off for a while. His presence was always comforting. On Melvin's part, he was just used to being prepared, being alert, and sleeping when he could. Thus was the nature of a traveling athlete. Even though his playing days were over, he couldn't break away from years of conditioning. And why would he have to?

"Ladies and gentlemen, welcome to New Delhi. The time here is now 6:36 pm. The weather is a balmy 92 degrees. We thank you for flying with us. Have a wonderful time in India's capital city. Until we see you again, thank you for flying American Airlines."

The clicking of seatbelts unlocking sounded like crickets chirping in the night. Melvin stood up and stretched in the aisle. It looked heavenly, but Padma would have to half stretch in her window seat and wait another ten minutes before she could scoot over into the aisle herself. But ah, that first stretch! She'd only managed to go once to the bathroom the entire flight, so she was surely stiff. It was nothing a good yoga practice wouldn't fix, and she thought since she had the time to herself tonight that it may not be a bad idea to stretch out before bed. What a lovely thought.

In contrast to the simplicity of sleeping through the flight, immigration was a whole other story. The waiting, the heat, the never-ending line — could one even call this mess a line? Padma had never traveled to New Delhi before. She did not realize the massive amount of people that would be cattle-driven to the immigration area.

"Don't lose me," she smiled at Melvin, trying to hide the panic.

"I won't lose you. Stay close," Melvin said. "This could take a minute."

Melanie put her arm around Padma and hugged her. Padma took a deep breath and decided to go with the flow. As Ashanti had told them, there was no other way to do it in Mother India. She was in control, and whenever you made other plans, she would remind you that that simply wasn't how it worked there. Padma had resolved not to worry or try to make anything happen and to allow all the energy of India to take her on the ride of her life. It was a little scary to let go that much, but it seemed to be the only way to do it.

And even though it seemed as though it might take another ten hours to get through the hoards of people, about an hour later, they were at baggage claim, where their bags awaited them.

"Easy-breezy," Padma said to Melvin.

"Easy-breezy," he replied, piling the suitcases on the cart.

"Hey, how come carts are free in every country other than the US?" Melanie asked.

"Hah, good old capitalism," Melvin replied, "Nothing's free. Not even your freedom. If that were true, we wouldn't have to pay taxes, have a passport to leave or get back in the country, or..."

"Okay, we get it," Melanie said to Melvin. "We promised no politics."

Melvin looked at his wife disapprovingly. "I wasn't talking politics. I was talking America, land of the free."

"Okay, Daddy," Melanie said a little condescendingly.

Padma took note Melanie was not, in fact, a morning person. Or was it evening? Anyway, Padma decided to defuse the situation by changing the story a little, she began singing the George Michael song "Freedom."

"Freedom....freedom...you gotta give back for what you take..."

"What?" Melvin inquired.

Padma's answer, which Melanie feigned a weak smile at, was to sing it again, "Freedom....freedom...you gotta give back for what you take..."

"Wait, no. Those are the lyrics?"

Padma laughed. She had to know. "What did you think they were?"

Melvin started to laugh as he pushed the cart full of suitcases out of the airport. He was embarrassed to say it, so he sang it out loud:

"Freedom...freedom...you gotta give me what you make."

Even Melanie laughed. The smiling trio suddenly found themselves outside of baggage claim, meeting a barrage of men holding up signs with people's names on them, all yelling out as they awaited their arriving party.

Padma's eyes frantically searched the sea of white signs, hoping to recognize one of their names. Finally, Melanie grabbed her hand and led her behind Melvin to a man with their name written on a card. He ushered them through the crowded area to his passenger van, which he had parked a little distance from the crowd. Once they got away from the business, he introduced himself.

"Welcome to New Delhi. I am Samir. I will drive you to your hotel. Are these all of your bags? Did you make sure to check the tags?"

Once they all verified the bags were good, they were loaded into Samir's vehicle, and they took off through the streets of New Delhi toward their hotel. And what a ride it was. Even though it was getting dark, Padma could glimpse a sea of people extending beyond the airport and into the streets. From motorized cars to pulled carts, from humans to animals, just about anything you could imagine being on the ride appeared. Samir drove like the ride was an Olympic event, weaving and creating the smallest of spaces for them to get through on their path. Padma thought at some point that she'd seen an elephant out of the corner of her eye, but by the time she turned to look back, a swarm of people filled in the space where their car was moments ago, and the image was swallowed up into the night. After that, she decided not to look backward again.

Finally arriving at the massive five-star hotel that they would spend the next two nights in, Samir unloaded their bags, waved, and wished them well on their journey, handing Melvin a well-used business card with torn edges and letting them know that if the group needed anything at all, to call him and he would come right away. Padma saw Melvin hand Samir some cash and was again reminded of how awesome it was to have someone else handling those little details of the trip. She figured at some point she would handle a tip somewhere for them in exchange.

The hotel lobby was something out of a travel magazine. With polished marbled flooring, a large water feature, gold accents, and large plant holders overflowing with hundreds of red roses, Padma felt like a princess. What a glorious thing that Rajesh had insisted that she get a room to herself so that she could bathe and relax in total luxury.

And luxury it was. Her suite came with a jetted tub, a shower big enough to fit Melvin's entire former team inside together, a sitting room that was larger than her living room, and a king-size bed with fresh linens, snacks, and a gift box just like the one she'd received from Ashanti a month prior.

Before she did anything else, she went to the window and peered at the city from her bird's eye view. There was so much to take in that she didn't know where to start. There was a stark difference between her hotel and some of the places they'd traveled through to get there. New Delhi certainly offered just about anything and everything. Would two days in the city be enough to uncover all of its beauty? Well, it would have to be because they certainly had other things on their itinerary to get to.

Padma sat down and picked up the gold box with the red ribbon. The same card with the elephant on the front stuck out, so she slid it out and opened it up. It was another sweet note from Ashanti.

Welcome to Mother India! I cannot wait to connect with you tomorrow for the start of our retreat. But for tonight, relax and unwind. I hope this helps you. Use it in your meditation this evening, and then please bring it with you tomorrow to our meeting at 10 am in the Shanti room just off the main lobby to the right. Love and Blessings, Ashanti

Padma tore open the box to reveal the contents of the gift from her teacher. Inside was a beautiful mala, a string of meditation or prayer beads. It was made of the same crystals that Ashanti had given her for her alter: rose quartz and clear quartz. It also had a red tassel with a small pendant in the image of the goddess Saraswati.

Padma decided to take a shower before doing anything else and to unpack a few items that would make her feel more relaxed. And it was the most beautiful shower she could remember. She luxuriated and allowed the cascading warm water to run all over her body for as long as possible before getting out. Once dressed, she took out her yoga mat and the contents of the altar box that Ashanti had given her at home to prepare a little altar, adding the mala beads that she had just received to it.

After a short, intuitive yoga practice, Padma picked up her mala beads and chanted to Saraswati, then took some silent time to meditate before journaling about her current thoughts and feelings. Everything at that moment felt magical and perfect. The anguish she had felt about coming to India, about hurting her mother's feelings, about missing or worrying about her children — about anything, was completely gone. And she knew without a doubt that this was exactly where she was supposed to be at exactly this moment in her life. The feeling was true and undeniable.

And even though she was pumped to be in India and had slept for most of the flight there, Padma fell fast asleep, sprawled out in her king-size bed, and did not awake again until six in the morning, just in time to prepare for the beginning of her first yoga retreat.

The only thing that would have made the trip any better was having Rajesh and the girls with her — if the girls were twenty-two and had their rooms, that is. Padma smiled. She could see that happening one day. Perhaps the whole family would retreat together to India. But for now, the trip was hers. And it would prove to take her to many places, not just geographically but mentally, emotionally, and spiritually.

The Invitation

"How wonderful is it that nobody needs to wait a single moment before starting to improve the world." – Anne Frank

Padma sat in a circle among the group of thirty others on the yoga retreat with Ashanti. They each held their new mala prayer beads in their hands as they were guided through a silent Japa meditation. Padma held her beads in her right hand and said a silent mantra, gently rubbing one bead at a time and repeating the mantra for each of the 108 beads. Her mantra was different from the others as Ashanti had given each participant his or her mantra before they began the meditation.

As Padma rolled her finger around the smooth crystal beads, she repeated in her mind, "I surrender to my Indian journey. May it bring me the understanding I seek."

Truthfully, that sort of scared her. Surrendering felt, in a way, like a defeatist attitude. It was difficult to understand, but still, she felt like giving it a whirl since Ashanti went through all the trouble of choosing it specifically for her. Repeating a mantra 108 times felt like it would take forever, but the meditation was over before she knew it, and Ashanti then opened up the circle so that each member of the group could introduce him or herself and say a little something about why they chose to come to India.

Padma listened intently as each person spoke. She tried to remember all of the names, but by the seventh person, she had already started to get confused. Her pre-mommy self would not have had this same issue. You lose some brain cells or memory capacity after giving birth. Padma had read this in a NY Times article about mom's brain and forgetfulness some time ago.

After Melvin and Melanie shared about their anniversary, it was her turn to talk about herself and why she came to India. Honestly, she had so enjoyed everyone else's story that she decided to keep hers brief and simply say that something was calling her to come and that she was working on being open to whatever that was and being guided by the Universe. Everyone seemed to like that, especially a plump woman named Sarah, who shared that even though she'd been to India several times before and that it had not been on her radar to come again, she felt called to come with this group for some reason. She, too, was allowing her intuition to guide her. Padma smiled at Sarah. She had a feeling that the two of them would be doing some things together on this trip.

After the beautiful meet and greet, the group headed out to embark on a walking tour of Old Delhi, the once magnificent walled city of Shahjahanabad, as it was called back in the 17th century. Ashanti told them to soak everything in and that they would indeed see just about everything that was on offer in the old area of the city.

She wasn't lying.

Before even making it to the iconic Red Fort, she almost got knocked over by a cow plowing through the crowded street and then witnessed not one but two accidents: one between a motorbike and small vehicle and another where a rickshaw hit a pedestrian. Maneuvering thirty people through the streets of New Delhi was a miraculous feat. Was it their fear that kept them together? Or just all the positive energy that they put out before embarking on their walking tour?

Padma had swirled around more than once to quickly try and recover and figure out where the path of her people went. And although they were never too far away, sometimes, in a flash, she would lose her walking buddy or the rest of the group for a moment right in front of her eyes, as if they just turned into the smoke of incense and then disappeared. No wonder Ashanti had paired everyone up for safety! Recovery needed to be quick, so she was constantly on guard. This was a high-energy walk and not some stroll. The sights, sounds, and smells kept her senses firing. She hadn't felt a rush like this since she'd gone to the local auction house with Payal and bid on several items, only to not realize she'd accidentally spent $1000 on a vase. It was just too easy to get caught up in the energy.

Before stopping for lunch, the group went to Raj Ghat, where the memorial to Mahatma Gandhi stood. It was comprised of a black marble base with an eternal flame at one end that marked the exact spot where Gandhi's body was cremated. The simplicity and serenity of the shrine sat in drastic contrast to the Delhi streets they had moved through to get there. And perhaps that was the point of it. Nestled into the extravagant sensory explosion sat a holy shrine to a man who successfully protested peacefully and inspired others around the globe to care about civil rights.

Ashanti instructed each participant to find a quiet spot to reflect on Karma Yoga, the "yoga of selfless action." She read them one of Gandhi's most famous quotes: "The best way to find yourself is to lose yourself in the service of others."

As a mother, Padma felt that she had the service part down pretty well. However, she was not sure she had found a deeper aspect within her by tending to her family. Taking care of them was the job of any mother, a job that she took seriously and honored. There most certainly was an expectation of recognition for the hard work involved with this type of service, and with Karma Yoga, there is supposed to be a lack thereof. So, did motherhood still fit the bill?

More questions: Was it work? Yes. And in the end, did it make a difference to her how things turned out? Yes. She was completely devoted to raising her daughters right, to be good people. And she did want them to acknowledge her at some point and for all the work she did in raising them. After all, what is the point if you don't receive accolades, she pondered?

Reaching into her pocket, Padma took her mala beads out and began to run them through her fingers, one at a time. Although she did not repeat her mantra from this morning, she felt it comforting to rub the crystals mindfully while reflecting on Karma Yoga, Gandhi, and service. It both soothed and focused her and allowed her to get lost in the process of considering what all of these things meant to her. She had lost track of time and had no interest in what anyone else was doing or thinking. In that moment, she truly felt pulled into her thoughts and considerations of Karma, the yoga of action.

Outside of her family, Padma had never really been of service without seeking something in return. She had not been involved in causes or even taken part in donations or assisting anyone underprivileged in her neighborhood. The more she contemplated selfless service, the worse she began to feel about herself. But, then again, this was the first time that this concept and practice had been brought to her attention.

How was karma a type of yoga? And why had Ashanti dove them into this deep self-inquiry on the first day in India? She caught herself wondering if dinner and drinks would balance out the day. But she dared not share it. Well, maybe with Melvin — during said drinks — whether or not they were a part of the scheduled trip.

Melvin was also deep in contemplation but with a smile on his face, wherein he felt completely at ease in his skin. Melvin's charitable contributions never seemed to run out. Whenever he found someone in need, he jumped right in with two feet without even thinking of himself. His mother had raised him to be that way, to look out for those weaker or in need, and to this day, he never needed to think but just act. Karma Yoga was his thing, and he hadn't even known that it was until now. He felt validated, but not in an egocentric way, but rather a contented one. He sat basking in the joy of knowing he was doing the right things in life. He was even more of a yogi than he thought.

Everyone in the group sat and pondered for quite some time about the nature of Karma Yoga before Ashanti brought them all together again in a circle on the grass. What she told them was a little shocking at first. They were headed to an all-girls orphanage for a seva or selfless service work. They were going to be stopping to pick up a special lunch and to bring the girls new pencils and notebooks for school. They were each given a stipend to also purchase one special small gift for a girl that they would be personally assisting that day.

Without knowing the little girl, Padma felt it difficult to think about what to give her. She thought about what her little girls might like, but they were still so young. She considered what her nieces and her friend's children were interested in, but when compared to the stark situation of life in an orphanage, most of those things felt superfluous and shallow. She attempted to put herself in the shoes of a little girl with no parents, staying in a home with other girls who had no family. What would she want if she were that little girl?

Truthfully, how was she to know the answer to this question? She tried not to judge herself too harshly and simply connect to the little girl within her. Eventually, she decided on a doll. As a young girl herself and an only child, she did know a little something about being lonely. Although she had parents, she certainly found herself many times feeling alone and having to use her imagination to get through the day. Her doll was her best play toy because she could pretend anything with her. She would talk to her, and yes, the doll would talk back, or at least she told herself it had. She would dress in different clothing, buy accessories, and change it up depending on the story that they were carrying out that day. Yes, a doll for any little girl, she thought, would be the perfect little gift. And the amount fits the stipend. She smiled, considering what it would be like to offer this gift to the little girl and how it might feel to that little girl to be seen and acknowledged that way.

Melvin had picked up a little purse with a yellow plastic flower on the front and had tucked extra rupees inside. Melanie had found a pretty stuffed lamb. Armed with their gifts, the group headed to the market to pick up the prepared lunches and take them to the orphanage for their afternoon of service. Padma felt inspired and eager to arrive and get to work.

As they rounded the corner to the orphanage, they could hear the girls outside in the schoolyard chatting and playing. They seemed busy with their activities of jumping rope and singing until they saw the group coming into the yard, and then all dropped what they were doing and ran over to them to assist. The girls were all smiling and hugging the group as they arrived, it was quite overwhelming. Before Padma realized it, a little girl had latched onto her hand and was walking in with her, smiling up with the most precious face and two missing front teeth.

"What is your name," asked Padma, "Mine is Padma."

The little girl smiled at Padma but did not reply. It dawned on her suddenly that maybe she did not speak English. And Padma was not quite sure which language she would be speaking in that area of India. She hadn't thought about communication being an issue, but it certainly was a consideration. Her parents had never spent much time teaching her the native tongue, so she had very little understanding of any Indian language anyway. She felt inept in connecting with the little one but decided that the universal language of love would suffice in this case and wrapped her arms around the little one as they walked along.

Skipping and giggling, the girls escorted the group into the orphanage's main hall, where they were greeted by some elders who pointed out where they were to put the items. Some conversations between Ashanti, her assistants, and the elders ensued. Padma and the others watched on as the girls danced and sang around them, completely comfortable and at ease. It was difficult not to notice that their clothing was simple and, in some cases, quite worn or a little too small. At the moment, they wore no shoes on their feet, having dropped the flip-flops and sandals at the entry to the pavilion where they were setting up for lunch.

Some simple table-and-bench seating was lined up in rows. There were a few longer tables set up on one end where stacks of trays suggested where the lunch line was going to begin. To Padma, everything appeared to need a good dusting, but there were no rags or cleaners to be found in the area. A few brooms sat at the far corners of the pavilion, but that would be the extent of any cleaning products. She dared not take it upon herself to grab them and start cleaning and instead awaited further instructions.

As she waited, she felt a tug on her hand and looked down to see the little girl who walked her in once again hanging on her arm, smiling up at her, toothless. Padma smiled back at her, then instinctively bent down and lifted the little girl, straddling her legs on her waist and holding her as if it were Nina.

The little girl threw her arms around Padma's neck and pulled her close. Padma could feel her little heart beating against her as she held on tightly as if her life depended on it.

Resisting crying, Padma decided instead to allow herself to feel the love for this little girl, the same love that she had for Nina and Zoya. She smiled and rocked her from side to side. And although she was smiling, a salty tear or two made their way down her face and into her neck.

Soon, Ashanti was bringing everyone back to circle up and pass out jobs. Padma, Melanie, and another woman in their group were given the job of preparing the girls for lunch, which required them to walk to the water pipe, wash their hands, and, if need be, anything else requiring attention. Melvin and some of the other men were to lift the heavier items and get them in place. Some others did grab the brooms to sweep up and did other various chores. Suddenly, everyone was flowing through the pavilion like an army of peace weavers.

The little faucet and small bar of soap worked well enough. None of the girls carried on like hers would have if they'd been asked to wash up. They lined up and, one at a time, washed hands, smiled, and awaited approval or assistance with other areas in need of a scrub. Several faces needed gentle washing to remove mucus and other kid crust. One little girl came up and quickly twirled around to show the woman a large streak of sludge along her backside. Was it mud? Poop? Her poop or someone else's? Padma thought it best not to ask the question and just went into mom work with Melanie, removing the little girl's clothes and washing her down. They needed to wash the clothing as well, but luckily, it was warm enough for her to wear her clothing wet, for there was no indication if she even owned another set. In the end, the little girl and all the others ran off and back to the pavilion, where they began to line up to receive lunch. Each one beaming ear to ear.

Honestly, it was a somewhat exhausting feat to wash so many little ones. Padma stood up and took a moment, but that was about all that she had. There was no rest at the orphanage, where it seemed every moment another task needed to be done, and this made being of service much easier for her, as there was no time to think anything through. At home, she could ponder in moments what she would make the girls eat, what to dress them in, and how they would spend their day. But here, it was simply go, do, and then do more. And when you are done, go and do more.

With so many helping hands, lunch ran effortlessly. The girls lined up and were given their specially prepared meals. Before eating, they all sang a beautiful prayer for their food and to the group for bringing it to them. And while the girls ate, Padma and the others hugged and held space for the little ones, who were simply joyful.

Cleanup proved just as exhausting as preparation for lunch. All hands were on deck again, as dishes needed to be washed, floors cleaned, and more hands and faces wiped down. But when they were done, Ashanti and her assistants brought everyone to sit in a circle on the floor and guided them that they would be bringing the girls back in to receive their special gifts and that each person could spend some time with the girls before they needed to head out.

The little ones came in and were seated by one of their group by the women running the orphanage, with a few extra girls seated by Ashanti and her assistants, as they had purchased extra gifts to accommodate everyone. But nobody needed to escort her little toothless friend to her because she bounded in and to her directly. Padma smiled. The little one hugged her around the waist, and she reciprocated, feeling a strong bond with her already.

One of the women began to instruct the girls on what was happening. Padma had no idea what she was saying, but Ashanti assured the group that she was conveying that they had each brought a special gift for them and that the girls would be sharing their names and appreciation. Then, when Ashanti gestured, everyone brought their special gifts out for the girls.

The eyes of Padma's little friend widened and sparkled with pure joy upon the sight of her doll. She looked at Padma and clasped her hands, yet awaited a gesture that she could take the doll. Padma handed her the toy, and with profound love, she pressed the doll against her chest and rocked it from side to side. Padma could not help but cry as she thought of the many dolls strewn about her home, barely acknowledged by Nina because of the plethora of other toys she became distracted by. Perhaps it was time to realign the priorities of raising her girls. Maybe fewer toys and more presence with those who loved them were most important. She was feeling that quite deeply.

Padma's little one stood up In front of her with a doll in her hand and pointed to her chest, saying, "Nima." At first, Padma thought she said, "Nina." Her jaw dropped open in disbelief. The little girl pointed to herself once again and repeated, slowly, "N-EE-MA." Padma nodded, pointed to herself, and said, "Padma." Nima threw her arms around Padma's neck and kissed her on the cheek before another little girl with a doll ran over to show Nima hers. Nima flashed Padma a quick smile before hopping off with her friend to play. It was all Padma could do not to fully break down in tears. However, several of them still made their way down her face.

Her thoughts were on her children when she felt the warm embrace of her friend, Melanie. The two women shared no words because, as mothers, they both understood what each other was feeling.

Ashanti assembled the group, which slowly began their leave of the orphanage. Silence and inner contemplation stayed with them on the trip back to their hotel, where the streets of New Delhi somehow seemed quieter than before. Snuggled into the comfort of their luxury hotel, each member of the group had time to reflect, journal, and rest before their evening meetup. If it had not been well into the early morning hours at home, Padma would have FaceTimed Rajesh. Instead, she sat in her room, gazing out the window into India. Day one, and she had already gone deep into the belly of the Mother and what true service meant. And somehow, she knew that she had already been changed, that a deeper level of understanding had been unearthed, and that service work needed to be a part of her life forever from this moment forward.

Wow! And this was only day one of the retreat.

That evening, as everyone shared their thoughts and reflections on Karma yoga, it was obvious that the significance of this day was masterfully planned by Ashanti, who shared that she was an orphan raised in America by white hippie parents who were themselves Karma Yogis.

"Know that to each girl that you connected with today, you made a difference in her life. Know that the profound love you gave them in just a smile or a scoop of rice brought them a feeling of being loved that they will cherish and never forget. And never forget the feelings you have felt today when you gave freely of yourself for the well-being of another. You could have all chosen a luxury trip of decadence and self-pleasure. But you chose this retreat for a reason. We were all meant to be here together and to witness and take part in the act of Karma Yoga. If we can harness the energy of this loving reciprocity and sprinkle it all over the world, we could truly have peace on earth."

Ashanti thanked everyone for their time and energy before instructing them on the time for the next day's start. It would be an early one, as they would be taking one of the famous Indian rails at 5 am.

Love & Loss

Five o'clock in the morning came a bit early. Was it the extreme energy of the previous day that made it difficult to wake? Or was the jet lag beginning to catch up to Padma after the first full and exciting day in India? She felt it was probably a little of both.

Melvin took one look at her and laughed. And while she thought she hadn't the energy to laugh back, Melvin just had something that drove her to smile even at the moments when she didn't think she could.

"You look how I feel," he said.

"Oh yeah? How do I look?" Padma joked back.

"Like you just flew halfway around the world, spent a full day walking and working in India, barely slept, and are on your way to a train before dawn."

"Okay, Captain Obvious," Padma joked, "just say I look like poo."

"No, no, you're gorgeous. You just look exhausted."

"Well, with having a colicky baby, I thought I understood what it was like to be exhausted. But India tired feels like a whole other level."

The truth was, India felt both uplifting and invigorating and humbling and tiring. She hadn't noticed this before on prior trips, but Ashanti had warned them that Mother India would bring them to places they'd never gone. Padma had just not realized this meant emotionally and energetically as well as physically.

Their day would prove to be another long one, as they began with silent meditation before breakfast and then on to the train station, where they would take the express train from New Delhi to Agra for a day of sightseeing around the great Taj Mahal. The anticipation of checking off such a sight from their bucket list soon shook each member of the group from their travel stupor as they reentered the enchanted world of Indian travel.

Padma had always been warned about the incredible overcrowding and general decline in the infrastructure of Indian railways. However, the Gatimaan Express train cut what would be an over three-hour ride to about half, making it a tolerable situation. It was with a pleasant and uplifting conversation that the train ride flew by, and soon, the group found themselves at their destination and more than ready to hit the town.

Agra's vibe was quite different than that of New Delhi, which felt as though one was plopped right down at the center of Indian culture. Agra's mass tourism created a melting-pot feel. In the span of the walk from the train station to their private tour bus that would take them to various sites in Agra throughout the day, Padma heard what sounded like German, Chinese, Italian, and Portuguese, among others she found herself perplexed by. Throughout the city, tour buses and various groups jockeyed for position, especially for parking at various sites. It was obvious that a short walk would have often taken less time than sitting on the bus, but she was certainly not complaining, as it gave her more time to chat and enjoy time with friends on their journey.

After a few stops, including Agra Fort and Itimad-ud-Daulah, aptly nicknamed "Baby Taj," the group stopped for a lavish lunch at a five-star hotel. The stark contrast between yesterday's day of service and Karma Yoga with today's comparative extravagance and luxury was not lost on Padma. Ashanti did not give any major instructions for the day other than to enjoy the sites, and frankly, Padma felt more comfortable in today's digs than the previous ones. Instead of deep feelings of the many levels of love, she felt today as waves of joy and pleasure. It was a welcomed change but not one that anyone dared speak of. The underlying tone of the visit to the orphanage hung still in the air, gifting them with a reverence for these famous sites.

"Ashanti," Padma said at lunch, "I am so grateful for this opportunity to travel to India with you. Thank you for nudging me."

Ashanti smiled and nodded. "I am grateful for your beautiful presence."

Padma decided to press her somewhat, even though she felt obliged to keep the day lighter.

"I'm curious about the drastic shift of energy from yesterday to today. Are we still considering Karma Yoga?"

Ashanti smiled. "I'm glad you are recognizing the difference. I feel it important to drop people right into Mother India, but of course, there are many, many different parts of her. Just like you, a Mother has many sides to her. She can both fiercely protect as well as nurture her family. She holds space for a life full of joy and happiness but also teaches lessons that challenge us to grow as a person. Some say that giving birth is the most painful thing that a woman can experience. But within minutes—seconds even—of holding your

191

baby in your arms, you no longer remember the pain and only witness the bliss of the moment. That is India for you."

"Wow, what an amazing way to describe her," Padma replied.

"India requires one thing of you: to open your heart. If you can stay there, your journey will be life-changing."

Padma smiled, for this, she already knew to be true, for her heart was broken wide open in just a day. Ashanti had not mentioned the connection or lack thereof to Karma Yoga, and she thought she would let it rest. Certainly, they were in very good hands, and she felt that she was being guided to be exactly where she needed to be as it was.

Upon finishing lunch and spending some relaxing time digesting on the grounds of the hotel, the group began to gather for their trip to the main attraction: the Taj Mahal.

This Muslim tomb is thought to be the greatest architectural achievement in all of Indo-Islamic architecture. Built in the 17th century by Mughal Emperor Shah Jahan, this structure, often misunderstood as a temple, is the final resting place of his wife, Mumtaz Mahal. The monument's combination of textures and hues created an unparalleled symmetry, thus labeling it a "modern marvel."

As a Muslim building, the Taj Mahal includes a mosque with an inscription from the Koran above the main entrance reading: "O Soul, thou art at rest. Return to the Lord at peace with Him, and he at peace with you."

After stopping to translate the inscription, Ashanti brought the group to an area to discuss the deeper meaning of the gateway.

"This gateway is said to symbolize the one that Mohammed took when he entered Paradise. As such, it is thought to be a transitional place between the world of the senses and the realm of the spirit.

"The Taj Mahal is said to be one of the greatest symbols of love in the world. The Emperor's wife, Mumtaz Mahal, died during childbirth. And it is said that she made him promise to build her this beautiful monument to their love.

"As you walk through the entry and as you take your time on the grounds, consider both the energy of love and of loss. Feel your way with both your senses and spirit."

Ashanti bowed and left them to discover the Taj Mahal on their own, but not before leaving them with a meeting location and time for their departure to the train and back to New Delhi.

Padma found herself suddenly missing Rajesh and her children immensely. She caught Melvin and Melanie embracing and kissing before heading through the entryway together. Many of the others from the group went forth in smaller groups or couples, taking pictures, smiling, and pointing out various architectural aspects. But she found it difficult to move forward, feeling tugged once again by the Mother's energy.

Mumtaz died giving birth to their fourteenth child. While she was not his only wife and the children would be raised by many other women who were like mothers to them, she found herself contemplating loss, thinking about her toothless little friend Nima and the other girls at the orphanage, and feeling the weight of a Mother's Heart after leaving her children behind.

Padma took a deep breath and went inside, slowly taking in the extravagant marble, arches, and gardens, each masterfully placed. At one point, she ran into a fellow traveler from the US, who found herself alongside Padma, sharing a gaze at the famous tomb at the southern wall of the court.

"When they say you can't put a price tag on love, I don't think they considered this," she said.

Padma giggled. Certainly, this was the upper echelon of gestures, but was it a true testament of love? Especially considering the rumor that Mumtaz prodded her husband to create the Taj in her honor.

"It's so over-the-top. But honestly, I am struck more by the events that led up to her death than the actual mausoleum itself. I'm trying to feel out dying in childbirth and leaving behind all my children," Padma said.

The woman smiled at her. "You're a new mom?"

Padma smiled back, "Sort of."

The woman nodded.

"For me, the opposite happened, I lost a child during childbirth," the woman shared.

Padma began, "I'm sorry..." but the woman waved her hand to stop her.

"No need. That is a very old story. But, as a mother, I can tell you that it was the most excruciating thing to have to endure. Being a mother is the biggest blessing and the most challenging thing you'll ever do."

Padma smiled and nodded. So true. She extended a more formal greeting to her American friend, "I'm Padma."

"Hello. I'm Norma," said the woman, who was more senior to Padma yet stylish and elegantly put together.

Padma had no idea of the woman's age but wondered if she was close to her mother's. She noticed Norma's maturity by how she carried herself, yet her humor was an obvious nod that she did not take herself so seriously. She noticed that Norma did not wear a wedding band on her finger, and it did not appear that she was with anyone else, but she did not want to pry into the stranger's life.

She and Norma walked along, sharing a light conversation about the Taj Mahal's many brilliant features. Norma offered to take Padma's photos on the grounds, and the two women sat and shared more time afterward.

"What do you love most about being a mother?" Norma asked.

"Oh, wow," Padma blushed, "What a question! Ah, well, I suppose when I look into my little girls' eyes, I see their future and potential, and I want to do whatever I can to create space for them to be whatever they want to be, whatever they are meant to be. I feel this great honor in guiding them in their journey of becoming women.

"Wow, tall order!" Norma commented. "I'm not saying that in any derogatory way. You are certainly committed to your children. Girls need strong women to guide them."

Padma nodded and smiled. "Yes, they do."

"But remember that those little sovereign beings have their journeys here and that sometimes you may not be a part of it. Sometimes, you may not even like it."

Norma's comment reminded her of her mother's feelings about her current journey, her journey into yoga and to India, and how terrified Uma was initially, yet reluctantly made space for Padma to seek out her way.

"My mother didn't want me to come on this trip," Padma shared.

"No?" Norma questioned. "Excuse my candor, but are you not Indian?"

Padma laughed and replied, "Yes, we are Indian. My parents left India when they were young. Although we visited a few times, it was not a big part of our life. There were some family issues, so they focused more on the American culture in my upbringing."

"America has a culture?" Norma said, both women laughing.

"Yes, capitalism," Padma shot back.

"Greed is good!" Norma said, quoting Michael Douglas's character Gordon Gekko in the 1987 movie *Wall Street,* which was not a reference that Padma was aware of. She knew it from the awkward look Padma was giving her. "It's a movie reference, never mind, you're too young," she smiled at Padma.

"When I look around here, I think of opulence and extravagance. Perhaps America learned that from these rich cultures."

"You know what is rich to me?" Norma revealed. "The deep spiritual legacy of India. The enormous connection to Spirit's presence in everyday life and the unending quest for spiritual knowledge and wisdom. To me, that is true wealth."

"I am being struck by that everywhere I go here. Yes, I've been to India before, but I never let her in. Now I'm feeling overwhelmed by that richness you're discussing," Padma said.

"I envy you. You see her with fresh eyes as if for the first time and inviting her in through your heart, despite your family's reluctance to do so. You are finding yourself, as your name suggests, despite the obstacles in your path."

This was the second mention of the deeper meaning of Padma's name since Ashanti had brought it up when she first talked with Padma about the retreat. And for a moment, she was back there, hearing Ashanti's words in her head: *I feel like there is something within you ready to open, and India can be the key to allowing that sacred flowering within you to bloom. I see you embodying the wisdom of your name on a whole other scale.*

Norma continued, and Padma returned to the conversation, "You know, if you look around here, at a Muslim shrine, there are lotus symbols everywhere."

Padma had not noticed the lotus symbols at all. Norma took a moment to tell her where she could find them. She certainly knew quite a bit about Indian heritage.

"If the Taj Mahal is Muslim, why did they use such a significant Hindu symbol?" Padma leaned in, intuiting that Norma would have an interesting answer to this question. And she certainly did.

"Yes, many have discussed this over the years. It is interesting to note that India was under Mughal rule for about 300 years, from the 1500s to the 1800s, and it was a very rich dynasty and one of the longest that ever ruled India. As the lotus is a deeply significant Hindu symbol of purity, wisdom, and expansion, it is a beautiful homage to a mixed cultural heritage. Instead of dismantling anything of a prior culture or religion, they incorporated it into their own. Although some consider this a little manipulative, I find it lovely."

Lovely, indeed, Padma thought.

"How do you know so much about India?" Padma asked Norma.

She smiled warmly and shyly dropped her head, "My husband and I first came here twenty-five years ago, and we both fell in love with the country and the culture. He taught anthropology, and I love travel, and it was truly a perfect match."

"And do you," Padma paused, seeking the right words, "I'm sorry for asking, do you have any *other* children?" Although she did not wish to bring up any hurt or pain, she felt that she could talk to Norma, and Norma certainly didn't seem to have a problem sharing with her. How odd that sometimes you meet someone and that perfect stranger can feel closer to you than some family members.

"Yes! I have a lovely daughter named Swati," Norma beamed at the thought of her beautiful daughter.

"Swati? That sounds Hindi, too!" Padma smiled.

"Yes, well, I have lots of stories I don't wish to bore you with all of them. But we adopted Swati from India when she was only four years old."

Flashes of her toothless little one immediately went through Padma's brain. Those lovely little girls at the orphanage are all seeking true homes. Norma, this angel, had been one of them.

"Norma! We just spent time yesterday at a girl's orphanage in New Delhi, and I have to tell you, it opened my heart even wider than I'd ever thought imaginable. Even though I have two little girls at home, I don't know how to say it..." Padma paused, searching for words. Norma did not jump in. She knew the words that Padma was trying to say, but they were not for Norma to speak for her. Padma would say them when she was ready. Instead, she simply nodded and smiled, awaiting whatever Padma wanted to share.

"Well, I don't know what I am trying to say. But I feel like I want to go back. No, like I need to go back. Something is there. I don't know what. Some connection."

Norma reached for Padma's hand and leaned over, gazing deeply into her eyes.

"When you know, you know."

The two women shared a long, loving gaze before standing up, hugging, and saying goodbye. Unfortunately, the time was coming to meet back with her group, and Padma needed to shuffle along. But what a gift to meet Norma and connect. Of course, thirty other Americans were in her group, but for whatever reason, she was meant to find Norma that day.

Diving Deep

"Yoga is a light, which, once lit, will never dim. The better your practice, the brighter the flame." - B.K.S. Iyengar.

"Mama, look," Nina said, twirling around in her ballerina tutu. Padma laughed at her little princess as she watched her awkwardly spin through the lens of her cell phone camera. Meeta had brought her to watch one of her children's dance recitals, and afterward, Nina had insisted on wearing a tutu of her own, mimicking her cousin's routine. It was quite adorable, and, just like that, Padma realized ballet classes were in their future.

"Look at you! What a prima ballerina!" Padma gushed. Of course, if that is what Nina wanted to be, that's what Nina would be if she had anything to do with it.

Meeta picked up Zoya and showed her to Padma on the screen. Although she had only been gone a few days, it seemed like her baby girl was already changing. She couldn't imagine how much more she would change while she was gone. Being away from the girls was difficult for her, and she realized she was constantly reminded of them throughout India.

After a bit of catching up, with Meeta ensuring that all was, in fact, very well at home, Padma was able to hang up without many tears. Certainly, she missed her family, but knowing they were in good hands made being away from them slightly easier. At least she could focus on what she was there to do, which was becoming quite apparent that it was more than just simple travel. Something deeper was brewing with this Indian trip, and she created more space for it every day.

The group had been given the morning off to refresh from yesterday's long travel, and Padma had more time to herself before meeting the group for lunch. So she took a short walk and quickly found herself nearing the orphanage. She didn't see any children outside, so they must have been in class. She picked up a samosa from a local street vendor and sat across the street, gazing at the orphanage. Something was calling her back here. Was it being of service? Was it the tugging of her mommy's heartstrings? She didn't quite know, but she felt a significant pull and knew she needed to honor and see it through. However, tomorrow morning, they were leaving New Delhi for Rishikesh on an over four-hour bus ride. So, if there was something here, she only had the afternoon to figure it out.

After lunch, Ashanti gathered everyone for a quick meeting to reconnect, give the upcoming itinerary, and answer questions. Afterward, some wanted to go shopping, others looked for an Ayurvedic treatment or massage. Melvin and Melanie said they'd wanted to be open and walk and see where Spirit guided them, and they offered for Padma to join them. But she already knew where Spirit, or her Higher Self, guided her.

"Ashanti, may I speak to you?" Padma asked as the group headed their separate ways.

"Of course! How can I assist you, Padma?"

"Well, frankly, I want to return to the orphanage today. I am being called to, and I am not sure why. Maybe I can clean up or assist somehow? But I don't speak Hindi."

"I love that, Padma. Hmm, let me think for a moment," said Ashanti, hands moving instinctively into the Hakini mudra, the hand gesture where all the fingertips touch, but the palms are open. This gesture is said to help one recall something. And it worked! Before even a moment had passed, it was as if that proverbial lightbulb went off in her head, and Ashanti snapped her fingers in the air and called out, "Sarah, Sarah! Can you come here, dear?"

The plump, smiling woman Padma recalled from the meet-and-greet came running over to Ashanti, ready to help.

"Yes! What can I do for you?" Sarah said, beaming ear to ear.

"I was just remembering; I think you speak Hindi, right?" Ashanti asked.

Sarah confirmed and giggled. There was a playful yet shy way about her that Padma found enjoyable and very real.

"Would you mind accompanying Padma to the orphanage today? You said that you were just happy to go wherever. How do you feel about that?"

Padma suddenly felt a little guilty about taking Sarah's last day in New Delhi from her and wanted to assure everyone that Sarah didn't need to come with her.

"Oh, no. Please, Sarah Ashanti, it is okay. I don't even know why I need to go back. I just feel called to be there and do something. It's not your thing to take on seriously. You need to enjoy your day."

Sarah took Padma's hand, giggling, "This would make my day!" she said with a smile that could not be faked. Padma found herself overwhelmed by Sarah's offer and began to cry. The three women hugged, and then Sarah and Padma headed off to the orphanage for whatever that would bring.

Along the way, they passed a bookstore where Padma noticed one of the books she read to her two little girls in the window: *Goodnight Moon*. When they went inside the store, Padma was relieved to find it as an English version, and she knew that she must bring it to the orphanage.

"Sarah, if I read this to the girls, can you translate it for me?"

Sarah giggled. "I love that book. I would love to translate for you."

With book in hand, the women skipped down the road to the orphanage and entered to find the elders and see where they could assist. The little ones were supposed to be napping, but as soon as Padma and Sarah walked in, they shouted and ran to them like a swarm of bees, buzzing around, giggling, and speaking all at once.

Feeling a hug around her leg, Padma looked to find her little toothless one, with her doll in the crook of her elbow, latched on to her thigh. She reached down and picked her up, bouncing her and carrying her over to the area designated as the napping place. And while Sarah gathered all the little girls around in a circle, Padma pointed to the book and the girls, gesturing to the elders that she wanted to read it to them. One of the women nodded and walked away, leaving Padma and Sarah with the little ones. She was shocked at how effortless it was to connect and find something special to offer the girls. But perhaps that is how things are supposed to work when they are the right things.

Padma showed the girls the cover of the book while Sarah read them the title. Some girls wanted to come up and touch the book, while others sat patiently on the floor, awaiting Sarah's next words. Padma gave them space to point, touch the book, or say anything that came up before moving forward, for there was no rush.

Padma opened the first page and read upside-down so that the girls could see the pictures. This was not an easy feat that everyone could do, but her old marketing days had prepared her for this, as she used to hold presentations in front of her and look down to read them to clients. Even though they had projectors and technology to put presentations up on the wall, she had learned from a mentor that some clients prefer more personal touches. It felt appropriate here in connecting with the girls.

Padma read, Sarah interpreted, and the girls watched intently. Some held tightly onto their toy, possibly afraid to lay them down and wake up to them being gone. Soon, more children lay down on the floor, fighting to keep their eyes open as the story progressed. Padma tried to ignore the one or two that were picking their noses. Kids do that, and she was not able to read and win their noses simultaneously. Her toothless little one sat at her feet, playing with the anklet that Padma wore on her foot.

As she softly read the book, the little girls began to fall asleep one by one. Once she was done reading it, even her little toothless one slumped over like a rag doll on the floor. As she closed the book, she realized that perhaps they had read the last page or two for themselves. It felt like a successful operation. Certainly, the elder women must be thrilled, but they were nowhere to be found. She imagined them all napping somewhere.

Padma smiled at Sarah, who smiled, then leaned in and hugged her. They watched the little ones asleep on the floor, one or two with thumbs in their mouths, some spread out like starfish, and others curled up tightly. The gentle sounds of their deep breathing filled the room as Padma and Sarah sat and watched them sleep.

Running her fingers through the toothless one's hair, Padma smiled. Little Nima is so much like her own Nina, without the love and support of a big family. Would Nima ever be a ballerina? What options would Nima have? Padma understood that it was hard enough for girls when they had loving and supportive families. Her heart broke, considering the challenges that these little ones had. They'd have to find the fortitude from within to work extra hard to figure out who they wanted to be and then somehow find a way to make their dreams come true alone.

These thoughts brought incredible sadness to Padma's heart. She would do anything and everything in her power for her girls. And she knew she couldn't do everything for all these girls. When she allowed herself to think about the larger picture, that this was but one orphanage in one city in the entire world, the enormity of the real issue revealed itself. So many children without families. So many children would have to do whatever they could to survive. What could she alone do?

Unclasping her anklet, Padma wrapped it twice around little Nima's and fastened it again. She smiled. That would be a nice little surprise for her when she eventually woke up. Was it real gold? Was that an actual diamond? Padma didn't care. She knew that Nima would glow when she awoke from her nap to see the anklet. That was a truly priceless thought.

The older women softly called the ladies into another room where they were having masala tea and offered a cup to them. Padma and Sarah gracefully accepted. Sarah asked the women more questions about the girls, specifically the little one who seemed so attached to Padma.

Hers was a particularly sad story. Little Nima was born to a poor family in a village close to New Delhi. Both parents became ill and eventually passed from tuberculosis, leaving Nima orphaned. Neither had received proper medical attention, which might have saved their lives. Nima was but an infant when her parents passed, and she may never have a memory of either of them. No pictures exist, and very little is known of them. The fact that she never became ill was astonishing, an impressive consideration of her little spirit's will. The women at the orphanage were as much a mother to her as she ever had, and because of her parent's history, many people who came to the orphanage might have wanted her to pass when they discovered the ailment of her parents, mostly due to superstition. It seemed that nobody wanted to end up with a sickly child.

But Padma saw no sickness in the little girl. Nima's precious eyes were filled with love and hope. And for now, that is what Padma would have to hold onto — the hope that someone would come along and adopt Nima and all of the other little girls there and all the little girls everywhere. And also all the little boys. Every child deserves to be loved by a family.

The next day, on the long ride to Rishikesh, Padma's thoughts drifted toward the orphanage and to little Nima. She sent her well wishes and imagined the sparkle in her eyes when she discovered the special gift wrapped around her ankle. She hoped Raj would forgive her for giving away a birthday gift that probably cost him half a mortgage payment. Maybe it was a stupid thing to do. But at the time, it felt like Nima needed it more than she did. Now, she was feeling a little funny about it and had to let go of her mind's judgment over a good deed.

The gifting of the anklet did make her think more deeply about the proper ways to be of service and what would make the most impact. Certainly, dropping off expensive gifts at every orphanage was not practical, nor would it potentially get the results that she was looking for. It may potentially even cause more problems. So, what would be the best way to help? Would fundraising be the best way? Her mind spun with thoughts and ideas as the road to Rishikesh stretched out before her.

Ashanti stood up and gathered everyone to talk more about Rishikesh, which was often referred to as the "Capital of Yoga." Thousands flock to the city every year for spiritual fulfillment and pilgrimage. Rishikesh is home to many ashrams where aspiring yogis practice the different styles of yoga traditions now made famous across the world.

Every year, Rishikesh hosts the International Yoga Festival, where thousands of yogis come to practice yoga from various presenters at the base of the Himalayas. It is a coveted event by many yoga practitioners, and although Padma's group was not going to be there at the particular time of the festival, they were assured that the streets would teem with yogis.

The thought of being in the "yoga capital of the world" intimidated Padma. She thought herself quite a novice compared to most others on her tour. As a relative newcomer to the practice, she did not share the depth of knowledge or understanding that many of the others did. However, she did have her family legacy of yoga with Nani, but she had not shared that with most in the group. It would be near Rishikesh that she might sneak off to the village where her grandmother had found her Guru, but she was somehow feeling less in need of pursuing that venture since coming to India. Now, she found herself having other feelings and thoughts and suddenly needing to heal that part of her family's past felt like a more insignificant focal point.

"In Rishikesh, we will dive deeper into our yoga practices, focusing on the type of yoga called Raja, or the Royal Yoga," explained Ashanti. "To most people, Raja is very similar to Hatha yoga, which we practice at our yoga studio and will also be practicing at the ashram. So technically, we are exploring two styles of yoga while in Rishikesh. Where these two styles of yoga differ is in the dedication. Hatha yoga focuses on postures, breath techniques, and meditation, while Raja is allocated for those who dive deeper into mind control and renunciation. For this reason, the practitioner of Raja yoga is considered the ultimate 'ruler' over their body-mind."

"I gave Melanie control over my body-mind a long time ago, so I guess she is the true Raja Yogi," Melvin said, provoking giggling throughout the bus. Melanie blushed and kissed Melvin, who took her hand and smiled proudly. Padma loved those two, especially Melvin's comedic timing, amid a deep discussion where, most likely, many on the tour were beginning to feel inferior to their quest.

Ashanti smiled and continued, "Well, give it a shot anyway, Melvin. You may be surprised that you haven't given up as much as you thought." Melvin nodded as Ashanti tapped his thigh. "So, this is not to say we will all achieve the ultimate control, right? We are on a quest here to unravel the deeper aspects of yoga through Hatha and Raja. Feel into what is right for you, always. But, permit yourself to immerse fully into the program at the ashram."

Ashanti began to pass out some papers to the group, listing chants and a timetable.

"So, these are some of the typical chants you'll learn at the Ashram. Well, let's say that you will chant. They don't so much teach them to you. So, I figured I would go over them with you here and familiarize you…"

Melvin interrupted Ashanti, "Ah, Ashanti, I think there is a mistake on my paper because this says the morning bell tolls at 4:30 am...Ah, did I miss something? I am on vacation!"

Once again, the bus erupted in laughter and a few groans. Ashanti nodded her head in appreciation of their truthfulness.

"I know, I know. Listen, don't get up if you don't want to. You can get up, freshen up, and then head to the main hall for a 5 am silent meditation. Or, skip that if you need to. I am not here to be your mother or your warden, except maybe for Melvin."

"I'll give you that role, gladly," said Melanie, referring to keeping up with Melvin while at the ashram.

"Now, don't you go and fight over me? There is enough to go around!" Melvin laughed.

Padma chimed, "If you need help, don't ask me. I will be hiding at that time, too."

"Me too!" yelled someone from behind Padma.

And then another, "Me three!"

Soon, they were all laughing again. Laughter Yoga is a real thing, and they were all feeling the mood-lifting effects. Ashanti didn't seem to be invested in getting back to the schedule for a few moments and allowed everyone to banter and chuckle. But when it was time to dive back in, she simply started chanting:

Om Namah Shivaya

The melody was slow and soothing. After two rounds, the group began to slowly join her, matching her cadence and pitch. One of Ashanti's assistants began to clap her hands, and soon, many others clapped in unison.

From somewhere, a tambourine began to clink to the clapping, and then there were some hooting and howling sounds that chimed in from others on the bus. The melody took an upturn, and the cadence quickened. Padma found herself clapping faster, chanting and sweating to the rhythm that finally intensified to a crescendo, then abruptly stopped.

Nobody breathed for a few moments. And then, in the silence, rang out Ashanti's beautiful voice, once again slow and soothing:

Om Namah Shivaya

The final sound of "*ah*" lingered for a long time, and she nodded to her assistants, who began to shake and rattle the tambourine and clap their hands, which signaled to others to hoot and howl and bring the mantra to another massive crescendo, that ended with clapping, laughing, and some crying.

Padma found herself completely hooked by the rhythm and energy. She felt physically and spiritually charged by their group chant like she never had before when she sang. Not even from the time she lost her voice singing with Payal at the Lady Gaga concert!

Ashanti hugged some of the people close to her. Padma hugged Sarah, who was sitting across from her on the bus. Everyone was feeling it.

"That is my favorite chant. Lord Shiva is known as the Lord of Yoga. You will see him everywhere in Rishikesh, as he is one of the main gods worshipped there, but especially by yoga students, who pray to him daily," Ashanti explained.

"You will see devotees of Shiva in the streets, setting up portable altars to Shiva with flowers, tridents, and incense. You'll see great statues of him by the Ganges and various renditions of him in most yoga ashrams. This will be a chant you will hear everywhere, but it is mostly about feeling it inside of you, permitting yourself to be your Highest Self, and to be guided by the Lord of Yoga in this quest."

The bus grew silent. The remains of the mantra lingered still in the air and for Padma, in her heart as well.

Everyone took their time to read through the rest of the chants and schedule, casually asking questions of Ashanti and talking amongst themselves. Padma was feeling into what would be right for her to do. Even though she loved the chant, in the back of her mind, she saw her mother crying. But then, she saw Nina smiling. She knew that whatever she was going to do while at the ashram was going to have to feel right to her and not for anyone else. But breaking that habit of pleasing her mother was so difficult, and she found herself second-guessing these ideas over and over as they grew closer to Rishikesh.

Their group had arrived after lunch, so upon checking in, they chose to walk a bit to a local restaurant. The streets of Rishikesh felt different than New Delhi. It seemed like hundreds of souvenir shops and restaurants lined the streets, proprietors begging the yoga students to come in and purchase from them. It was a bit overwhelming. How many bags, harem pants, and scarves can one person own? And after a while of "window," or windowless shopping, it all started to look the same anyway.

So that they didn't overcrowd one spot, the group split into different places for lunch. Melvin, Melanie, Sarah, and Padma sat at a table together, ordered, then sat back with some masala tea while they waited for their food.

"I cannot wait to practice tomorrow. My body is stiff from that bus ride," Melvin shared.

"I was thinking about taking the later evening class," Sarah added. "If we get back in time, and I can make it, that is. Although, if you want to stay here and talk, I love that too." Sarah added a giggle, then nervously drank her tea.

Melanie and Padma shared their similar thoughts about giving it a whirl tomorrow at 4:30 am and taking the evening to slowly move into the schedule. After lunch, they wanted to head back to the ashram, settle in, and maybe relax on the grounds before heading to bed early.

"That sounds lovely, too," Sarah giggled. She just seemed thrilled to be alive and open to just about anything.

Melvin, who was already nodding off from his tea, agreed that perhaps that was the best choice of schedule.

And before they knew it, they were all tucked into their rooms, quietly moving into the evening, falling fast asleep and dreaming of yoga pants.

Yoga of the Mind

"Meditation is the eye that sees the Truth, the heart that feels the Truth, and the soul that realizes the Truth." - Sri Chinmoy.

The sound of the train was getting louder as it approached the station. Suddenly, with a whistle, Padma shot straight up from bed, only to realize that this sound was the temple bell ringing, not a train pulling into the station.

Wearily, she looked around her darkened room, trying to make out the shadows to determine where she was and what she was supposed to be doing. 4:30 am had come quite quickly, just as Ashanti had warned them it might. Although Padma knew it was up to her to choose her schedule, she wanted to make the best effort to push herself to get up for meditation. Now, if only she could make her way to finding a light.

As she made her way to the meditation room, Padma did her best to take in the sights of the ashram, but it was still quite dark before sunrise. But from what she could make out, she knew that she would be in awe of later, once the sun rose to highlight the rippling currents of the beautiful Ganges, lined with temples amongst the Himalayan mountain backdrop.

It's funny how loud the simple sliding of a foot on the floor sounds during a silent meditation. Padma had waited as long as she could before moving her legs because she was losing sensation in them. As she gently moved her tight leg out and away from her body, she realized that the sound it made mimicked that of a needle on a vinyl record screeching to a halt. Knowing she had to tuck the other foot, she waited a few moments longer, and when someone in the room coughed to mask the sound of her movement, she quickly adjusted.

Now comfortable again, Padma regained her ability to focus on being present, yet not in pain. This proved to be trickier than she thought as suddenly everything in her body hurt or felt uncomfortable. I mean, where did the pain in her knee even come from? She never had pain in her knee! Well, not until sitting for silent meditation at the ashram in Rishikesh. Had she been at her home in North Jersey, she mused that, more than likely, she wouldn't have felt a twinge anywhere.

Coming back to her breath and focusing inward, she noticed her eyes darting about, even though her eyelids were closed. What was she looking for? Why were they doing that? She tried to make them stop, but it wouldn't work. Finally, she focused them toward the tip of her nose, something she recalled one of the yoga teachers saying in class. Before that comment, she'd never noticed her eyes darting about when shut. But her mind had a way of constantly maintaining a story that she played out, and her eyes were watching the said story. Focusing the eyes on one spot did help. But she still felt herself fighting to relax.

Incompetence filled her, and suddenly, she felt the urge to cry, realizing all she was missing: She missed home, the creature comforts of her palace, and her loved ones, who were all seemingly doing just fine without her.

What am I doing in India?

Why wasn't I more grateful for what I had at home?

Why is this all coming up now?

Fighting off tears, Padma took a slow, deep exhale out of her mouth, and a whimper fell out with it. Embarrassed, she opened her eyes to look about. Nobody else in this large room, full of at least a couple hundred bodies, seemed to notice. But while her eyes were open, she took the opportunity to look around at everyone else. They all appeared peaceful and contented — from those wearing the clothing indicating that they were yoga teachers in training to the vast plethora of different folks from around the world joining in meditation to her travel group. For sure, she was a failure, and she was certain that she was the only one in the entire room.

The time meditating was excruciating to Padma. From the physical discomfort to the mental agitation and the emotional response, she could not wait to run out of the hall and get some fresh air.

When the silent meditation was finally over, Padma exhaled, followed by a tap on her shoulder. She turned to see Melvin sitting there. He placed his arm around her.

"How you are doing?" he asked, concerned.

That gesture was all it took. Padma's tears could no longer be contained and began spilling out and down her cheeks. Melvin carefully led her outside to a spot where they sat down on the ground. He waited patiently while Padma cried. Melvin held his friend's hand until she processed all of the emotions that were flowing out and took another deep breath, signaling that she was okay.

She wiped her tears with the edge of her shawl, looked at Melvin pouting, and hugged him.

"Do you want to tell me what's going on," he said gently.

She took a long sigh, searching for a way to communicate her feelings. "I'm not sure I can put it all into words," she said.

"Okay, paint me a picture," Melvin said, encouraging her through their normal bantering.

"Ah, you always know how to make me smile, Melvin. Thank you."

The two shared a knowing gaze.

"That was hard," she finally admitted.

"Yes," he replied, head nodding, then wiping his sweaty brow. "I didn't think I would ever get comfortable."

"You too?"

"Agh, my back, my neck, my legs, it was like all of a sudden I felt ninety years old, and every football injury that I ever had reared up and began to ache."

The two laughed. Padma concurred.

"I looked around at one point and felt like everyone else was extremely peaceful, and I was the only one suffering," she admitted.

"Well, rest assured that wasn't the case. I was a lot less than peaceful," he told her.

They were complaining about physical sensations, but they were both aware that there was more to it than that. What lingered underneath was more the issue than anything that was on the exterior. Padma knew what her stuff was but wondered what Melvin's might be. Didn't he have it all together, after all?

She took another deep breath and shared with him that she missed home. She missed everything about home. She was feeling quite homesick. He nodded but didn't respond.

"I'm wondering if I made a mistake coming here," Padma said, digging in the dirt with her fingers as she spoke, careful not to make eye contact with him or anyone else for fear of being seen as the incompetent yoga fraud that she truly was.

"I mean, what was I thinking? Everything at home is perfect. I have a great husband, two healthy children, family, and friends who love me. Oh, and I have a bathroom with hot running water, like all the time, whenever I want hot water, it's there…"

She trailed off. Was she being petty? She thought not. Just honest.

"I miss my bed," Melvin finally said. "My feet are hanging off this tiny little yogi ashram cot. I can't even stretch out."

With that, Melvin fell backward onto the ground and stretched out his entire body like it was the first time he had ever stretched it in his life. He began to groan with pleasure and roll on the ground. Padma giggled and decided to join him, rolling on the ground, laughing, and enjoying the deep stretch. Now, she didn't need it like him. He was a big guy, and the little yogi ashram cot worked just fine for her petite body. But, boy, she got what he meant about the comforts of home.

After rolling on the ground laughing, they finally sat upward again. They were filthy, and that made them both laugh even more.

"Oh dear. I doubt the cold spigot is going to get all this dirt off," Padma said.

"No, I doubt that it will. I now understand the look of the traveling yogi," Melvin said, referring to the yogi nomads who wander about without a house because the earth is their home, and wherever they plant themselves serves as their bed for the night. For these devout yogis, their spiritual quest has trumped all else, and they have taken to the renunciate lifestyle that Ashanti spoke of. You see them throughout the streets all around the Ganges and Himalayas.

Although she was now laughing, the urge to cry sat right below the surface for Padma. This brief respite certainly was needed because she was ready to Uber to the airport and go home. Wait, she wondered, *was there Uber in India*? She felt she should find out just in case.

"Hey, is there an Uber in India?" She asked Melvin.

"If you are Ubering somewhere, take me with you," he said. "Or drop me off at the nearest Hyatt, at least."

"Oh, I was close, man. Just before you came by, it had crossed my mind. Head to the airport and take a red-eye home, I will be there tomorrow with my family. Not that they need me or anything, they seem to be doing just fine."

"Ah, is that it? Feeling unappreciated?" Melvin asked Padma.

"No, that's not it either. I don't know what 'it' is. I just feel lousy. I feel inadequate, like an imposter. I'm not a yogi; I am a mom who is raising her children, and I took off for India on some spiritual quest when, in actuality, I am fine. My life is great. I don't need all this," Padma said, waving her hand around, referring to the entire interworking of the ashram, the retreat, and everything it entailed.

"I want to scream," she said.

"Well, you can scream. Or, you can pick your little ass up and come to yoga with me," Melvin said, standing and offering her his hand.

Twisting her mouth, considering the offer, Padma looked away, then back again. Melvin waited patiently, and eventually, she reached for his hand and allowed him to lift her. He towered over her tiny frame. What was she complaining about? He had to be way more uncomfortable than her.

"So, we are going to get through this together," he said to Padma, shaking her hand.

"Yes, but," she paused, "we make a pact that if it gets too much for either one of us, the other has our back, and we Uber or we Oxen or whatever it is that people ride around here, to the nearest Hilton, which might just be hours away, but will be worth it for the hot water and king-size beds."

"Deal," he said, both vigorously shaking hands.

Padma looked at herself. She was a dirty mess. "I am going to at least put on different clothes for yoga, and I will meet you at the yoga room. I can't practice like this."

The two parted ways to change and clean up then found each other again at the entry to the yoga area, where they left their sandals in a sea of other sandals and headed in for yoga practice. Padma's mental state fluctuated, but she was determined to push through with her friend at her side, at least while she still could muster enough energy.

Padma and Melvin set up near the back of the practice area, closest to the exit. It felt like a worthy location for the two misfits, who were both ready to bolt if necessary. Padma noticed many of their group spread about the area, all on their mats, patiently awaiting the instructor. While there were fewer people at the yoga class than at the meditation that morning, there were still quite a few bodies ready to practice. The gorgeous spot was outside on an enlarged patio-type area overlooking the river. They all seemed physically and mentally content and relaxed in their loose-fitted yoga clothing, looking like the perfect yogis. Melvin lay down on his back, relaxing. She took the time to simply look around and take everything in.

As she settled in, the River Ganges came to the forefront of her mind. This massive river that ran from the Himalayas downward through India was more than a waterway. Many thought of Ma Ganga as a goddess, one who forgives sins and cleanses. Never still and always in flow, the Ganges River was the first thing in Rishikesh that she was able to somewhat understand. For just as within her, who knew of the many mysteries and secrets that lay in the depths of the mighty river but the goddess Ganges herself?

She pondered the thousands of people who, over the millennia, had bathed in the Ganges, asking for their burdens to be released. Did the river still hold the energy of all those tears after all these years? Or had her mighty waters tossed them and squeezed the impurities like a huge washing machine?

As Padma closed her eyes, she visualized kneeling in the waters, crying and releasing whatever she was carrying, even if some of the root causes of her emotions were unknown to her. She saw her tears reach the waters of Ma Ganges but not entirely merge with her. As with oil and water, even though they were together, there was a distinct separation of the two water sources. Padma felt as though the river would never be able to transform her tears. Yet she cried and cried until the tears sunk deep down into the waters, eventually disappearing entirely.

Padma took a deep breath and opened her eyes. As she visualized the strength of that ritual, she completely understood what drove so many people to walk into those waters every day. She felt lighter now just from that simple visualization. She would have shared all this with Melvin but had to shift her awareness back to the yoga space.

A large altar with a dancing Lord Shiva, what is known as Nataraj, faced inward from the river. The energetics of the feminine waters danced behind the metal statue of the masculine, balancing the dualistic energies incredibly well. The notable energy of water and fire coming together also struck Padma as she gazed at the images. Incense wafted from Shiva's altar, and Padma realized that this was the energy of air making its presence. At her next glance, the fresh flowers at the base of the altar represented the earth element. Padma noted that now all four elements were present at the altar.

Wait, aren't there five elements?

Yes, the element ether, the omnipresence of an intangible yet undeniable energy that flowed through all matter, that was most certainly present, too. Padma could feel it. And she felt as though all of these elemental energies created a complete and harmonious sacred space. As she gazed at the altar, she couldn't think of anything else that was needed.

Once the yoga instructor came into the area, everyone sat up and prepared for practice. Padma thought she had nothing to lose, so she decided to throw away any anticipation and be open like the river and go with the flow. It turned out to be a good plan. Although she was familiar with many of the postures and breathing techniques in the practice, the way that they were taught was different to her, and the instructor's broken English made it difficult to understand all of the cues. She noted the Sanskrit being used to reference different parts of the practice and that many students seemed to understand those words. She caught a few here or there but mostly had to follow others' movements a beat or so behind. This communication barrier kept her in sharp focus, which assisted with removing other invading thoughts that may have distracted her.

Instead of feeling defeated by the challenges she met during the class, Padma felt like she was learning something new, and her mind felt engaged in that process without feeling inadequate. She wondered how Melvin was doing. He was sweating a lot. And it seemed he came out of postures quicker than she to wipe his forehead. Heat aside, Melvin seemed to be holding his own in the class. But she had already learned not to make judgments based on perceived looks after the morning meditation.

Overall, the yoga practice went a lot smoother than the early-morning meditation. And suddenly, she found herself a little less needing to Uber out than she had just a couple of hours earlier.

When the practice concluded, Melvin looked at her, sparkling with sweat, leaned in, and revealed how very famished he was.

"I could eat my yoga mat," Melvin said.

Padma laughed. "Well, that makes sense. We've been up for several hours, and I've lost any steam I gained from that warm cup of water with lemon we had earlier."

"Did I hear her correct? Is breakfast in another hour?" Melvin moaned.

"I fear you are correct, sir," she concurred.

"Agh, Okay. I am heading back for another cold shower," Melvin pointed to her while walking away, "I'll find you later."

Padma waved at him and decided to find a place there to sit and spend more time connecting with Mama Ganges. A lovely soft spot in the grass, surrounded by plants and multiple colored flowers overlooking the water, would do just nicely. The area was on a slight embankment, allowing her to sit upright easily without needing a meditation cushion or chair. It was warm out but not unbearably hot to her due to a slight breeze that seemed to move through her hair as if Raj were blowing on the back of her neck while he ran his fingers through her hair.

Unlike earlier this morning, she now found herself completely at peace and gazing softly at the river. She allowed her eyes to focus on a spot and half-closed her eyes. This type of meditation, she would come to understand, was called Tratak, meaning gazing point. In Tratak, one uses the eyes to look softly at a particular thing and allow that to be the focus of the meditation. This served Padma well, and before she knew it, someone was tapping her on her shoulder to go in for a meal. What felt like a few moments turned out to be just about an hour. Now, *that* was meditation!

My style of meditation is just a little different than what they teach here at the ashram.

The remaining time at the ashram felt about the same as this first day for Padma. She found the morning silent meditations almost intolerable, while her tratak by the Ganges after yoga felt like the real deal, and she often found that she could stay there much longer than was the allotted free time if it weren't for being famished and in need of sustenance. There were only two meals a day served at the ashram, and while they could go out to the restaurants for more food if they chose, Padma wanted to try her best to stick to the program there and see where it would bring her.

Melvin had given up the program on day one. He decided to stay there with the group but headed out multiple times seeking food, Ayurvedic massage, and anything more pleasing than what was offered at the ashram. They started calling his ventures "breakouts" between them. Melanie sometimes joined Melvin and sometimes stayed back. Padma was attempting to dive into the renunciate lifestyle as much as she could while at the ashram, knowing full well that this would not be a long-term lifestyle for her.

However, she found herself seeking out more solitude as the days went on and feeling less need to engage in social activity. She even forgot to check in with Raj one day and came back to her room later to find several missed calls. Instead of being upset with herself for forgetting, she embraced the energy of Mother Ganga, let it go, and flowed on. Instead of being overrun with guilt, Padma decided to be completely present with her family when she did talk to them and to exude as much love for herself in the process.

The idea of love as it related to self was brought up on the second or third day at the ashram, and this hit home for Padma. In all of the roles that she played: mother, daughter, wife, etc., the focus was on loving others. Yet when she thought about loving herself, it felt foreign — selfish even.

"You yourself, as much as anybody in the universe, deserve your love and affection," Buddha read Akasha, one of the yoga teachers at the ashram during class.

The thought of this captured Padma. In his instructions on living simply, the Buddha felt it important to remind his students of this particular aspect of love. As they were guided through the yoga practice and brought back to the concept of self-love several times, Padma realized that she lacked this quality quite a bit in her life. What she had replaced with self-love was harsh judgment. She had created monumental criteria for what being a good mother, daughter, etc., was, and in the process, had become her own worst critic when it came to implementation. The people closest to her continued to provide her with support and assurances, yet she ignored them to listen to her inner critic. It was not serving her well. It had created more anxiety over unattainable goals. How she treated herself lacked a lot of love.

But how can I learn to love myself like I do my daughters?

At the moment of this thought, the yoga teacher came by and asked her to squeeze her quadriceps muscle on the front thigh.

"Use the muscle to support you. After a while, you won't need to consider contacting it," she said, floating off to the next student.

That's it! Love is like a muscle. If you don't use it, it becomes atrophied. When you use it with enough consistency, it becomes second nature.

Wow. What an epiphany! That evening, Padma decided to splurge and go outside the ashram with Melvin and Melanie for a big meal and some extra dessert. After all, she determined that time spent at the ashram as a yoga aspirant deserved an extravagant reentry to the real world. The good news was that being a simplistic yogi and consuming good treats were both acts of self-love.

On the last day at the ashram, Ashanti came to Padma to see if she was still interested in going to Nani's ashram before they left the area.

"Hmm, good question," thought Padma. "You know, part of me thinks it would be interesting, but I also feel like I am gaining so much of my wisdom following your lovely programs that I don't need to go there anymore."

"Do you think that you will have any regrets once we leave? Or that you left a stone unturned in healing the family wounds?" Ashanti asked Padma curiously.

"Can I meditate on that question?" Padma asked her teacher.

"Sure, do you mind if I join you?" Ashanti asked.

Padma smiled and shook her head, placing her hands on her heart and appreciating that her teacher wanted to be with her. She took a deep breath and gazed softly at the mighty river, watching it flow. She pondered Nani, the Guru, her mother, and their family's history.

Suddenly, an image began to emerge from the water. A feminine figure in white robes ascended. Although water shimmered like diamonds as it rolled down her robes, she was dry, smiling, and holding a pink lotus. The woman walked across the water, and each time she took a step, she left a pink lotus behind in her footprint. She walked toward Padma and stopped at the water's edge before sitting inside a large lotus that appeared at her feet.

She was the goddess Saraswati, but her face was fluid, like water, continually changing in form. At one point, she appeared with the face of Padma's Nani. The next moment, it was her mother, Uma. As she continued to watch the form mutating, she became Nani again, then little Nina, and then Zoya. The fluidity of the changeable face became each woman in her immediate family before finally morphing into Padma's face. But it didn't end there. The goddess became her many friends, one by one, and her extended family members like Raj's mother and sisters and more. Eventually, the little girls at the orphanage in New Delphi began to show up in the goddess' face, including her little toothless friend, Nima.

Saraswati was at once her particular form and all women. The goddess revealed the "Oneness" sought by spiritual seekers and proved an interconnected web of energy that all women share as life-givers. She lost a sense of time as she continued to witness generations pass, ancestors rise, and the original bloodline of all women appear. This vision was nothing short of sheer ecstasy.

This beautiful energy of the Mother goddess, the protectress, the nurturer, the lover, the friend, the grandmother, and all of the forms that a woman takes at various times of her life were all wrapped up in one complete form. It was the goddess Saraswati.

And while Padma longed to stay with the vision forever, eventually, the feminine image rose from her lotus, walked backward into the depths of the water, and descended until the only thing left was a small ripple of water. And then, eventually, that too vanished into the flowing energy of the river.

Padma took a deep breath and bowed her head to the divine vision, the river, the mother, and herself.

A sense of completeness wove into the fabric of her being. She knew instantly that she needn't travel back to Nani's ashram for answers or closure because wherever she went, she was complete.

She opened her eyes and shook her head 'no' to Ashanti, who smiled and nodded, affirming Padma. There would be no extra excursion necessary.

The vision also confirmed for Padma that she had a bigger calling, one that would assist women. She knew she had the means to be of service. She also felt she was being called to be a voice or a helping hand for all women. But where should she start in such a large world with much need?

On the way back to her room, a pink lotus flower appeared on the path in front of her, very out of place. Padma picked up the flower and walked forward, not being lost that her vision had manifested in reality.

The poignancy of the lotus flower in her vision then hit her: her name and its true meaning. She now understood that she was a key to bringing women together and uplifting them. She also understood that she was going to have to trust that the roots of what may be dormant in the murky depths of the water would continue to climb upward toward the light, eventually be seen in full glory again.

The lotus. Padma.

Death Becomes Her

"Death is not an ending. It is a transformation. Death is the threshold of this life. Beyond it is something else, some mystery." — Deng Ming-Dao.

The quickest way to travel from Rishikesh to Varanasi—believed to be the world's longest-inhabited city—is by plane. This Indian retreat included a variety of transports. So far, they'd taken a plane, bus, train, and taxi, and now they were flying off from the foothills of the Himalayas in the north, southward to the holy city of Varanasi.

Truthfully, Varanasi scared Padma a bit. She was told that you look death in the face there every day. Ashanti shared with them that it was estimated that about 20,000 people arrive there annually to die and be cremated due to the belief that this act will end the cycle of one's reincarnation and the soul will achieve full liberation. To Padma, that was a huge thought, as if Varanasi was a black hole, ready to swallow up anyone who dared get too close.

Padma usually preferred not to focus on the horrors of death but rather the beauty of life. Other than her grandmother, who passed when she was still quite young, Padma had not lost anyone close yet. She could not bear the thought of losing anyone at the moment either, especially since, as a new mom, her focus was on creating and sustaining new lives. And yet, she was told that death was an important aspect in the cycle of life and that without it, how could one truly appreciate what they had in the present?

The idea of reincarnation was not something she'd thought deeply about in the past. Although she understood the concept, her family kept conversations relatively light, and religious events focused mainly on celebrations. This trip to Varanasi now availed her the first opportunity to allow herself to consider her thoughts about death and dying and, ultimately, the path and final destination of the soul. It was a lot to drop into on vacation.

The four-star hotel Ashanti picked in Varanasi was a wise choice, particularly coming from the modest accommodations at the ashram and moving to the holiest of cities associated with death. Melvin was more than pleased to spread back out in a nice, big bed, and for Padma, the hot water and western shower were more than welcome. It also felt important to have a safe place to land where they felt comfortable at night — especially since the daytime activities seemed to press some uncomfortable buttons.

Ashanti told the group that their trip to Varanasi was bringing them to the style of yoga known as Jnana, or the "Yoga of Knowledge." But instead of this being like a college course for yogis, she explained that for the Jnanin yogi, true wisdom was associated with realizing the real from the illusionary. She went on to describe the six accomplishments that the Jnanin, who is liberated but remains in his/her body, would have:

"First, we have tranquility or Shama in Sanskrit. This is the ability to remain calm even in the face of adversity. I work on Sharma daily with my children, especially my youngest son, Todd. That kid likes to get into things. I have to keep my eye on him, or he will have the entire contents of our pantry on the floor in bubbles from laundry detergent," Ashanti told them. Everyone got a good chuckle out of that. It was quite relatable to anyone who had a toddler.

"Second is serene restraint or Dama. This is the curbing of one's senses, which habitually crave stimulation.

"So, like you want to eat the whole bag of potato chips, but you don't," Melvin jumped into everyone's approval and laughter.

Ashanti pointed at him, "You got it!"

"Well, if you mean I got the whole bag of chips, you'd be right because I did that on night two at the ashram. But if you are referring to restraint, I think I have to work on that a bit more," Melvin admitted.

"Don't we all?!" Shouter Sarah.

Everyone laughed again. Padma admired how Ashanti and the group could keep heavy things on a lighter side.

"Okay, what's next," Ashanti checked her notes. "Ah, cessation. This is Uparati in Sanskrit. It is the abstention from actions that aren't relevant to maintaining the body or the pursuit of enlightenment. So, Melvin, this comes after restraint. And, if you already missed the boat on that, well, then Uparati will be a little further away. But never fear! You can always work on these, and one day, you may find that the very thought of potato chips is no longer a thing for you."

Melvin chuckled, "Okay."

"Come on, Melvin, that's just number three. We have three more to go!" Ashanti said to a roar of laughter. "Listen, you will like the next one: endurance or Titksha."

"Yes! Finally, one that I can master: Endurance!" Melvin said, pounding his chest.

Padma had to keep wiping the tears from her eyes from laughing so much. Her stomach muscles were working as much as if she'd done several rounds of breath of fire!

"So, with Titksha, this is the stoic ability to be unruffled by the play of opposites in nature, such as heat and cold, pleasure and pain, or praise and censure. So yeah, it's the ability to stay calm amongst the storm of duality constantly raging at you. And I think of it as when you have two athletes or opponents trying to get under each other's skin, attempting to throw the other person off their game. Right, Melvin?"

"Yes, Ma'am," Melvin responded.

"Yeah, see, how we can all feel these complicated yogic ideas in our everyday life?" Ashanti asked the group.

"It makes them more available for me," said Padma.

Ashanti smiled and nodded to Padma.

"Okay, two more guys and gals. Number five is mental collectiveness. We call this Samadhana. It's concentration and the discipline of single-mindedness in all situations—but specifically concerning education."

"So focus," Melanie offered.

"Yeah, focus to the 'nth' degree," Ashanti added. "Then, finally, we come to the final accomplishment, which, in my opinion, should be first: faith. Shraddha is a deeply inspired, heartfelt acceptance of the sacred and transcendental Reality. 'Faith,' yoga scholar Georg Feuerstein said, 'is fundamental to all forms of spirituality, and must not be confused with mere belief, which operates on the level of the mind only.'"

With a gaping mouth, Padma lingered on those final words. Discerning the difference between Jnana, Karma, and Raja yoga was a tall order. This brought up a lengthy discussion of the five types of yoga they were there to experience through India herself: Karma, Raja, Hatha, Jnana, and Bhakti, the last of which they'd yet to discuss in detail.

As Ashanti edited down the styles of yoga, Padma noted in her journal the following:

Karma is the yoga of acting selflessly, without concern for outcome or recognition. Raja is the type of yoga that compels the yogi to dive so deeply into controlling his mind through renunciation that he's considered the "ruler" of his/her body-mind. Hatha, the yoga that focuses on postures, breath techniques, and meditation, is most practiced in the West. Jnana is the yoga of knowledge. Last but not least of all styles, Bhakti is the yoga of devotion that seeks to merge with the Divine, often through chanting.

Among the group, some felt that Jnana reflected the ultimate ideal of Karma yoga. As a people-pleaser, Padma understood how Karma yoga could be misunderstood. She had considered why she attempted to accommodate others and had found that there was a seed of needing to be appreciated involved. A true Karma Yogi did not come from that type of need. But instead of feeling her normal, inadequate self, Padma took a moment to admire how far she'd come in a short time already. She was sprinkling in that self-love wherever she could.

So, Jnana yoga they'd contemplate as they pulled into the city of the dead. But not before Ashanti shared another quote from Georg Feuerstein's book *The Yoga Tradition* regarding Jnana yoga:

"Philosophical study on its own is said to be like 'dressing up a corpse.' It comes alive only through the desire for liberation, and that desire must be deeply felt and not merely based on casual fascination or delusions of grandeur."

The thoughts of Jnana yoga and the discernment of the real from the unreal put Padma in a pensive mood. She was well aware that she, along with her mother, preferred to keep things lighter. She knew that Varanasi would push her out of her comfort zone a bit. And she wasn't sure how ready she was for it.

That night, Padma slept like, well, the dead. In her plush private hotel room, she spread out and luxuriated. She found the time to chat with Raj and the girls over FaceTime, took a long, hot bath, and slid to bed early. In the morning, she even had time to try to do something with her hair for the first time since they'd landed in India. Between the extreme heat and humidity and a busy schedule, sheather threw it up in a ponytail or wrapped it with a scarf. Frankly, she rather enjoyed her simple pin-back hair of India to the blow-dry and straightening at home. Yet, with her extra time this morning, she felt compelled to do "something" with it. Maybe because of all the thoughts of mortality, she allowed herself more time this morning.

After all, you only live once. Well, depending on your thoughts about reincarnation.

However, the humidity proved that doing anything with her hair was a complete act of futility. So, after about two minutes of walking outside, she took her scarf from around her backpack and twirled her hair around it, tying the knot under her hairline like a pro on the go.

Today, the group was to walk through the maze known as Varanasi and visit the many ghats or steps that descend to the

Ganges. Here, the river is primarily used for bathing—both ceremonially and not. The level of toxicity in many areas along the Ganges, particularly in Varanasi, has changed the once pure waters into an unhealthy place to wade. When pressing Ashanti for a more clear answer to the toxicity, Padma was not pleased with her reply:

"Well, from various bacteria. From human and animal waste to remnants of the remains of the burned bodies."

Yikes! Not going in there! I doubt I'll have a recurring vision of Saraswati in this area of the Ganges.

As Ashanti explained how many rituals continue here despite the potential dangers, Padma kept her thoughts to herself. She informed the group that they would not partake in bathing rituals due to these concerns about the waters. But, of course, she could not keep anyone from stepping in if they felt compelled to, as many people do.

Padma reassessed her feelings on this matter. On the one hand, moving into the mighty Ganges felt significant on a spiritual level. But on the other hand, Raj's voice screamed in the back of her head, telling her to stay clear and not to take a chance on obtaining any bacterial infections.

"One of my friends has a father who is an Indian doctor, and he told me not to go into the river. And they're from this area," Sarah shared with Padma.

Padma nodded her head in agreement.

As the group walked along Varanasi and out toward the various ghats, they witnessed many people swept up in the holiness of Mother Ganges, unaffected by thoughts of contamination. Padma mused that the embodied divine goddess energy flowed down from just a short distance away in Rishikesh. All signs pointed towards Varanasi being a spiritually heightened place, yet she was having a difficult time feeling it as such. What Padma felt was apprehensiveness and unease. When she mentioned these feelings to Ashanti, she told Padma that it was part of Varanasi's job to make one feel uneasy.

Death is everywhere. Funeral pyres line the Ganges, making mortality a constant thought — be it conscious or unconscious. With a constant concentration on the end part of life, Padma realized how little this was discussed in the West, especially living with a doctor whose duty was to save lives. Most of their conversations ran around living, building their family, having goals, and healing from sickness. She didn't ever remember one conversation with her husband or any of her friends or family about death or end-of-life wishes. This pervading theme thrives in Varanasi. Padma wrestled with a fleeting, worrisome thought of a soul leaving a body and accidentally inhabiting hers. Of course, this was irrational, but once the door had opened to all thoughts of death and dying, her mind didn't seem to discriminate. The progress that Padma had recently prided herself on suddenly felt diminished here in Varanasi, and she knew at once that this was one of the ways this town would trigger her. She also knew this awareness of this issue would be a major key in finding greater ease moving through this part of the trip.

Padma contemplated if she believed in reincarnation. What did she truly think happened at the time of death? And, for that matter, what was the soul?

Life, death, mortality, and soul were the thoughts all swimming in Padma's mind as she walked the smoky streets of Varanasi. There were no shops selling harem pants or OM scarves to distract her down by the cremation areas. And she certainly had no interest in food, at least not while walking the ghats. She couldn't envision dropping into Varanasi as a mere tourist destination. This holy city, where so many came when they were close to death, was considered a final resting place and an opportunity for the soul to ascend.

Around the corner of another spot, they came upon a body dressed in saffron-colored cloth, decorated with flowers, being brought down to the Ganges in preparation for burial. Everyone in the group was quiet and sat on the steps to witness the body being lovingly placed down by the holy waters and dipped in. The group of men that carried the body brought it down towards an area that was prepared with wood on a platform in the sand and took time to place it there properly. What they said to each other or the body couldn't be made out from where they sat. But Padma noticed that there were no somber faces amongst them. They'd come to release the body of a loved one, and they seemed quite content with the situation.

Padma glanced over towards her friends and noticed that Melvin and Melanie were clasping hands tightly while Melanie leaned her head against Melvin, seeming to wipe a tear from her eyes. Padma, too, felt emotional witnessing this sacred act of releasing the body, although, at the moment, she was not brought to tears. She felt that her friends were grieving something deep at the moment and chose to continue to give them the space that they needed to be with these feelings.

It was some time before the men staged the body in its final place and then lit the pyre. The crackling wood began to smoke, and it was not too long before the body was fully engulfed in flames. Padma felt herself holding her breath, at one point realizing this and releasing it with a huge sigh. More than a few group members walked away from the cremation ceremony, but she noticed that Melvin and Melanie were still there, both crying fully now. Witnessing this emotional release in her friends permitted her to cry for the first time in Varanasi. She felt herself crying not just for the person being released but for all who had come to Varanasi seeking the ultimate passage into death, with the hope of the soul's release from karmic baggage. She didn't know how she felt all of this, but it did not matter. She allowed it all to come nonetheless.

Ashanti tapped Padma's shoulder sometime later and motioned for her to join the group at the top of the steps when she was ready. It seemed that she was gathering them to move to another location, and the group had somewhat dismantled due to personal experiential needs during the ceremony. But before she moved on, a woman sitting next to her spoke gently.

"The smoke is going towards the Ganges, this is good," said the woman sitting next to Padma.

"I'm sorry?" Padma asked.

"When the smoke from the body moves to the water, the soul has been released. This is good. This is happy."

Padma looked at the woman with much gratitude. She smiled and nodded to Padma, who smiled back. She then placed her hands in prayer and bowed to the woman. She giggled at Padma and nodded before smiling back at the funeral pyre. This was the first time Padma had witnessed an aspect of death as a positive outcome. It felt odd but not oddly welcomed, and she was very appreciative to have had the small yet significant interaction.

Under Ashanti's loving presence, the group entered one of the larger ghats.

"Spend time here reflecting, meditating, or holding space for whatever comes up. I'll be right over there," Ashanti pointed to an area by the water, "if you need me to talk, come get me. But first, I have something personal to attend to."

Padma did not feel like conversing with anyone. She already felt overwhelmed with reflection but chose a nice spot where she could watch the water and the many small boats gently floating and bobbing about. There were a lot of people moving about this area, too. There was no short supply of people-watching. But what caught her attention most was Ashanti's stride directly toward the water, where she walked up to her knees, opened her bag, and removed a small satchel. She watched as Ashanti took out some flowers and laid them on the water, then slowly began to pour what appeared to be ashes from the satchel into the water.

Ashanti had not shared anything about this ritual act with the group. Padma noted that it was personal, and she would leave it so. But she found herself captivated by the image of her teacher releasing what she imagined were the final remains of someone or something significant to her into Mother Ganges and then slowly retreating to the spot where she told the group they could find her. Ashanti didn't appear upset by this act. It was with confidence and grace that she performed her ritual and then walked away, not looking back.

Taking a deep exhale, Padma looked up to watch the wafting smoke from the funeral pyres rise upward and dissipate into the sky. The thick smoke seemed to always linger near the ground, but she was more interested in watching It move up and thin out. She imagined that when the souls left the bodies, they got thinner and more dispersed the higher they went. She invented a tratak meditation on the air of the pyres and visualized the energy shifting as it expanded. The hypnotic motion of the boats gently bobbing in the water, with the smoke dissipating into the sky, felt oddly calming in this somber place.

When she released her meditation and began to refocus on the happenings at the ghat, Padma noticed the many smiles on the faces of the people in the water. The look of happiness among those who chose the city as a place of purification was more apparent to her. These faces were not sad about death. The people of Varanasi seemed to be celebrating it. Yet, the contrasting colorful flowers and joyous people against the burning bodies and sheer presence of death were surreal. At home, death is scary and unhappy and something that most people try not to talk about. In Varanasi, death was but another part of life, a cycle to be honored.

Even though Padma thought that she'd already done plenty of reflecting, she found herself lamenting even more, wondering how she would take the eventual death of a loved one when it occurred. Dealing with grief is a reality. She counted herself lucky that, at her age, it had not come up yet. But considering it could happen at any moment, she had to wonder if she would be able to release the loved one with love or scream in agony with attachment. She thought it would be the latter, yet hoped for the former. This gave rise to more reflection on the nature of death and her personal beliefs.

Questions like: What happens to the soul when you die? Is there an afterlife? Heaven? Hell? What is reincarnation? Do we come back to another body with no memories of our previous life? And, if so, what's the purpose of that?

The more she reviewed these questions, the more questions arose. She continued: What, then, is the purpose of our life? Since everyone eventually dies, what did we come here to do? And why do some people never really figure out just what that is?

The totality of a person's life comes down to the moment just before death; she realized when there is either an acknowledgment of having accomplished what one was meant to do, sadness in dying an unfinished life, or having lived one devoid of love and happiness. She may not have known a lot, but she was sure that she did not want to be one of those people who died depressed and lonely, wondering what the whole thing of life was about. She wanted to be someone who, at the end of life, had a deep inner knowing that they'd positively impacted the world. And she wanted to die surrounded by loved ones.

Padma took a deep, long, surrendered breath. And with it, she let go of her racing mind and the many thoughts. She was realizing how easy it was to get caught up in her head again, and that was starting to cause a bit of needless anxiety. She claimed moments of deep breathing to center herself back in her body, in the present moment, into where she was now and what she was doing here. It did not take long to regain her presence, and then she felt much better than she had all morning when her mind dizzied with definitions and answers.

Padma then began to notice members of her group approaching and, in some cases, moving into the Ganges with flowers and releasing them into the water. Melvin and Melanie walked in together, released a flower, and smiled at each other. As Melanie rested her head on his shoulder, they seemed to watch the flower float away. She imagined that their grip on each other's hand was tightening.

She then realized that Ashanti had been giving out the flowers. She approached her to find out what was occurring, and Ashanti explained that she could place the flower in the river as an offering to Ma Ganges but first suggested she take a moment and reflect on an aspect of her life that she was ready to release.

"Within all of us is a place of darkness or shadow. Everyone has something that they need to let go of. Death is but transformation. So, as you release that aspect of yourself to Ma Ganges—allowing it to essentially die—you are creating a transformation in yourself, creating space for it to change into something greater, something lighter," Ashanti explained.

Padma shook her head.

"I don't know if I can do this," she told Ashanti.

"Nobody says you have to," Ashanti answered sweetly.

Yet, she knew that she needed to. After all, when would she have the opportunity to release and honor the death of her lower self in Varanasi again? So, she picked up a flower and walked slowly toward the river.

First, she released her breath. Then she released her body. She did not realize how tensely she had been holding it. She took a moment to stretch and shake about, then turned her gaze to the flower in her hands. Closing her eyes, she imagined that part of herself that sometimes feels inadequate, not good enough, or like a bad mother; that piece of her that judges herself harshly becomes anxious and sometimes even unraveled; she imagined that part of her on one of the funeral pyres being released into the river. How could she truly be a good mother and raise smart, intelligent women if she didn't feel confident in her skin? It was time to transform that old self and release her into the mighty river.

Padma took a moment, silently apologized to her husband, slipped off her shoes, and walked into the river. Bending down, she gently placed the orange flower on the water's surface and watched it float off, bobbing up and down with the current. And when she was sure she'd completed that old story, she turned, as gracefully as Ashanti had, and walked away, not looking back.

She sat back down on the steps of the ghat and felt a new sense of peace and contentment. The truth was that she was never really the anxious, imperfect mother she imagined herself to be. That was something that her mind had created. It was an illusion. Now, at this moment, she knew with unwavering faith that she was truly much more than that. Suddenly, she realized how much of her higher self she had been hiding away and how much of that true self she had kept small. Even her role as a mother was so much more than the role she played at home. And although it was probably her favorite role, even that was not who she truly was.

Padma sat and watched the endless pouring of funeral smoke wafting upward, revealing a deep truth: life may be impermanent, and yet, there is no death, only a change of energy. She knew that a part of her old small self died that day in Varanasi, making way for a spark of newness to rise in its smoke, like the Phoenix that rises from the ashes. This new self felt more true to who she was. She felt invigorated and empowered.

And, she mused, if she did manage to die of a bacterial infection from the Ganges, well, at least she was in the right place to do it. She laughed. Death was not really that scary. It was not fully living a life that scared her the most.

Hopelessly Devoted

"You will face many defeats in life, but never let yourself be defeated." - Maya Angelou.

The two days in Varanasi went quickly. Soon, the group was back on a plane to New Delhi. Varanasi was like Las Vegas: what happened there, stayed there. Melanie and Melvin never spoke to Padma or anyone else on the trip about their grief over the baby they'd lost or the ritual they did to release that pain. Padma didn't tell Raj about stepping into the river and never needed to do so due to illness. Ashanti continued to keep her ritual private.

After all their travels, from the opulence of the Taj Mahal at Agra to the yogi sanctuary of Rishikesh and into the deep dive of the "cycles of life" at Varanasi, New Delhi felt like a peaceful home. Although the streets teemed with bikes, cars, trucks, and animals alike, and going from point A to point B felt like a live video game, it was no more difficult than Manhattan during rush hour. Okay, minus the oxen and other mammals on the road. Or at least her last jaunt into the city never exposed such things.

The group was given an open day to explore or relax before meeting again to begin their final yogic path of Bhakti. Padma and several others agreed to take an informal walking tour of New Delhi and let spirit guide them. And so she and several other friends set out to enjoy the day in perfect trust.

They began with a full breakfast at their hotel before heading into the robust streets. Their group first stopped to try a Falooda, a local favorite they had somehow missed until that point. And yes, even though they had full bellies, it felt like, in the short walk, they'd earned the right to this snack. Falooda consists of noodles, milk, almonds, rose syrup, and spices. It tasted like a creamy rose milkshake, but one that you needed to eat instead of drink. Melvin ate one in a few gulps and then purchased a second one for the road. Had he tasted it? She wasn't sure. Melvin seemed to inhale his food.

"You never know when you will get another meal," he told the group, who laughed at his remark since food was easily found anywhere along the way. Melvin just liked food. And there was no crime in that.

Sarah mentioned to the group that there was a great place nearby called the Chandni Chowk and that they should check it out. This way, they could shop for anything they wanted before heading home. Padma already had a suitcase full of gifts, but she was confident she would find even more fun tokens at the market and was game for the trip. While deep conversations and religious ceremonies may not have been in her family's blood, shopping, almost anywhere, certainly was.

So, with great enthusiasm, they headed out to the famous market on their last free day in India. They decided to split up and ride rickshaws. And wow, what a stupendous idea that was.

Padma and Sarah laughed the entire time the driver wove through the traffic, sometimes against traffic, and, more than once, nearly colliding with a motorbike or bus. They had to laugh because if they didn't, Padma felt she might have a mild heart attack from the stress of the ride. She recalled the agonizing studying and practicing she'd done to receive her US driver's license at the age of 17 as she caught sight of a family of four without helmets carrying a large satchel of goods careening through traffic like a snake wrangling away from a captor. The youngest, of about five, was doing the driving.

They'd long lost sight of the others with their rickshaw drivers. Staying together for the journey was an impossible task, yet miraculously, they all arrived at the market around the same time and, thankfully, all in one piece. At least they thought all the pieces were still there; they hadn't checked. Everyone was giggling like little kids. After their drivers warned them to be careful of pickpockets, which they claimed were even more dangerous than the ride to the market, they all entered Chandni Chowk hand-in-hand, ready for whatever should come.

This market area was closed to large motor vehicles, making walking a little safer. Still, the plethora of people on bikes, scooters, and whatever else they could manage to fit into the area created a chaotic atmosphere.

Padma recalled that about 32 million people lived in Delhi.

At least thirty million people must be at the Chandni Chowk market today or en route.

Sarah wanted to get an Indian soccer shirt for her nephew, and Padma thought Raj might enjoy one as well, so they headed toward a shop that looked like it supported sports teams. Melvin came with them to "authenticate the merchandise," which was just his way of getting involved in something sports-related.

Once Melvin approved the quality of the merchandise, it was haggling time. Most people in the US do not understand that haggling is just a part of Indian life. Shopping is negotiable, and not haggling is impolite. This was one Indian ritual that her parents had taught her and that they were proud of. It was not unusual for her mother or father to haggle like warriors in battle, only to laugh like children at their conquest later. She loved to shop, and haggling made it that much more fun.

"How much?" Sarah said in English, even though she was perfectly capable of speaking Hindi.

The man picked up a calculator and showed Sarah a price: 2500. Her face said it all. Melvin stuck his head forward to see the price, then shook his head side to side.

"No. No way. Too much," he said to the shop owner, who then threw his hands in the air, said a bunch of things in Hindi, and, after a moment of sulking, went back to the calculator and presented Sarah with a new offer: 2200. That would be about US$26, which Sarah thought was an okay price, but Melvin chimed in before she could say anything:

"2000 rupee. No more," he said, gesturing with his hand, sliding it out as if to indicate it was marking the top of something.

You could have heard a pin drop in the busy market. Well, maybe not a pin unless said pin was the size of a boulder. Everyone in their group, including the shop owner and nearby shop owners, waited to see who would be the first to speak. "The first to speak, losses," is what they say in sales circles. Melvin bit his lip hard. Sarah had to close her mouth with her hand so that no words spilled out. Padma smiled. She loved this part.

The shop owner made a fist as if he wanted to punch Melvin, but faking anger was also a part of the rouse. Everyone there knew that this was the first purchase of the day and that if the shop owner wanted a good day of sales, he would have to make a good deal on the shirt to kick it off. The worst thing that could happen for an Indian shop owner was the first potential sale to walk away. That meant bad luck and little sales until they corrected the energy.

"Okay," he finally said, feigning disgust. "2000 rupee. But only for the pretty woman."

Sarah gushed. The shop owner snook a smile behind Melvin's back as he pridefully walked away. Once she had her shirt in hand, Padma then asked to see another shirt for Raj.

"Same price?" She asked the shop owner.

He looked at the other local shop owners, who were all still watching, waiting to see what the group would purchase next. Melvin had disappeared around the corner, and Padma awaited his response to see where her next move would take her.

"Where you from?" the shop owner asked Padma, who appeared to be Indian. But the question caught her off guard, and she had to pause and consider what to say. If anyone else had asked her that at any other time, she would have said the United States. But she understood that what he wanted to know was what area of India her family was originally from — and that her answer would hold great weight as to whether or not he would agree to offer her the same price he had for Sarah.

Padma smiled and replied, "Kerala," a province in the extreme southern part of India where Ashanti had said she was doing her next yoga retreat. She was betting that the man had little thought about Kerala, which was much better than mentioning a location close to New Delhi, where he may have had bad feelings.

He paused, then smiled in the way her mother often did. She knew that tell: Even though he wasn't in love with giving her the shirt for the same price, he was going to. And she was correct. Shortly thereafter, she was walking away with the shirt for the same price as Sarah. Both women smiled, knowing that they'd gotten a smart deal at the market and that the shop owner would be happy that his future sales were smiled upon.

Within five minutes, Melvin and the rest were noshing on Chikki, a sweet treat like brittle made of seeds, nuts, and sugar. It was a perfect "walking through the market" snack, and they took turns breaking off pieces and handing them to each other as they walked.

Some of the owners were quite aggressive in their tactics to get them into their shops. The more they pushed, the more Padma wanted to walk away. Melanie had a way about her that graciously acknowledged them and moved on without offending. Padma would often smile and nod her head, then move onward. If she stopped to look at something too long, the shopkeepers descended, and then it took several minutes to peel herself away from them. No, it was best to have eyes on all sides of your head and keep moving unless you saw something of particular interest.

They stumbled upon an adorable shop with handmade dolls that would make excellent gifts for the girls. The female owner was polite and bowed to them as they walked in. She spoke very good English and explained that the dolls were made by the women of her village, sweatshop-free, cruelty-free, organic, and vegan. 100% of the money from purchases went back to support these women and their families.

Padma purchased three dolls and gave the woman full price without haggling. Frankly, it didn't feel like a haggling situation, and

Padma was more than happy to pay the asking price for the artisan dolls. After wrapping the dolls in a cloth, the shop owner simply bowed and thanked her. It was a quick and easy purchase that made Padma feel even better than the one she'd made for Raj.

"Why did you get three dolls?" Sarah asked Padma as they walked out of the shop.

"What?" Padma asked, then saw she'd gotten three dolls instead of two.

Why had she done that? As if instinctually, she'd purchased the three dolls.

Sarah stopped and grabbed Padma's arm, shouting, "Wait, are you…" and pointing to her stomach.

Immediately, Padma shook her head and told her friend no. There was no chance of another pregnancy for her at the moment. They'd taken care of that. Sarah didn't press her further, but as both women walked on, Padma silently wondered why she had purchased three dolls for her two girls.

Why did I do that?

Did I buy one for myself? For Mama? Payal?

Although all of those would have been good answers, in her heart, she knew that none were correct. In a flash, her little toothless friend at the orphanage, Nima, came to mind. But alas, she'd already gotten her a doll last week. Certainly, it didn't make sense to get her another doll. Or had it?

With a deep sigh, Padma tucked the dolls in the bag and walked off with Sarah. She had no answer for the extra purchase, only that it was an instinct. For now, she would leave it alone until the Universe decided to reveal the real reason to her in the future.

Later that evening, the group got together to share a peek at all the goodies that they'd purchased at the market. Ashanti and the others who went in different directions all came to see the treasures of Chandni Chowk market. When it was Padma's turn to share, she simply pulled one of the dolls out of the bag and mentioned getting the girl's dolls. She was still trying to determine why she'd bought the three dolls and decided to avoid the discussion entirely. Nobody seemed to notice what she'd done except Sarah, who was still giving Padma her space about the whole thing. After it was none of her business, Sarah had an intuitive feeling that Padma would realize it as a significant purchase one day.

When Padma returned to her room that night, she took the dolls out and lined them up on the dresser. She knew that the one with the pink dress was, undeniably, Nina's. Zoya would then get the doll in the green dress. The third doll, in the blue dress with gold embroidery, was slightly more lavish than the other dolls. And she was starting to feel a hint as to what it was. But she dared not think about it too hard or too long, for there were too many variables in that story. And it would have to wait until she had time to talk it all over with Rajesh.

For the time being, she decided to put it to bed and then herself to bed, too, turning out the lights and getting into the lavish bed. That night, she dreamt of haggling at the market, eating snacks with her friends as they walked through the streets of New Delhi, and then saw the third doll seated in its rightful home.

The next morning, the group met at breakfast before their day of diving into Bhakti Yoga, the "yoga of devotion." Ashanti explained Bhakti as a devoted love and a merging with the Divine through that expression of love. She said that the most common type, Bhakti, was done by chanting the names of God. She mentioned some famous Kirtan artists some in the group may be familiar with, such as Krishna Das, Jai Uttal, and Wah! These artists had made a living traveling around the world, often putting the ancient Vedic chants to modern rhythms and guiding others in group singalongs. Padma had heard of these events through the yoga studio but had not joined, mostly worried about her mother's potential reaction. But all that old story felt like so far in the past now and, frankly, insignificant. Not that she didn't care about her mother's feelings. But her Indian journey had been incredibly healing for her, and through it, she released the heaviness of the past and the things that didn't serve her highest or truest self. There was no need to worry about that anymore.

Ashanti explained to the group that they were joining in a puja celebration at a temple in town dedicated to the Goddess, Durga. She handed out beautiful red and gold scarves for each of them to wear and asked them to bring their mala beads to the temple, where they would join in with the rituals and chanting.

The temple was a short walk, and when the group arrived outside, they found many people were moving in and about. It was obvious that there would be a need to find a place for their group to meet up later and for a location to drop off personal items to free them up to walk about the temple. The group found a spot to the left of the front entrance under a tree to put all of their shoes and backpacks. Ashanti's assistant stayed outside with their items while the others went in for the puja. Sarah gifted her a beautiful scarf to put on the ground to sit on while she waited for them indefinitely.

The chanting vibrations flowed out of the temple with wafts of incense. The melody of the mantra to the goddess rang out repeatedly from those who had entered to honor the great Mother goddess, who is associated with strength, protection, motherhood, destruction, and war.

Twice a year, on Navaratri, The Nine Nights of the Goddess, Durga, in her three forms, Kali, Lakshmi, and Saraswati, are honored for three nights each. The story goes that Durga was created to kill the powerful demon Mahishasura because no other gods could destroy him. This fun festival sees dancing, singing, and merriment, all for the goddess in her triad.

Although it is not Navaratri at present, this particular mandir always honors Durga and holds regular puja for her and her disciples. One of Ashanti's many connections made her aware of a special gathering this evening, allowing her and her students to attend. Ashanti thought to herself how often Spirit put the retreats together for her.

As each attendee entered the temple, Ashanti placed a bit of red kumkumam powder on their third eye. When it was Padma's turn, she smiled and looked upward as Ashanti pressed the powder on her forehead. Of course, she'd had this done for many Hindu celebrations at home, but she'd never given any thought to the reason for it. For her, it was just a part of dressing up. But, to yogis, this simple gesture is done to awaken the mighty third-eye chakra. It is also specifically connected to Durga, as most depictions of her have this special powder on her third eye, symbolizing her awakened, self-realized being.

Inside the temple, Padma saw women, children, and men sitting around a large statue of Durga, swaying to the sweet chant. Although the Sanskrit words had little meaning to her, they seemed to speak to her spirit in some way. Candles lit the room that was otherwise mostly darkened. And as the hundreds, thousands, of candles flickered, it created an illusion that the goddess statue was alive and moving. As the sweet floral scent of incense moved throughout the space, Padma found a spot to sit among the other followers and adapt to the rhythm that had the room moving as one being.

After some moments, a woman tapped Padma on the shoulder and handed her a chant sheet. She took the sheet but quickly realized that none of it was in English. She could not understand Hindi or Sanskrit but still placed her hands in a prayer mudra and bowed to the woman in deep appreciation.

From across the room, she could make out Melvin and Melanie sitting side by side, chanting and swaying. She wondered how they knew the mantra, and it did not appear that they had a chant sheet—let alone one in English. She closed her eyes and tuned into her breathing. She allowed herself to get lost in the sound and energy of the temple, which felt alive. As she turned more deeply into the words being chanted, she smiled. Still unaware of what was being said, she was eventually able to find the repeated words and tune into their sound and vibration.

There was no way to know how long she had sat in this deep concentration, but eventually, she too found herself chanting the mantra of the Devi, unaware of when she began but crying sweet tears of love and appreciation as she continued with the chants.

Was it the sense of community? Was it the energy in the mandir? Or was it the goddess herself that filled Padma's heart? She was not sure. She did not care. All that mattered at this moment was the feeling of love that pervaded every word, every breath, every vibration.

Soon, a tabla player began a rhythm, and the mantra slowed and stopped. Padma searched to find the man who was playing the double drums. He was seated on the floor, legs crossed, eyes closed, as he played a rhythmic beat that began slowly and progressed to a faster and more chaotic one. And the louder and faster he played, the louder the crowd grew, clapping and hollering.

Some in the room began to stand and dance about, allowing their arms and feet to move to the rhythm of the drum in an ecstatic trance-like state. Padma could see that Ashanti had joined those standing and dancing, and so she began to clap and holler for her friend and teacher, who displayed fluid movement that she could only dream possible in her own body.

Soon, most of the temple population was standing, hooting, clapping, and hollering to the crescendo of a drum. Padma found herself enthralled in the moment, not even sure what her body was doing but going with the divine energy flowing through the space.

And then the room fell dead silent. Not a person moved. Padma waited, not holding her breath but breathing more deeply than ever. Then, suddenly, the tabla player began to drum again, creeping up louder and faster to a second crescendo that came at the end with an intense gong strike! The reverberation of the gong rang through the room and into her body. Padma stood, feeling the intensely powerful silence that awaited at the end. Everyone in the room seemed to feel the same, and the silence hung for some time.

In that silence, Padma again had a vision of the goddess Saraswati, quite similar to the one she had in Rishikesh. Here she was also standing on a large lotus flower in the water, dressed in white, only now she was holding onto an infant in a white cloth. The goddess stepped off the lotus, walked toward Padma, handed her the baby, and then floated back onto the lotus. In her arms, Padma could see an unknown baby girl snuggling contently into her bosom.

This was her confirmation, for she had already had a vision of the future. It was the baby she would adopt, the little girl she would provide a home for, and the owner of the third doll she had purchased at the market.

Without thinking, Padma stood up and walked out of the temple to her shoes and backpack. Kara, Ashanti's assistant, stood up.

"Padma, is everything okay?" She asked.

Padma reached out and hugged her deeply, then looked into Kara's eyes.

"Everything is more than okay. Please don't worry about me. There is somewhere that I need to be. I will meet everyone back at the hotel later."

She waited for a smile-and-nod confirmation from Kara to turn and run out of the temple grounds at top speed. She ran down the street and right out of her shoes, which she had to go back for and pick up. But this did not slow her down, nor did the traffic and the chaos of Delhi. Padma ran and ran and ran. She somehow knew exactly where she was going or was to being led by the goddess as she turned down a familiar road, the street where the orphanage sat.

Standing outside the orphanage, she took a moment to catch her breath. Dripping with sweat, Padma took several deep breaths, put her shoes back on, and slowly crossed the street to the orphanage, where she went inside.

The building was quiet, and for a moment, she questioned if she should be there. But from down the hall, she could hear the muffled voices of several people, and so she followed it until she came to an office where a couple sat, signing papers and where little Nima stood nearby.

Her intense smile and assured knowingness faded instantly, and Padma gasped. The sound startled the group, and little Nima jerked her head and, seeing Padma, ran to her, throwing her arms around her legs. But Padma stood still, unsure of what to do since it was apparent that her little toothless one was already being adopted. And while that was a good thing, a beautiful thing, It was not what she had envisioned or thought that the goddess was leading her to see.

The couple turned to see their now-daughter embracing Padma. The woman smiled and came to Padma, extending her hand.

"Hello, I'm Mona. My husband, Rob, and I are adopting Nima. I see that she seems to like you a lot."

The woman spoke perfect English, and Padma softened and smiled but with tears in her eyes. Hadn't she just had confirmation that she should adopt little Nima herself? Full of confusion, she extended her hand to Mona and shook it while wiping tears with her other hand.

"I apologize," Padma said, "I am happy for you and for little Nima. She is a special little girl."

"Thank you, we think so too," Mona acknowledged.

Rob came over and extended his hand to Padma. "We live in Chicago. Do you live in the US too?" he asked, assuming so due to her familiar accent.

Padma nodded her head. "Yes, a short plane ride from you. I'm on the East Coast."

"Perhaps we can exchange contacts and meet sometime when we are back home? It may help Nima to know that you are nearby."

Of course, Padma couldn't say no to that. This seemed like a very beautiful situation. She looked down, and little Nima, who smiled up at her, still clenched the doll that Padma had given her just a week ago, although much more worn than it was from all the sincere love being given her.

Padma smiled and picked up the little toothless one, hugging and rocking her. And although she knew that she would not understand a word that she said, she spoke to her nonetheless.

"Little sweet Nima. You are so loved. I wish you nothing but happiness with your new family. You are so loved. And I will never forget you." And with that, she kissed Nima and sat her back down on the floor.

After a brief contact exchange, Padma found herself back on the streets of Delhi, wondering aimlessly, confused by the vision and inspiration that now seemed out of place.

Surely, the energy of the Mother had come to her throughout India. She felt in her heart a strong connection to that protecting energy and that she was being guided to adopt a baby girl. Although there were many other little girls in Indian orphanages and orphanages all over the world, she was now disillusioned by what she thought was a clear vision of her future. Perhaps she misread the signs. Maybe there was something even more profound that she was missing altogether.

When she returned to the hotel, she made her way to her room and shut the door. The light on the telephone blinked, alerting her that there was a message. She realized she had taken off without much to leave her friends to go on. Had she worried them?

The first message was from Melvin. "Hey, what happened to you? We saw you get up and leave the puja. We hope you are okay. Give us a call. We are in the room packing."

The second was from Ashanti. "Padma, I understand you had somewhere to be. Just checking in to see if you need anything. I'm in my room if you need me, or I will see you in the morning for our first flight home."

The third was from her mother. "Padma, calling to say have a safe flight home. I have been thinking of you and hoping you enjoyed India. Love you, my dearest daughter."

The fourth was from the front desk, simply alerting her of the checkout time and that her room bill would be under her door that evening.

Alas, there was no call from the orphanage explaining their mistake. Nor was there word from the goddess saying, "Oops, my bad."

Padma took a deep breath and sat back on the bed. She had little packing to do for the morning, so she thought she would make the necessary calls to ensure her fellow travelers that she was okay. The only thing she shared was that she felt compelled to go back to the orphanage one last time before leaving India. It felt rather superfluous to explain in detail, particularly since she was so confused about the events that had propelled her to run, top speed, barefoot across half of Delhi.

If Raj could see my feet now!

Padma's journey through India was difficult to put into words. She imagined that she would tell people the bullet points when she arrived back home. But how would she convey the deep sense of love or understanding of her true self, the healing of wounds that she didn't know that she had in the first place, and the renewed sense of gratitude for her life that she found there?

Her little toothless friend's adoption did not negate or invalidate everything that had occurred on the trip. But this confusion left Padma feeling let down. Wouldn't adopting little Nima have been the perfect ending to her new story? Wasn't this her deeper purpose?

Mother India certainly knew how to take one on a ride. And now, it was time to return to her life at home. And Padma was more than ready to do so. She was more than ready to get back to her beautiful family and home, back to her babies, and back to her perfectly curated life. How she was going to integrate the question mark at the end of the trip would be something she would tackle at a later time.

Re-Entry Can Be Bumpy

"Brace for Impact." —Captain Chesley "Sully" Sullenberger (2016 film "Sully").

Padma hugged her children as if she would never let them go for even a moment—ever again. After an insanely long journey back to the US, Padma was finally in her home with her family, and all that she wanted to do was snuggle them and sleep. Lucky for her, it was about bedtime.

The four of them all cozied up in the same bed, which would be a treat for the girls on this special night when Mommy came home from her big trip. The feeling of finally being in your familiar bed, the smell of your sheets, and the comfort of your favorite pillow are all things that need not be described. Anyone who has ever spent time away from home understands the luxurious re-entry to one's boudoir. Of course, in other ways, re-entry can be a bit bumpy.

Case in point: Padma took a leisurely peek at her home the next morning. After being away for some time, she thought she'd be more excited to cook for her family again in her kitchen. And she was happy to be cooking for them. Except the kitchen was in complete shambles. The pantry lay just about bare, leaving little for her to cook. The dishwasher and sink both sat full of dirty dishes that would need to be washed and put away to make room for any more. Her spices were strewn about haphazardly so that she needed to sort them for cooking. And where were her dish towels? It was as if, well, as if a man and children had been running the show the past two weeks.

Ok, right, she recalled.

After taking nearly an hour to organize her things back where they "belonged," Padma took a long, slow exhale. Now, she could assess what was needed and prepare a grocery order. Thankfully, she had a frequently bought item list in her online grocery account, so she easily ran off a quick order to replenish the necessities and get that going. This would be needed as the kitchen was only the first of the rooms in the house that she'd reorganized, and she felt that she would be spending equal time in each of the others, putting things back together.

Now, the "old Padma" would have been carrying on about this in her head. But the new-and-improved Padma decided that Rome was not built in a day and that she could take her time working through things. She was quite grateful for everyone's help taking care of her family while she was gone. But who puts cheese in with the fruit? Or plugs the toaster next to the sink?

While she took a moment to wash her favorite tea mug that had been recently used as a cereal bowl, Nina came bounding into the kitchen and wrapped her arms around Padma's legs, immediately flashing her back to the last day at the orphanage as her little toothless friend hung to her in the same way.

Padma bent over, picked her daughter up, and kissed her repeatedly on her face, neck, arms, and anywhere else that she could get. Nina giggled and tried to wiggle away, yet secretly loved the attention she was receiving from her mommy. She swung her little arms around Padma's neck and squeezed tight with all her might. Padma was simultaneously impressed with her daughter's strength and slightly concerned that Nina may soon prove stronger than her.

"Honey, loosen up, you're choking mommy!" She managed to get out.

Nina released her grip and giggled, thrusting several hard kisses back on Padma's face and neck, forcing Padma to now giggle and try to wiggle away.

As she enjoyed the moment with her daughter, Raj slipped into the kitchen holding Zoya.

"Whoa, what is this?!" he laughed. "Am I missing all the love and fun!?"

With that, he went over and also began to thrust kisses on both his wife and his daughter. For her part, Zoya banged her empty bottle against her father's head, also giggling.

Rajesh recoiled, also impressed by his little daughter's strength.

"Ouch! Okay, okay. Breakfast time, indeed," he said, placing Zoya in her high chair and preparing her bottle.

"I can do that," Padma said to Raj.

Instead, he kissed his wife and continued, "I got it. We've been doing this dance every day while you've been away. It doesn't take that much time for me to for me to handle it."

Padma was impressed. She had figured he would be handing the girls off and running out the door to work. She was not going to argue with this welcomed change in morning priorities. She turned her focus back to Nina.

"And what do you want for breakfast?" She asked her daughter, who always had an opinion about food.

"Waffles!" she screamed.

"Of course," Padma said.

Raj laughed. "You asked her."

"Indeed I did," Padma replied, heading to the freezer only to find no frozen waffles — and then to the pantry to see they were also out of the mix.

She gently told her daughter that there would be no waffles this morning and awaited her subsequent outburst. Instead, she received a gentle "It's Okay, Mommy" from Nina.

That was certainly a new type of reply than she was prepared for. Padma took a moment to see what she could offer her daughter that might be a pleasing replacement. Again, stocks were quite low.

"Well, how about some cereal today? And I promise to make you waffles tomorrow?"

Nina nodded and hopped up on the chair, awaiting her cereal. This opening gave Raj a chance to take his wife and twirl her around, dipping her for a quick kiss. Nina clapped. Zoya banged her bottle. Padma smiled and hugged her husband.

"I missed you," she told him.

"Not as much as I missed you," he replied, gently kissing her neck.

It was good to be home. Some things had changed, but perhaps for the better. Certainly, things had changed within her. And she now understood that her outer world was a complete reflection of her inner world.

A good night's sleep had proved not only refreshing but clarifying. While the goddess had not visited her again, she awoke with another level of clarity that hadn't come while in India. All was not lost. She was still on the right track. She had just been watching for the wrong train.

"I want to talk to you about something later, Okay?" Padma said.

"Okay. Important? Serious?" Raj asked.

Padma smiled. She didn't want to worry him. "Kind of, but not in a bad way."

He smiled and kissed her again, relieved. He had heard stories of women going off on trips, finding themselves, and coming back only to want a divorce, although he couldn't recall where he'd heard that.

"Okay, it's a date. Let me kiss all my girls and get off to work. But I will see you all later for dinner. I promise."

With that, Raj kissed and kissed and kissed the girls and then slid out the door. Once he was gone, Padma again turned her attention to the home to determine what needed to be done and what could be left for another time so that she could spend some quality time with her girls while they were young enough to still want to spend the time with her.

That night, after the girls were tucked safely into bed and the downstairs was decently cleaned up, Padma sat on the couch with a warm cup of tea. She held the mug in her lap, crossed her legs, and closed her eyes, focusing intently on her breathing. She'd promised herself that when she got home from India, her yoga and meditation practice needed to be an active part of her day. Since she hadn't had the time that morning for them, she took some time now as the quiet home lent itself nicely to meditation.

It did not take long for Padma to reach a calm, meditative state. By focusing on the inhalation and exhalation of her breath, an effortless space of presence was available almost instantaneously. She wondered if Mother India, being still such a part of her energy field, was at the heart of this ease. Or was she too exhausted from the plethora of energy that ran through the house that day? She missed that even though it was a busy day; it was a perfect one that she wouldn't have changed at all.

The girls were even more beautiful and loving than she remembered. She spent hours with them on the floor, playing with various dolls and toys, rolling around, kissing them, and listening to Nina's endless stories about the time she'd had while Padma was away. Her love and gratitude far surpassed any annoyance about where to find something that Raj or the aunts may have placed in a different spot.

As she sat in meditation, she realized that she'd never opened her heart to another place like she had to India on this trip. From the first day of Karma Yoga discussion around Gandhi's shrine to the final day of Bhakti at the Durga mandir, Padma's heart expanded somehow even more than she had thought it could. Like her namesake, the lotus flower, she felt a blossoming and an opening within her that was undeniable and unshakeable. Being a wife and a mother was the highlight of her life. Yet, she felt an aspect of that expanding and blossoming into a fuller and richer aspect of motherhood than she had originally thought possible.

She had been so deep in contemplation that she hadn't heard Rajesh come in from the hospital until he sat beside her and kissed her cheek. She smiled and gently opened her eyes, falling into his arms for cuddling and support.

"How was your day? I'm sorry that I'm late and missed dinner," Raj said sweetly.

Padma smiled and looked up at her husband lovingly.

"I understand. It was a good day. How about you?" She asked him.

He took a deep breath. She began to notice that often, after work, he took a deep breath.

"It was a good day. Saved some lives today. Didn't lose anyone. So it was a good day," he replied.

"I'm envious that you have a passion to help people and a job that allows you to do that," Padma told him. "How does that make you feel?"

Raj shook his head. He hadn't contemplated the positive aspects of his profession in a long time. The day-to-day of hospital life often had him questioning his choice rather than appreciating the good work that he did.

Raj kissed the top of Padma's head and rubbed her shoulder. Her hand stroked his knee and patted his thigh. A quiet contentment moved through her being for the first time in a couple of weeks.

"Yes, I get to help a lot of people. It is a good thing. Sometimes, I wonder if it will ever stop – if the amount of people who are sick or hurting and needing help will ever stop. It can feel quite overwhelming some days. But I am glad that I get to do what I do. I can't think of anything else more important than helping people."

"I agree," Padma said wholeheartedly. She did not want to rush into the discussion with Raj, yet it was the only thing on her mind other than her pure joy and happiness with her life and loving her family.

"Do you miss working?" Raj asked his wife, knowing well that she had a deeper underlying meaning for her comments and questions.

"No," Padma said. "I thought I missed my work, but I don't. I wouldn't change being a mom and spending time with my girls for anything at all."

Raj smiled. That was exactly what he wanted to hear. Although he supported Padma with whatever she wanted to do, he was very happy to have her home raising the girls full-time. He saw every day the many things that can happen when children are left unattended or without safe boundaries. Although he knew that accidents would always happen, he rested better with the knowledge that his family was together and safe at home.

"But..." Padma said, voice drifting off.

And there it is, he thought. What was on his beautiful wife's mind tonight?

"But..." he echoed.

Padma sat up and turned to face her husband. She smiled. He smiled. She waited. He raised his eyebrows. Why was she being so coy?

"Okay, hear me out," she said.

"Of course," he replied, patiently impatient.

"India was phenomenal in so many ways. First of all, I feel complete about my family legacy concerning Nani and her yoga practice. I know that I respected my mother's concerns while also learning why my grandmother loved the practices so much. I feel much closer to my grandmother and my mother because of this entire journey. And I feel like I healed something within my entire feminine ancestry by being in the Motherland."

"Wow," Raj said, "That is something quite extraordinary."

Padma nodded, hoping that he would still be as enthusiastic as they moved through this entire conversion.

"Yes! It was and is spectacular. I saw my mother today, and I told her about some of my experiences, and she smiled, and we had good talks. She sees that I came home to my family and that I can integrate yoga practices into my life without canceling out the other things that are so important. It was a good talk, and it felt good to put it all to bed."

Raj nodded, still awaiting the rest of the story to reveal itself. She was stalling, and he decided to just wait and let her reveal it as she was ready. He would be the rock for her.

"Yes, yes…" Padma said, trailing off. She took a moment to put her hands on her solar plexus, her power center and took a couple of deep breaths while gazing into Raj's eyes. Finding a greater sense of inner strength, she continued.

"Remember I told you we went to an orphanage?"

"Yes."

"We met some really beautiful girls who were awaiting families. The whole experience touched my heart in a very profound way. I mean, first, it gave me clarity about what a beautiful life we have together, and I am truly blessed. We have so much and are so privileged…"

Shaking his head, Raj jumped in, "Well, I wouldn't call us privileged…"

"Yes, Raj, we are privileged. You grew up with a mother and a father who are doctors. You rarely had any worries as a child. Growing up, you had seven cheerleaders and eight mothers supporting you, which allowed you to become the successful man you are. Can you imagine for a moment if you had no family? Who would you be if you grew up as an orphan? If you didn't know anything about being a doctor, having financial security, or being successful modeled for you? What would your aspirations be? Who would you have become? And, would you be fulfilled with what you had manifested in your life?

"I don't have an answer for those questions," he honestly told her. "This is the first time I've ever had to think about them."

She didn't have to say, "I told you so." She understood the sudden realization he was in because it was how she had felt throughout India.

"Raj, I don't want you to feel bad. You had," she paused, "you have a great life, and you continue to work hard in a profession that helps other people. And you do it with love and care. You are an amazing man and father. But me,"

Raj interrupted his wife, "You are an amazing mother and woman."

She nodded.

"Yes, I am. And the thing I am most proud of in my life is being a good mom to our girls. There was such a strong connection to motherhood in India. I felt drawn to empowering goddess energy that aligned with a higher purpose regarding Mothering. At first, I thought maybe it was guiding me to adopt this little girl. She was so precious, and we had this connection," Padma said.

Raj listened even more intently.

"I even had a vision of the goddess handing me a baby…"

Raj jumped in, "…you want to adopt a baby!?"

Padma took a moment to move her head. First, she turned it side to side, meaning "no." Then she moved it like a wave from side to side as if to say, "I'm not completely sure." Then she took a deep breath to continue trying to explain.

"Well, I thought I did. I thought I wanted to adopt a baby, but then I started thinking about all the little girls and boys out there needing families, love, and support."

"Padma, you cannot adopt all the babies in the world. Of course, you know that."

She nodded her head. She knew that. It was not an acceptable reality, but she understood it to be valid.

"Yes, I understand I cannot adopt all the babies. But, I was thinking about all the resources that we have, between us and our families and friends. And I want to start something bigger. I think I want to open a facility…"

"…a facility?"

"Well, I am not sure what the word is yet. Not a school, not just an orphanage…"

"…an orphanage?" Raj mimicked.

Padma stopped talking and stared at her husband. He had to know that she was serious about this. Usually, he was more patient with her and didn't jump in to finish her sentences. This conversation must be making him quite uneasy. And she most certainly wanted his support.

Eventually, he got the hint and made a zipping gesture to his mouth. They both smiled. Padma took another deep breath before returning to the story.

"Raj, let's open a place where children with no families can live, receive health care, and acquire ongoing support about their life journey. We can counsel them and assist them in learning about the many options they have to reach their highest potential. We can show them that they are not alone, that they're supported, and that they're loved."

Raj took a deep breath once his wife stopped talking. Where should he begin?

"Padma, I love your passion for this idea. I love you. But honey, we don't know anything about running an orphanage or any type of facility. This could take years of fundraising, research, and…"

"Okay, then we should get started on it now," Padma said, taking a play from his book and cutting him off.

Raj pursed his lips as he looked at his wife. Padma knew this look well. She was at once back in the Chandni Chowk market, haggling with one of the male shop owners. And the first one who spoke lost. What her husband did not know was the amount of patience she had gained. And with her newfound sense of purpose, she could wait him out all day long.

Raj wiped his hands over his face. He couldn't fathom the amount of work such an undertaking would need. But he did know something, and it was a place to start.

"Okay, so, I remember some time ago, my mother did some pro-bono work for an organization not far from here. You would have to talk to her and find out. But, they were a non-profit that helped orphaned kids. Maybe it's similar to what you are proposing."

Padma's eyes widened, and she clasped her hands in front of her heart, holding her breath.

"So," Raj continued, "I think it would be beneficial to make an appointment to talk to someone there, to find out how things work, and maybe volunteer there to learn the inner workings of the organization."

Padma threw her arms around her husband and squeezed him tightly. Yes! She was feeling all of that. Of course, she may be creating big dreams, but she had to start somewhere. Knowing that she would be assisting others and being of service, she knew, was key, but connecting it with her mother archetype, the protector and nurturer, and with Ma Durga, well, this was what she was looking for.

"Raj, that is a great idea. I love the idea of volunteering and learning and being a part of something already in place. And maybe someday we can do something with our family and start our place for kids." She paused and put her hand down, taking a more serious tone.

"I know how this all sounds, and perhaps I'm getting carried away, but I want you to know that this is not just a passing idea. I discovered in India that I feel a very deep calling to support children, and I want to teach this to our girls. I want them to be involved in helping others from a very early age. And I want to teach all kids valuable tools like yoga and meditation, and how it can benefit their lives, help them focus, relax, and…"

There was no stopping Padma. She was on a roll. So Raj started giggling at his wife's enthusiasm, not to slight her in any way, for he was truly tickled by her. Padma stopped talking and threw her hands on her hips.

"What?"

"Have I told you how much I love you lately," Raj said.

"Then why are you making fun of me?"

"I am not making fun of you! I am here to support you and your dreams. And I love that you dream big. I just want to be the pragmatic, realistic voice here. Slow down. But don't stop."

Raj leaned over and gave his wife a long kiss on the lips. She fell into his arms without hesitation. As they made love that evening, she felt the goddess strongly with her. She felt powerful yet soft, forceful yet open. Raj felt this, too. India and yoga had changed his wife. And he liked it. He liked it a lot.

Emergence of the Devi

"The Goddess doesn't enter us from outside; she emerges from deep within. She is not held back by what happened in the past. She is conceived in consciousness, born in love, and nurtured by higher thinking. She is integrity and value, created and sustained by the hard work of personal growth and the discipline of a life lived actively in hope." —Marianne Williamson.

Many years later, on the eve of the opening of their boarding school for abandoned and neglected girls, Padma reflected on all the tireless work that had gotten them here. As Nina and Zoya put the finishing touches on one of the classrooms by sorting out school supplies and putting together backpacks, she smiled with pride. Her girls would never know what it felt like to be forgotten or abandoned, but their empathy for others who had been was unshakeable. Even though they'd grown up with complete love and support, her work over the years had taught them, especially by her example, how to empathetically be of service to others less fortunate. Either of them would kindly give the shirts off their back to someone else without hesitation. And both shared Padma's particular passion for supporting and lifting women.

Uma fiddled around in the kitchen, fussing over some baked goods for the grand opening in the morning. Her mother-in-law and Raj made an inventory of the supplies in the clinic. Many of Raj's sisters and their nieces and nephews busily arranged the bedrooms, placing fresh linens on the beds. Even her father fixed a few last-minute things around the building like a skilled carpenter. Her entire family was a part of this grand miracle that would, Goddess willing, help thousands of young girls find their way in the world. Watching everyone happily assist made her beam.

Padma walked to the main entryway, a large open room with vaulted ceilings, a chandelier, and a large painting of a beautiful goddess on a pink lotus flower dressed in white, holding out a baby. The image took her breath away. Her vision had finally come to life. And it had only taken thirteen years.

Now, for many, thirteen years may seem like a very long time. But not for Padma. Every day of that time, she awoke, tended to her family, and then spent an hour in meditation, focusing on the vision she had, the vision of the goddess extending the baby to her. And over the years, the vision expanded. The more spacious she allowed her mind and being to be, the greater the vision expanded. So, when it came time to make connections, fundraise, seek out lawyers and accountants, and even work with the state government, well, it fell into place effortlessly and easily. Yes, it was thirteen years of consistent work, but it was rooted in a very focused yoga and meditation practice.

From the main entry, Padma walked down the hall and into another room: the yoga room. Yoga and meditation would be a part of every girl's day. In their own home, she started to teach the girls simple poses named for animals like frogs, cobras, cats, cows, and downward dogs. She bought kids yoga cards with fun animal-inspired pictures of the postures, and she would let the girls choose which ones to practice each day. They loved this new "game" that they played with Mommy, but as the years went on, they learned to appreciate the yoga practice in a much deeper way, eventually finding their styles of yoga to practice regularly. All four of them took time to meditate in their house. This helped set up an energy of openness and connectedness for the day. Raj told Padma it even helped him with concentration during his surgeries.

Ashanti had graciously volunteered her time to teach a yoga class each week at the boarding school as a part of her karma yoga practice. Although she was not certified to teach yoga, Padma felt confident enough to teach them short, daily meditation lessons herself. She knew that this would be one of the many highlights of her days as the Mum of this school.

Her office sat across the hall from the yoga room. She took a moment to look inside. It was probably the only room still left with boxes to unpack and walls to decorate. That was fine with her. She would take her time to prepare it and make it a safe place for girls to come and talk with her. But up until now, she hadn't had the time to put it all together. Payal had picked out most of the items for her, ordered, and shipped them. She would be by tomorrow morning to help unpack and set up. She thought she would leave it to her as a gift. It was her project, after all. Padma was simply the gracious recipient.

But there was one thing that Padma had unpacked. She walked to her desk, where a single framed photograph sat, and she turned the frame around and picked it up. It was a photo of her and

Nima from the orphanage in India. She stroked the edges of the frame and smiled. Her little toothless friend was now about to enter Northwestern University. No longer toothless, this fierce woman was majoring in Psychology and planned to be an active part of the school just as soon as she could bring her skills there. They'd never lost contact and had remained close over the years. Her adoptive parents had raised Nima very well, and Padma considered her a third daughter. Padma would never be able to communicate just how much that little girl inspired her to be where she is today.

She sat the photo back on the desk and opened the one box sitting on top. Smiling, she gently pulled out the doll she'd purchased in India at the Chandni Chowk market so many years ago. Intuitively, she had purchased three dolls that day. It had sat on her home altar all these years as she focused on creating this space, and the doll served as a surrogate for all the little ones who would come and whom she would mentor and serve. Still looking as good as it did the day she purchased it, Padma placed it on her desk next to the picture. Payal would understand the significance of both of these items and integrate them into her magical office space in just the right way.

"Mom?"

Recognizing a voice behind her, Padma turned to see her eldest daughter, Nina, walking toward her.

"Hello, beautiful daughter," she said, hugging her.

She could feel the waning hours draining the last bits of energy from her daughter and realized that tomorrow would certainly be coming early. With the town's mayor attending the ribbon cutting at 9 am, it was time to get home and rest in preparation for the big day.

Padma held her daughter's hand and led her into the hallway, where they quickly met Raj and Zoya, who were also coming to find her and call it a day. Together, the family walked to the main entry, where the rest of the extended family was now slowly filing out. Uma and Swarup walked up to their daughter and dangled a fresh set of keys in front of her, just as they'd done the day that they gave her a brand-new Toyota on her eighteenth birthday. If it was even possible, they were both even more proud of their daughter today.

A single tear ran down Padma's cheek as she accepted the keys to the building from her parents. Together, they walked out and locked the door behind them.

As Padma turned to leave, she saw her entire family awaiting her. All smiling, wearily so, but smiling nonetheless. Her heart broke open even wider at the image of her great family, all a part of this fabulous new endeavor. She placed her hand on her heart and felt more tears, happy tears, come down her face. Her father put his arm around her. All that she could muster at that moment was to tell everyone, "Thank you."

Just before getting into the car, Padma turned one last time to look at what she had created. This would probably be the last time it was this quiet there, as beginning tomorrow, girls would be arriving from all over the area. She gazed at the sign above the entryway:

The Lotus Sanctuary for Girls

She smiled before stepping into the car and driving home with her family.

Padma had finally come into the full and deep understanding —and embodiment—of her name. To the Tibetan Yogis, the mantra *Om Mani Padme Hum* translates to OM, the Jewel in the Lotus. It is a call to profound wisdom, where we can expand into knowing our true selves without being sullied by the mud we are surrounded by. Growing upward toward the light, we are reminded that we are both the lotus and the light.

Padma wanted to be a light for all the girls in the world to know their full potential. And to understand that, in the end, the things that matter most are being a good person, a person who honors and respects all life, being loving and open to love, and finding the light within to drive you upward to your highest form and Highest Self.

In her practices, she had come to realize this and much more. She also understood what the invisible force was that drove one upward when the mud felt so thick that the idea of breaking free felt hopeless. This divine force was *Shakti*, the feminine creative energy in nature: the goddess. Whenever she faced difficulty or a situation felt heavy on her, she went to Durga or one of her many forms, and she found strength in the Mother. She would be that strength for her girls and all of the girls that would come through The Lotus Sanctuary for Girls.

No one ever said that motherhood was easy. But the one thing that everyone does agree on is that one's mother is one of the most significantly impactful energies in a person's life. There was a time when Padma felt an inadequate mother, but that was all in her mind. Her ego had created an illusory feeling of not being good enough. Now she understood the undeniable truth: She was not only good enough, but she also would be a driving feminine force assisting hundreds of children to create lasting positive change in their lives…

As Padma relaxed that evening, she rested in a quote she received in a card from her now not-so-little, formerly toothless friend:

"*A hundred years from now, it will not matter what my bank account was, the sort of house I lived in, or the kind of car I drove... but the world may be different because I was important in the life of a child.*" — Forest E. Witcraft.

Other Books by

Rev. Dr. Tracey L. Ulshafer

The Accidental Yogini: Kristin

The Tia Brooks' Trilogy:

Butterfly
Wolf
Raven

Co-Authored Books:

Love Initiation: Learning the Language of Soul

Stories from the Yogic Heart

Yoga in America

Made in the USA
Columbia, SC
02 December 2024

48200531R00154